THANK YOU FOR BURNING

JUDD WILLIAMS

ISBN 979-8-35094-457-0
eBook ISBN 979-8-35094-458-7

"Coal has always cursed the land in which it lies. When men began to wrest it from the earth it leaves a legacy of foul streams, hideous slag heaps, and polluted air. It peoples this transformed land with blind and crippled men and with widows and orphans. It is an extractive industry which takes all away and restores nothing. It mars but never beautifies. It corrupts but never purifies."

Harry M. Caudill, from *Night Comes to the Cumberlands* 1922

Dedicated with love and hope to the children of the future

CONTENTS

CHAPTER 1

JAN 15, 2016
JULIA, MT BAKER, WASHINGTON

Julia slowly closed her eyes and gently, arms outstretched, fell backwards onto a pure white snow drift. The powder was so light she barely felt her fall end. Smiling sweetly at this she swung her arms and legs making a snow angel. The dry powder tumbled back down over her arms covering them to the elbow. She inhaled slowly through her nose letting the cold dissipate and the clean air deep into her lungs. She was thrilled by such a delicate cedar scent and an exhilarating breath of nature. Lying in stillness, dreaming the past and the future – the rocks and the hills – all the people who have existed there. She remembered Albert Einstein's thought "a human being is part of the whole, called by us universe." She felt warm insulated by her cradle of snow and stillness. Time slowed to match her breathing.

Above this clearing she had spotted marmots and mountain goats high up on the glacier. She had heard the wolf call and the pack respond. Even the memory sent a shiver of delight down her spine. She blinked snow from her long dark lashes to closely examine a cedar branch. She watched how precariously the flakes came to rest and how generously the dark green needles seemed to welcome them to their new home. Her breathing was the only sound other than the quiet gurgle of water beneath the ice encasing the nearby waterfall.

She stood and looked up through the arched black branches supporting the snow. High against the gray sky a female snowy owl wheeled around. Her majestic five-foot wingspan traced a spiral toward the tree above. Yellow eyes locked on landing, talons forward covered in puffy white feathered gaiters and body centered, her wings and tail feathers flared open. A final forward push of wings braked as she landed delicately overhead.

The sky exploded in powder cascading off every branch avalanching from above. Snow buried Julia back into her snow angel. She jerked up leaving her tasseled wool cap stuck in the snow, blew the snow out of her mouth, wiped her face, got up and brushed off the dusty coating from her hunter green parka. She looked up, grinning. As the indignant owl glided off she retrieved her hat, shook it off and adjusted her wool scarf.

Regaining her footing and upright posture she spied a drifting feather. Unlike any she'd seen before it radiated delicate spines out from its base like a bottle brush. The tip flattened to a plane. An elegant light gray design against the white looked like Northwest Haida art motifs. She twisted it slowly in wonder and used the shadowed trunk nearby for contrast to examine it closely. Her breath made every bit of it tremble. It barely had any weight of its own. Holding the spine tight she felt it press against the air. She carefully unzipped her parka and opened a space in the inside pocket over her heart. Gently she slid in the feather.

She lifted her knees high to walk down into the well around the tree trunk nearby and retrieved her caribou hide snowshoes. She planted them flat on the snow, laced and tied them over her boots. The dimming flat light of winter sunset reminded her to head home. She side stepped up to the clearing and built a walking rhythm over the light powder. She picked up her pace to beat the coming darkness. Winter days were too short. Even with the reflecting brightness of snow clouds blocked the light as darkness embraced the woods.

She began singing songs from her childhood and some bits of Woody Guthrie folk songs that came to mind. She had a strong, pretty voice, happily sharing her songs with the forest. She remembered Snowshoe Thompson, the mailman who delivered US Mail to the gold miners and high Sierra folks and sang to his memory. She picked up the trail along the streambed and followed it between iced outcroppings and dense cedar growths.

Deer originally made this trail. The cedar forest gradually opened to the snow-filled streambed. She carefully navigated through snow hummocks that covered the rock. Evergreen trees, Noble, Pacific, Silver firs and Mountain and Western hemlocks marched above the rocky cliffs in the gulley. They retreated from the frozen waterfall's edge and snowy shapes finally unveiled the rock of the streambed. Ice covered the smooth lip of the falls as water cascaded into a black pool below her.

Now she could see the sun setting low in the sky, watermarking the silver haze as the trail opened onto a promontory. In the distance a sliver of the Nooksack River's dull reflection and below the hamlet of Glacier. Here the trail split off from the stream toward her cabin and she took a final look up the magical canyon to the north face of Mount Baker. Julia lived in awe of the majestic mountain and thought how small she was on its slopes. Mount Baker or Kulshan anchors the Northwest corner of the Cascade Mountains.

Picture perfect on all sides; she is a stratovolcano. Like sister Mount Saint Helens she is active with plumes escaping at times. From the stormy mystery at the peaks to the placid beauty of Mirror Lake she offers a visual feast. Views to her North of Chilliwak and Vancouver in Canada and Mounts Glacier and Rainier above Seattle to the south are spectacular. The Twin Sister peaks buttress her flanks to the southwest. Mount Shuksan's crags rise to greet the dawn on her east. Her slopes wear a cover of snow and ice equal in volume to all other Cascade mountains combined. One of the snowiest places on earth, she once recorded ninety feet of snow. Glaciers descend thousands of feet from her rock peaks before reaching the treeline.

Julia's snowshoes squeaked on the dry snow as she walked the remaining mile on the trail away from the creek to her cabin. Arriving at a clearing ringed by trees in the heart of the woods she looked to her cabin on the far edge. Built of logs with rustic windows it seemed a part of the forest. Her ghostly garden beds buried in drifts were just outlines with some spooky stakes poking out and her aged Subaru dusted with snow. She took off her snowshoes and smacked them against her cabin to loosen the snow then hung them on the wood pegs set in the bark wall. Filling her arms with split pine from under the eaves she pushed the door open with her back and went inside.

The cabin's exposed log walls were dark, even once she turned on lights. She kept her wool hat and gloves on while laying the wood for her woodstove, struck a match, and lit the splinters she had piled up. Instantly flames engulfed the logs inside. She closed the iron doors with a medieval clang and spun down the damper to tune the air flow of her fire. Gradually the iron warmed, clanking at each new energy level. She took off her hat and gloves.

Eventually water in the kettle set atop the stove boiled. She made tea in a squat iron Japanese pot. After it steeped she poured herself a cup. Heat transferred into her delicate hands gradually warming them back to comfort.

She went over to her bookshelf to see if she could find the quote stuck in her head and as she reached up the feather floated gently out of her open parka toward the floor. She caught it as it spiraled down and held it up once again. She took a photo from a small display holder made with a stone base and an alligator clip vertically attached by a cable, opened the jaw, and clipped the stem of the feather. It stood in delicate defiance with amazing structure and volume. She blew gently and watched the downy base flutter.

She looked through several of her books before she found the quote she had been trying to recall. "A human being is a part of the whole called by us 'Universe' a part limited in time and space. He experiences himself, his thoughts and feeling as something separated from the rest, a kind of optical delusion of his consciousness. This delusion is a kind of prison for us, restricting us to our personal desires and to affection for a few persons nearest to us. Our task must be to free ourselves from this prison by widening our circle of compassion to embrace all living creatures and the whole of nature in its beauty." She smiled thinking good old Al, always inspirational.

She connected her cell phone to the speakers and played old bluegrass and old folk songs, 'Peace Like a River' By Elizabeth Mitchell, then some hammer dulcimer music from her playlist. She took a mason jar container with a wire spring lid out of the refrigerator and admired the dark red beet soup inside. Then into a saucepan and onto the woodstove. There was a loaf of dense dark bread on her counter, and she sliced off a couple of pieces. Bringing it over to her wooden plank table and serving herself the borscht she closed her eyes, sat very quietly and still for several minutes, her usual grace. She enjoyed her dinner alone listening to music.

After cleaning up she got a novel and sat in her Stickley rocker and read. Around eight o'clock she went outside and started up her aged Subaru. Back inside she finished the chapter and put her book down. She dressed for her shift as a nurse at the Belle Clinic, grabbed her backpack and autoharp and went to the car. Now it was warm inside and the windshield clear. She didn't like running it but knew from experience not to skip preparations with temperatures below zero. She tuned into NPR for her drive to Bellingham.

Driving carefully, in low gear, she navigated her steep, long snow-covered driveway, through the hamlet of Glacier onto the road along the Northern Fork of the Nooksack River. She thought of how the middle fork drops through slots in the rock and over boulders and joins with the north and south to run out onto the fertile plain below. Thousands of acres of raspberries, blueberries, and blackberries drink the waters and spring from this soil before the Nooksack winds through Ferndale and empties into Bellingham Bay.

Her ears perked when she heard Cherry Point named on the radio. The announcer talked about a huge facility to welcome coal trains from the Powder River Basin in Wyoming and load it aboard mammoth ships to markets overseas. Her mood darkened; this was wrong. She gripped the steering wheel and her body tensed.

Waterways are the lifeblood of a place, feeding creatures in and out of the water. They float the ships of commerce in and out with the tides. The Salish Sea in the northernmost US had become a siren calling to the coal industry's desire for a tidewater loading facility to send coal to Asia. The watery part of the 'Fourth Corner' boundary between the US and Canada is drawn in a way that splits the Strait of Juan de Fuca and allows ships from both sides to navigate on their national waters. To accomplish this boundary took decades and a small bloodless war.

Cherry Point sits on this curious northwestern notch on the US map, just below Vancouver, B. C. Before there were Europeans, Asians, or Russians the Lummi people of the Salish Sea fished, hunted, and enjoyed the bounty of nature there for centuries.

The town of Ferndale sits just inland from Cherry Point and hosts ten thousand residents. Ferndale is the replacement of the original logger's name, Jam, applied after the big logjam on the Nooksack River in 1872. Modern Ferndale is American as apple pie, its streets lined with beautiful hanging baskets of flowers and flags. The economy evolved from fishing and trapping, to lumber harvesting, to agriculture and dairy. Then oil refining and aluminum smelting drove the economy.

Julia had spent countless hours writing and protesting the coal train when Cherry Point was first proposed. So many people had joined together from all parts of the community to keep it out. It was like having a second full time job.

Then the developers poured money into funding candidates, like Wayne Henson. She remembered his huge yard signs all around town. It didn't work but the money they could spend was intimidating. She felt anxiety continuing to build as she heard her world was again in the crosshairs. The radio made it sound like some mythical epic set far away.

She loosened her grip on the steering wheel letting blood return to her knuckles. She focused on trying to relax her jaw. 'Breathing and calm' she said to herself. She smacked the dashboard in rage and frustration "Fuck!"

Her heart sank as she remembered all the work it had taken to block it the first time a couple of years ago. Fear rose up that she might lose this round. Only when the Lummi tribe had won the legal challenge with recent court protection for their fishing rights did the Army Corp rescind the terminal permit.

Her former lover, Ted, had helped them show the scale of enormous coal ships to carry mountains of coal. His data helped convince the Corps of Engineers who were deciding the issue. His expert testimony had added another dimension to the broad popular support and legal strategy. Everyone who lived there, and all her friends joined them. Some of her kayaking friends staged a floating protest of the terminal site. Even with that it had been such a close call.

Her mind filled with memories of all the local outreach, doors knocked, postcards sent, and rallies. What more did they need to do to keep the terminal away? Maybe Ted had been right, coal owners would stop at nothing, and a protest was just noise, a temporary setback.

Her drive followed the river north to where it opened to the broad plain into Bellingham. She looked northwest to Cherry Point, just beyond Ferndale and north of the Lummi Nation off Rainbow Road. Recalling visits with her dad to enjoy the rocky shore watching the crabs skitter around the rocks and the funny bull kelp. It held a very special place in her heart although no longer pristine. Smelting and refining had taken its toll over the years.

Just before graduating high school, she'd thrilled riding with Ted on his motorcycle as he raced along the shore roads. He was expert but still it was scary going so fast. She remembered their sensuality intimately. He was a powerful lover and they drove each other to distraction. It was so fresh and exciting she could barely wait for their next opportunity.

She and Ted had Lummi friends who would bring them crab right off their boats and build a little fire on the beach to cook it. He had a wealth of mountain stories when he'd open up about his life on the Blackfoot res and hiking Glacier National Park. They hiked together on adventures in the wild. Then her car accident and she'd lost her taste for risk. When she needed him he had left for his Montana home leaving her feeling abandoned. Ted didn't slow at all, just continued racing. She had retreated into her love of nature. She wondered how he was these days.

She drove past the Auburn Rest where her mother lived and through the empty streets to the Belle Clinic. More of a Victorian house than an urgent care facility it was on a corner lot in a residential neighborhood. Parking her car on the old split concrete driveway aside the house she entered through the back door. She hung her backpack on the hook and set her autoharp in the alcove near the kitchen. She took off her parka, put her gloves in the pocket on one side and her hat on the other. Then took several deep breaths and then shifted into work mode. She put on her scrubs and nametag. Walking down the hall she said hi to Dr. Alice, the resident MD, who was at her desk working.

At the front counter Julia saw Carol, with a hearty frame and curly thick blond hair, gently dancing back and forth listening to some music on her headphones. Julia came around so Carol could see her to say hello. So began her nine to five graveyard shift, usually a quiet affair. Carol took out her earbuds and gave Julia the updates from the last shift. Carol opened a bag of potato chips and pointed them at her. "You want some?" Julia declined and opened her book; Carol went back to dancing.

Things were slow for the first hour and then a burn case came in, throwing everyone into action. Alice came to the counter after treating the teenager. "It wasn't too bad, just a brush against a wood fired stove; kids heal so quickly." In and out.

Julia asked Alice and Carol "Have either of you heard anything about the Cherry Point coal loading terminal coming back?"

"Nope." Carol answered. Julia filled them in on the news.

Alice was disturbed "Oh hell. That is awful." She went back to her office muttering angrily. Carol resumed her dance.

Julia put down a book she'd been reading, trying to keep calm, and asked, "Hey Carol, what do you think about this?" Carol listened as Julia read to her from *Alice in Wonderland* "I wonder if the snow loves the trees and fields, that it kisses them so gently? And then it covers them up snug, you know, with a white quilt; and perhaps it says "Go to sleep, darlings, till the summer comes again. ""

Carol replied obliquely. "That's real nice, Julia. Very sweet." She shook the last crumbs from her potato chip bag into her hand and slapped them into her mouth. Absent-mindedly wiping her greasy hand on her uniform, she reinserted her earbuds and resumed swaying to the music.

Alice had heard and added "Julia, you are a delicate flower. Come here and I'll catch you up." They went over all the details of medications, and ordering supplies. "You know they've been doing a major upgrade to the road out to Cherry Point. I think maybe it's to carry trucks to build the coal loading terminal. These guys never take no for an answer." Alice looked exhausted.

"Keep an eye on things, will you?"

Julia watched her lay down and pull up her blanket. Julia said. "No problem, I'm on it." She pushed the old button switch with the mother of pearl inset off and pulled the glass doorknob to gently close the wooden door.

Here I go again Julia thought and rededicated herself to engage in the fight to keep coal out of the Cherry Point waters. The first thing would be to find everything she could about the new terminal plan and who was behind it. Then she would be calling in the troops for another battle.

CHAPTER 2

JAN 15, 2016
TED, GLACIER NATIONAL PARK, MONTANA

Ted, a tall outdoorsman with black hair, wide forehead, strong jaw, high cheekbones, and a Glacier local, heard distant thunder rolling among the peaks, and reflectively pressed his razor-sharp trekking poles and crampons into thin ice at the summit of Mount Jackson, rooting himself.

He turned his head to see sunbeams that played on the jagged ridges of the Eastern faces of the five other peaks that broke ten thousand feet in Glacier National Park. He studied Jackson Glacier below, what was left of it, reflecting the sun. Tiny ice needles stung the narrow band of exposed skin. He pushed up his balaclava to seal against his goggles and cover his face.

The ridge he stood on divided not only east from west but the entire watershed for the continent. What his Blackfoot mother had called 'the backbone of the world.' Cold wind coming off the prairie to the east meeting up with the western moisture from the Pacific on this ridge.

Stretched out below him the Jackson Glacier was small, like a wizened grandmother. Everything looked smaller than when he was a kid, and fragile. The twenty-five-acre bite of the Blackfoot avalanche in 2007 had taken away a quarter of what was once the biggest glacier in the park. Shrinking the homes for the Pica, Mountain Goat, and the Bighorn Sheep. Just not enough snow for them to live here anymore.

His heart ached in awe of this grandeur, the panorama of mountains with cliffs, snowcapped peaks, crags, lakes, forests, and meadows. It stirred a fierce desire to protect it. Temperature rise due to human use of fossil fuel energy was melting these glaciers before his eyes. He was enraged to see all this nature where he had grown and still lived, his birthright, these glaciers, and all that depended on them, melting away. The peril to ecosystems and all the creatures in them was a clear, present danger.

His father told a story that there were one hundred fifty glaciers before this was a park, when the Civil War was fought. Now the park had only twenty-five. Since they had been there together only twenty years ago, he'd seen the Blackfoot Glacier shrink so much it separated from the Jackson Glacier. They would be gone at the current rate of melting; a total loss by 2030, if not earlier.

He began his descent into the rushing wind, his crampons holding him onto the icy knife edge of the summit ridge toward Blackfoot Mountain. Each step of steel on ice balanced his hold on the ridge. He arrived at a pile of rocks where his gear was pinned down. Crouching against one of the larger rocks he unstrapped his Black Diamond crampons. Fixing them onto his pack he noticed his breakfast food scraps were gone. The crack in the rocks he had filled with them hoping to see a pica or golden-mantled ground squirrel was clean.

Shouldering his backpack he tensioned each strap, forming it to his body. Methodically untying his skis, clipping into their bindings, and then securing their safety straps he stood up. Locking the ice with his poles and leaning forward he weighted his skis. He felt the sharp edges slicing the icy crust. Slowly he launched down the steep pitch balancing gravity against gusting wind. Soon he was racing.

Moving across the snow-covered saddle between peaks he was free from the difficult footings on the loose rock. His movements became more relaxed. His expert use of edges kept him from skidding or grazing edges on exposed rocks. The saddle had barely enough snow to connect the snowfields. Skiing beat walking on rock he thought. He pondered how to act to heal the glaciers, what could any man do?

He fell into the rhythm of poles and strides across the crust and began making good time. The snow bowl to the east contrasted to the naked rock cliffs along his route. He came to an outcropping at the cliff edge of the drop-off. When he'd been ten years old clambering around the rocks to look down into a large bird nest in the rock below, he was showing off a little climbing move he hoped would impress his father. Swinging around to reach a crack in the rock face his weight broke the rock off under his foot. Between holds, he was unattached to the face and began to fall. Time stopped, he was airborne, his connection to the mountain broken.

His father had caught his wrist in a viselike hold. Swinging around the rock face he'd seen fear on his father's face. It was permanently etched in his memory. His father dragged him up over the ledge to safety. As he recovered, a Golden Eagle soared up from far below. It grew larger as it circled up toward them. It circled just below them and then flew straight at the undercut, flaring its broad wings expertly. It grasped the nest with its talons and two eaglet chicks popped up. She obliged them with regurgitated pica. He'd felt excitement at seeing the magnificent bird, terror from his slip, and gratitude for his father. He had a lifetime of memories of this place.

His father was a man who talked low, slow, and never said much. He'd done what was required of him his entire life and often more. Freedom was his most cherished value. He'd endured and overcome many trials to stay independent and take life on his own terms. He served in the Army's Tenth Mountain Division in Afghanistan in 2001 for Operation Enduring Freedom. When he came home in 2003 living with him became difficult.

His father had ceased to enjoy life since his wartime experiences. To get away Ted enlisted in the Marines.

Ted skied past the outcrop on the saddle and onto Blackfoot Mountain. This place reminded him that his father was half and his mother full-blooded Blackfoot. When the ground began to tilt up he stopped and drank water, then put climbing skins on his skis and continued. On the upslope the slow patient work of polling began. Now the sun was warming him, and he adjusted his gear to keep from overheating. Every aspect of this place, the ridges, snowfields, and peaks each stood proud in their being. He looked for the switchover as he rounded Mt Blackfoot. Keeping off the rock and on the snow, he was able to ski again easing his long eastward descent toward Two Medicine Lakes. The work was continuous, each movement on the snow deliberate. He was thankful for good visibility. Rock ridges, cornices, and snowfields marked his line down from the highest elevations.

He was traveling along the backbone of the continent where waters shed east to the Atlantic, west to the Pacific, and north to Hudson Bay. This vertical mountain range for the Blackfeet was the Old Man's Sliding Ground. One of the creation stories they used to describe the genesis of the world. Thousands of vertical feet of rock slope covered with ice and snow with avalanche ribbons running straight down; shearing through the trees to the angle of repose were the sliding places of their stories, places where The Old Man came for fun.

His mother's father, Mountain Chief, came to their home when he was born and shared stories for hours with his mother. They said Ted cried with such force that, at the end of his visit, he'd said "This baby is one of our people. He will be called He-Mah-Ta-Ya-Latkake, or in English, Thunder Rolling From The Mountains. It was a name she'd hidden in her heart. She didn't share it with him until he'd come back from his service in the Marines.

She'd lived with the Blackfeet and in his father's white world as well, going easily between the two. Her voice was like singing, and she knew many stories. As he reminisced, the cadence of his stride soon matched her voice. From this percussion one story, the Death of Four Snakes in Fire, came alive in his mind. He heard her voice in his mind telling the Blackfoot tale.

"In a time before time; the snake gods were good friends to men. Then they turned into giant monsters who ravaged the land, the sky, and the sea. They grew into oppressors of people. They ate up all their gold. The Sun decided to free men from the tyranny of the snakes. He blotted out his rays and darkened the sky. When they looked up, he struck them with lightning. They burned up writhing and screaming and were no more. Where they died became the Black Hills and all the gold they had eaten was left there for the people."

He descended into the tree line as the sky darkened. Enjoying gliding through the silence of the forest out of the wind. After long hours of effort, he could see the Two Medicine lakes below him. Thunder followed him out of the mountains. He felt satisfied with the distance still to go and his lead over the storm coming down from the high peaks. Ted's quest to heal the glaciers, as Thunder Rolling From The Mountain, had begun. He felt the urgency as a prophet sees the revealed truth. As he crossed a snow bridge it collapsed as he reached the other side.

CHAPTER 3

JAN 15, 2016
JC, SPURLOCKVILLE, WEST VIRGINIA

JC, a swarthy young man with hard angular features, pronounced eyebrows, and tousled dark brown hair, leaned down and grabbed his overstuffed frame backpack. Pretty much everything he owned was inside. He took a last look around his bedroom taking in the dirt frosted and cracked windowpanes, the rattle of the counterweights in the jambs, iron bed frame, sagging mattresses, and yellow age-stained pillows with threadworm blankets. He inhaled the stale smell that never changed. He coughed then exhaled deeply. This would be easy to leave behind. He stepped into the living room and dropped his pack against the wall near the front door. He took his tired parka off the hook and then put it on before collecting the cardboard box from the shelf above the coal-burning fireplace and walking outside.

One last thing before he could leave this valley; he needed to head up the familiar road to his grandmother's house to say goodbye. He walked past yards strewn with abandoned appliances, tattered trailers, and homes peeling and patched with despair. This had been his life, and these were the homes of his youth. He turned at the edge of town and his climb became steeper. He stopped to catch his breath and felt his pocket for his inhaler. Small frozen garden plots tucked into the hollows of the landscape, sharing the space with rotting cars. As he got farther up the mylar snack wrappers blowing in the gutters petered out, replaced by an occasional old can or bottles frozen in the cold ground.

Soon the uneven pavement broke apart into a rutted gravel road. He passed between the naked winter tree and the old graveyard with its angled sooty headstones casting shadows on the snow. He avoided looking at his sister and parent's markers and the freshly dug hole, a waiting grave for his brother. Centuries of stones that marked lives lived in more civil days.

The bare branches arched over the road parted before a clearing. JC took in the mountain top panorama. Across the horizon rounded peaks and valleys shaded in purple and blues rose and fell in every direction. He turned his gaze to Grammy and Pappy's log cabin sitting just beyond the crest of the road. It stood fixed like a barnacle to the stone of the mountain in the clearing under an enormous Chestnut tree, wind blowing through the naked branches.

The scene here at the cabin remained unchanged throughout his childhood and seeing it brought a flood of memories. The mountain had seemed eternal. The old well with its bucket set off on the stone wall and on the other end of the house the crescent moon of the wooden outhouse and the porch. A battered antenna with wires leading inside next to the power lines were the only reminder he was in the present.

In the eighteenth century his family settled here. This mountain home had endured and anchored his family through time. Centuries ago, his family's entire village simply left coal mining in England and relocated to America. Chasing hopes for a better climate with dreams of better fortune. Even then the easy farmland in the Virginia plain was taken so they kept moving. It was hard going. Up the Potomac River to Harper's Ferry and then following along the Shenandoah River to find a home they traveled over the ridges and valleys of the Allegheny Mountains and onto the

Plateau until they found this place. They cleared the forest and joined the native Moneton Indians already living there and grew up with the country.

Unlike the Appalachian mountains' orderly orientation to the Atlantic, West Virginia's ancient texture folded in every direction, scrunching mountains together like walrus hide. Even the glaciers couldn't tame this land and affirmed its isolation as the Appalachian Plateau with hollows and steep valleys.

They'd brought with them their songs, opinions, and way of life from the borderlands of northern England. Building this simple cabin, a dream come true, with all their friends and family gathered round them. All his fond memories of family picnics and joyful holidays filled with laughter and warmth were formed here. It was hard to leave these memories, but he needed to live and this place offered him only death and pain.

He remembered as a child looking off the back porch across the top of the apple orchard at the tree-covered mountain. Verdant supple greens in spring, dense and dark shadows in summer, and the riot of color in fall. Winter white with snow or sometimes crystal ice sparkle covering the entire mount like liquid silver. He would run off the back porch and through the orchard down to the streambed with sister, Loretta, and cousins to hunt salamanders and explore the watershed.

Now beyond the cabin he stared down into the pit left from a mountain mastectomy. Dull shades of gray and black defined horizontal strata of the cut. Exposed and scared by vertical drill stitches imitating a Frankenstein scar. Terraces of a lifeless moonscape with shattered bedrock shoved aside at the bottom of blast lines. Jumbled mine tailings seemed to be ominously advancing, leeching poison as they came.

Curiously towering over the desolation of the pit anchored to the rough stone terrace were two four-hundred-foot-high wind turbine towers. Their blades turned steadily in the wind. Cherry red navigation lights atop the nacelles warned aircraft away. A hopeful, if alien, presence in the midst of despoiled nature. Sentinels guarding the grave of God-given natural wealth. Despoiled forever all for a narrow seam of coal long since burned up leaving ash in streams and smoke in the sky.

He startled as the hounds bounded directly toward him; he called them by name as they playfully jumped on him. Uncle Luke whistled from the woodshed to call them back. He was busy stacking split firewood but gave JC a wave with his leather paw. The faded American flag was flying proudly off the porch blowing in the restless winter wind. Colorless desiccated leaves of maple, oak, ash, dogwood, and hickory swirled in little vortices and then fell to the ground. Aunt Mary looked out of the kitchen window and noticed him. She pushed her hair away from her face with the back of her forearm and waved too.

He picked his way up the front path and could see Grammy dozing in her rocking chair through the wavy glass pane in the window. One of the beautiful crazy quilts she hand-stitched covered her lap. He noticed the glint off her thin gold wedding band looped loosely around her bony finger in the last low rays of sun. Her chin rested on her chest and her mouth was open. A small woman worn down by love and loss dressed in a simple wool sweater and shawl.

Storied wrinkles spread across every bit of her face. She had braided gray hair in rings around her big ears with unruly whisps flying out from the nape of her neck. Her teeth were usually in a bedside water glass, but he could see that she had them in today. They looked so out of place, so shiny white and even. He saw her startle when he stepped onto the planks of her porch, so he knocked on the unlatched screen door to give her a moment to collect herself. She'd always seemed ancient to him but now she just appeared frail.

She didn't rise but lifted her arms embracing him from her seat. He wrapped his arm around her, holding the cardboard box with his brother John's ashes with the other. She looked at it and gently took it with her arthritic hands, "John, he loved you and your sister more'n you can know." He leaned in and gave her another hug smelling her woodsmoke and mothball scents. Her heavy knitted black shawl had holes and had a dusting of white near her neck. She placed the box in her lap on the quilt.

After a few minutes she spoke "Oh, you are my honey child. I wish this weary world wasn't so heavy on you. Set yourself down and rest your bones." JC took the wooden chair across from her. "It grieves me sorely that your brother has passed. My prayer is that he is our kin's last human sacrifice to King Coal." She took a moment and spoke slowly. "I know you are fixing to leave us," and looking up into his brown eyes, "no future here for you. With yer asthma you'd never get hired for any job in the mine, even if there were to be one. All this hooey about bringing coal back is shit, no future here for you baby, that's for certain." She turned her head from side to side. "No sir."

JC felt uneasy as he pulled his brother's wedding band and small gold cross from his pocket. He placed them gently in her waiting hands. Silence overwhelmed them. Finally, Grammy spoke. "Fetch me that wooden box there, atop the fireplace. Bring it over and give it here." JC walked over and collected the box; it was much heavier than he expected.

She opened the battered dark walnut box so he could see inside. Chipped toy lead soldiers from the civil war, coal scrip from a company town, an old watch, and a military medal were among the trinkets and keepsakes nestled in the green felt lining. Grammy took the tarnished star with cloisonne emblem inset and elaborate purple and maroon ribbon from the box. She clasped both of his hands and said "This here's the medal they gave my lovely Clem at the end of the war. He done right by his men and the government done right to give it to him. His earthly race is run." She replaced it and took out a silver pocket watch and gave it to JC. "I want you to have it now; as you are twenty-one, he'd want you to be the one to have it. So's, you'll remember us and where you come from. Now is your time, you are young and strong. Go to where you can succeed." She beamed at him through her aged eyes. "See them notches at the numbers?" JC felt the cover and saw thin black grooves on the case radiating out on some of the roman numerals around the face.

"Well, the notch on the one hour is to remind him of me and when we got hitched." She grinned and her eyes sparkled, "Can you imagine me as a cute little girl with long braids?" she crinkled her whole face with a spritely smile. "The two is when your mother was born. The seven is when we got this cabin." She closed the box gently. "The eight is when your mother got hitched and nine is you and Lo and the ten was your little brother. And the eleven is when my Clem retired at the railroad." JC smiled at her and closed the cover on the watch and saw 'Clement Craddick' engraved on the cover.

"You are a special one, you know you are. There's things in this world for you to do, things with purpose and helping the world be better'n when you got here. Now's your time." JC studied the stopped watch and looked at the fancy engraved patterns on the cover and felt its weight. "Thanks Grammy. I loved Pappy and I'll keep this to remind me." he patted his pocket. "Remember when I was a little rug rat? He'd pull on my ears with his toes through his stocking feet when I'd crawl up to him on this carpet. I couldn't stop crawling to him, but my ears hurt when he'd pinch them with his toes. He'd laugh and laugh."

"He sure did, surely did. "She relished the thought. "You go now. Git. There's nothing here but ash and dust. You belong out where you can grow. You don't want to sink your roots in this sad place." She gave him a last smile and slowly dropped her wrinkled chin down onto her chest. The box of John's ashes in her lap deepened as the center of gravity.

He turned to leave when she suddenly burst out in a rage, "Digging coal done cursed our family! From Dwert River to Blair Mountain to Matewan and now again coal cursed us. Right here too. Our mountaintop blasted to a pit of hell; our crick filled with its broken bones. Blasting and squeaking tractors all damn day long drove me nuts." She started rocking, pressing her hands on the box. "And not just our home, the family too. Losin' your sister, Loretta, broke your father's heart. He poisoned himself with the alcohol, pain, and sadness." She looked down at the box, "Workin' the mine broke your brother's back. They didn't do right by him. The drugs for pain turned out to be the road to the Fentanyl; that killed him." She fixed her gaze on JC. "You didn't get off neither, you got the asthma."

His heart ached; he'd miss her. He stood for a moment in silence as she slowly rocked. Then leaned over once more to hug her, "I love you Grammy." With that he stood and walked out the door.

His uncle met him on the porch. "Your brother, John, was a good man. Just unlucky to be working for Lockerby. Still, he was one who got out of the explosion alive. Some men weren't as lucky." He put his hand on JC's shoulder. "Now he's gone. A hard-working man and loyal to all of us. I'm sad it ended this way." His aunt came around to where they were standing. She gave him a long hug. She was perfumed with cooking aromas of cinnamon, nutmeg, and cloves. She cast her dark eyes down so he wouldn't see her tears and handed him a bag filled with apples, some jerky, biscuits, and a plastic tub of her spiced apple butter. She wiped her eyes and soaked him into her memory. He hugged her again and they said goodbye.

JC's journey began down the road past his brother's yawning grave to the train yard. The sun set behind the mountain. He crossed the tracks, ducked through and around a couple of hoppers, then found a graffiti-covered boxcar with an open door close to the engine. He took one last look at the station and the creek running out alongside the tracks.

Heaving his pack up over the cold steel edge he shoved it into the car and scrambled in himself. One end was filled with machinery crates but there was space enough to stretch his legs and lean on his pack. The pallets under the machines smelled like fresh cut oak. He reached into his pocket for a lemon drop and felt the watch. He studied it with his fingers scouting for the thin notches.

JC heard the muffled squeal of steel wheels and felt the clumsy cascading jolt of the train locking the cars together. He heard the stationmaster call and then the train slowly pulled out of the station. He thought about his grandfather, Clem, or Pappy, and how much running this little train yard had meant to him. He took such pride in every part of the operation, the rails, the schedule, and every detail on the engines. He thought about the times he got to see him at work. The wooden shack with the enameled sign, Mud Road Station. It was his castle and command center.

When he could he'd visit Pappy and wide-eyed take in the kerosene lanterns from the old days with red Fresnel lenses and wire bow handles for signaling the trains. Galvanized buckets of rail spikes sat against the wall and heavy switch levers piled in the corners. Rusted crossing signs and metal number tags decorated the walls. The holy center: the telegraph and switch desk, was always ready for work with worn and true clarity. Dust would fly up through the floorboards when trains went by. He remembered his coughing fits after that.

The engine gave another tug, and he was on his way. Again, Grammy's voice filled his mind. Stories he'd heard on her knee or sitting on the hooked rag carpet. He could almost hear her voice, "Coal first come to our folk in England back in the 1700s. T'warnt no big deal; just pick, shovel and barrow. Then it come to be everythin'. Cockermouth & Workington Railway come in and by then the whole town was diggin' coal or bakin' bricks to shore up the mine shafts. Oh, there was jobs; most of 'em bad. Workin' the mine wasn't much of a life, never seein' the sun or sky. Everything dirty. Folks stopped fishin' salmon, too dirty in the Derwent River for fish. Everyone just minin' coal. Soon coal's the only thing.

Then the owners an everybody else took to look down on us mining people like we was dirty animals. Slaves fit only for their black pits dug into the earth. Times were black but we were proud and so we turned it around. We took pride in being able to survive the mines and live the hard life in such a place. But we knew it weren't a life. We had the chance to move to America and we took it. All of us just up and left." She loved telling the old stories.

JC looked out the open door of the car at the night sky through the trees. He briefly spotted his favorite constellation Orion flickering on and off behind the bare trees. She'd tell the story about the Moneton Indians and learning woodcraft from them. But by far her favorite was about the wedding. When the family first settled in America, the bride from Pinchgut Creek and he from Whiskey Springs when James Monroe was President. What a fine man the groom was, tall, lean, and sinewy. His weather-beaten look had some anger, and hardness.

The capture! Just like President Andrew Jackson took his bride, Rachel, and terrified her husband. Mostly play acting but the wedding ceremonies started with his groomsmen riding up from their home to fetch her. Grammy always delighted in embellishing how her family rode out to stop them. Cutting down trees to block the road and piling vines on the turns to slow him down. Once the groom and his men broke through, they rode up shooting in the air and hollering; quite a sight to see. Then everyone formed up in two lines and all met in the middle like for a dance except on a signal everybody raced for 'the bottle', a ceremonial prize. Her family won and passed the bottle around through her party. Of course, then they passed it on so everyone had something to drink. Afterward everybody had squirrel stew. What a lot of fun it was. Both families had a lot of kin folks, so it was a big party. Hopeful newlyweds in an unspoiled paradise, almost heaven.

The rhythm of the rails rocked him, and he drifted off to sleep wrapped in his ancestors' lore.

CHAPTER 4

JAN 15, 2016
JC AND WRIGLEY, WEST VIRGINIA

The train rocked and the steel wheels squealed as they went around a sharp bend in the track. JC opened his eyes and saw they were crossing a ravine on a high trestle. It quieted as the track straightened and he fell back into his dreaming.

JC felt vague and contrary emotions; tired and excited to be leaving but still sad over his brother's death, Grannie, and the life he'd loved as a child. He yearned to go anywhere he could breathe freely.

He pulled out his sleeping bag and tried to get comfortable for the night ahead. The train rocked and jerked around the twists and turns. He rested his head on his rolled-up parka and listened to jingles of the safety chains, clicking over the switches and the rhythmic knocking on the rails crossing trestles. Rail cars sounded a strange hollow note of passage, occasional car horns, and the long blast of the train horn. Warning bells at crossings and squeals around tight turns became his soundtrack.

JC awoke with the sun and stretched. A little stiff but excited to be on his way west. He was thinking about getting out of his sleeping bag when the train slowed around a tight turn and a puppy flew into his car, huge dark gray head, sweet black eyes, and paws like saucers. It landed with legs splayed then got up clumsily. Running over to him the puppy gave JC a big lick on the face. JC laughed at the tickle of his sharp tongue when a backpack landed and a wiry thirty-some clutching a KFC bucket heaved himself into the boxcar. His freckles were just as red as the art on the bucket.

"Name's Red, that's my dog." He came over and collected the pup. "Who're you?"

JC was taken aback by this invasion but looked up and said "JC, I'm heading to Bellingham."

"Where're you from?" Red asked pointedly.

JC replied, "Little town near Spurlockville, off Mud Road." As a wave of homesickness and thoughts of Grammy swept over him, he reached unconsciously into his pocket touching the watch. He wondered if this was a good idea after all.

"Where's that at? Bellingham?"

"Way in the Northwest. I've got family there." The puppy had returned and was nuzzling JC, who uneasily studied Red's hatchet face and shifty eyes. Red didn't look at him but talked anyway. "He likes you." Red poured some water into a paper cup and gave it to the puppy. "That's a expensive puppy. He was at the park, and I grabbed him. Hoping I'll find a buyer soon, he's a handful. Since then, I've learned all about Carney Coorso." The puppy slopped it up and then ate the cup while his metronome tail whacked JC's feet. Red smacked him and said "Bad dog. Now how am I supposed to give you a drink?" The puppy came back over to JC.

JC grabbed his giant head with both hands looking into its big eyes and asked, "What kind of dog is he?"

"Carney Coorso, a Gladiator dog!" Red pulled the puppy back. "Italian massive is another name, see those cool stripes, still a puppy but look at the size of his paws." Red got his bucket of KFC and began eating a drumstick. Holding the bucket toward JC he asked, "Want some?"

"Sure, thanks." JC took a cold greasy thigh from the bucket.

Red finished and gave the puppy the bones, and watched as he devoured them. "Eats like a goat." As if to emphasize the point the puppy began to consume the KFC bucket. Red kicked at the puppy, who dragged it out of reach.

Red began a tug of war with a sock. The puppy was holding his own, whipping his head from side to side. "I'm from Vulcan, you know, on the Tug River? Hatfield McCoy feud and all.

He looked up at JC. "My town is so fucked up. There's no road to get out. Just this crap swinging bridge over the Tug. Even to get anywheres I had to crawl under the train cars. Can you believe that shit?" He took a knit cap off his head and his greasy red hair flopped down on his shoulders.

The puppy came over and settled into JC's lap. "What's his name?"

"Uhm, it's Billy, like Billy goat I guess!" Red was surprised and laughed. Then he looked pleased with himself. "Come here Billy. Come on." The puppy ignored him.

JC wasn't happy sharing the car with Red as he reminded him of the dealers that sold his brother John the drugs he'd overdosed on. Easy going and charming, smiling while they sold poison. He began to think of a way to move to another car just as soon as he got the chance. The puppy started rolling around on his back snapping at a fly batting his giant paws. 'Billy' was a lot of fun and his antics distracted JC.

Red fumbled in his pack and pulled out a vape pen. He began smoking and offered JC some. JC said "I can't. I've got bad asthma and I'll just end up coughing." Red looked at him with suspicion.

"I've also got this Fentanyl." He reached into the liner of his cap and pulled out a thin plastic envelope. "It's the real thing. Pretty cheap too."

JC felt his skin crawl and shifted uneasily looking for an escape. Fentanyl overdose had killed John just a few months ago and here it was in his face. "No, thanks." Red persisted "C'mon this is the good shit. I swear. Cheap ticket for a fancy ride."

JC got more agitated, breathing more shallowly, "I said no." His anxiety triggered his asthma and wheezing he took out his inhaler.

"Your loss man." Red returned the baggie to his cap lining and slowly started to mellow as the high kicked in. He took some more vape hits, blowing the smoke towards JC. JC went into a dry coughing fit that just wouldn't stop. He recalled times they would go on until he could barely breathe at all and had to be hospitalized. JC tried to slow his breath so as to not waste his inhaler too soon. Red finished vaping and with heavy lidded eyes, leaned against the machine crate.

The dog had not left JC's side while he had been vaping. "That puppy likes you." Red slurred as he nodded off. JC continued coughing. Looking out the door he saw flat frosted farm fields everywhere. It was so different from home.

The next morning JC awoke to a foul stench and saw the puppy had pooped in the car. Red was still asleep. He got up and threw it outside. He kicked some hay around to get the rest. The country had flattened to fields. He saw some station signs and knew they'd crossed into Ohio. It was still a long way to get to Chicago. He looked at Red and considered changing cars but decided it'd be easier to wait for a stop.

JC recalled his brother John's death spiral. JC's eyes filled with tears as he recalled how many times he'd tried to help him get straight. Attempting to reason, cutting him off, threatening to stop helping him if he wouldn't help himself, none of it had worked. John had been injured at Lockerby's mine explosion years back. He'd said, "So many problems with my back now. The docs got me all this Oxycontin. It was good, I needed it to block the pain of my back injury so I could keep workin', but then they kept giving me more. I think I didn't need as much as they gave me.

Soon it took over. I needed it. I couldn't work, wasn't there for my wife, and finally I couldn't stand it and needed something stronger that didn't require a prescription. Somebody offered Fentanyl. I felt just fine again but it started to own me. If I can't get it outside, I get it delivered by USPS from a lab in China. Only problem is it's hard to know how much to take."

JC had spent hours just hanging out, waiting for John to regain consciousness. When John finally awoke John would yell and tell JC what a bad brother he was, not helping, and how working in the mine was so great. JC had to drive him everywhere to get help. How hard it had been to even know what to do.

John would be so desperate, apologetic, and vulnerable and then so hard, harsh, and cruel. He stole anything he could sell when he needed a fix. Pretty much anything of value JC had owned John had pawned at one point, even their guitars. JC had to go buy back his own stuff so often the pawn shop took pity on him and sold at the price they'd paid for it. The worst was that John had lost himself and his hopes and dreams. Just like their father, John was lost. He was reduced to getting the next dose and nothing else mattered. Not his own family or their close brotherhood was enough to save him.

On a particularly low and honest day, John told JC, "Your hair hurts, it controls your life, you need it, you can't work, you can't stand yourself. One day a cop came to the door and asked me 'Have you looked at yourself?' I tried looking in the mirror but had to stop; it made me so depressed."

John had also confided in JC about the demons beyond the physical pains that drove him. When Lockerby's mine exploded John was trapped with his crew. The blast of dust made it impossible for him to hear or see. When John's hearing returned, his high school friend, Jim, was calling to him. Jim was buried to his waist in rock. John crawled over and tried to drag him out, but the pain was too much for Jim. Digging away the rock with his bare hands, coal dust streamed in over them filling the void.

Jim had started laughing in the dark. Jim asked "You remember *My Sweetheart's a Mule in the Mine*? He'd tried singing but dust went deep into his lungs, and he began coughing violently. John watched, helpless and in terror, as the black dust slowly, inexorably covered his friend. While John held Jim's hand dust covered Jim to his hardhat. Too late for Jim, the rescue crew had arrived and pulled John out on a stretcher.

Now John too was ashes, filling a cardboard box in Grammy's lap.

JC's recollections were disrupted as the puppy came over and wagged one of Red's dirty socks at him. Relieved at the distraction, JC picked up the end and they commenced a game of tug of war. He was surprised how strong the puppy was and how determined. Sometimes the puppy would jerk it free and JC would have to chase him around. Both were happy to have a playmate. After a while he made a small well in the plastic tarp covering the machines and poured some water in for the puppy to drink.

Red jerked awake. "Where are we?"

JC didn't know but offered, "I think we're following the Ohio, and just went through Cincinnati. Maybe Chicago by nightfall." Red got up, pissed in a corner, then returned to his stupor. JC and the puppy continued to play.

Later Red woke up, querying, "You got any food?" JC shared his biscuits and jam with Red. "Have you got anything else? I'm hungry," the train slowed, and the brakes squealed, "Look there's a McDonalds! I could use an Egg McMuffin. I'm going." He threw his pack out onto the gravel siding and sat down on the edge of the car. The puppy came over and looked as Red jumped down and ran back to get his pack. Red ran alongside the train signaling the puppy to jump. "Come on Billy, come on jump!" The puppy paced up and down the opening of the boxcar looking at Red but then turned to look at JC. He went over and sat in JC's lap and didn't take the leap.

"Hey, JP, a little help man, push him out here." JC didn't move. Red looked at JC angrily then yelled at the puppy "Get out here you little shit! Come 'ere you stupid dog. Godd…" The train blasted its horn covering the rest of Red's words as it slowly sped up.

Red was gone. The puppy shoved his head under JC's arm to get him to pet him, then gave him a lick. JC was surprised how happy he felt. By the time the train pulled into the Chicago rail yards the puppy had a new caretaker. JC remembered Chicago Cubs stories his father told and of the puppy's wiggle and waggle. Putting them all together he renamed the puppy Wrigley.

CHAPTER 5

JAN 18, 2016
JC MEETS TED, EAST GLACIER, MONTANA

Wrigley's hard head poked out from under his parka like a baby in a Snugly. They'd already been waiting on the rail siding at East Glacier for a couple of hours and he began to wonder if his train was really coming. Train hoppers had said that this spot, littered with cigarette butts and empty cans, just before the platform was where to wait. They'd said he could catch the train on the fly as it slowed around the bend. If it sided out or switched cars it'd be easier.

The sun was dropping low on the mountains to the west. He was a lot further north than expected. It was winter and he felt alone and out of his depth. His geography wasn't great and he hadn't planned this route. The other train hoppers were a rough lot. Though their advice had been welcomed, he hoped he'd seen the last of them. Much older scruffy, unwashed, and haggard men. They had been eying his backpack too often. They made him nervous. As he'd left to check on something, one of them snagged his drinking bottle, retreating into the safety of his trio, daring JC to do anything about it. JC was relieved when they'd moved on. Wrigley was spending half his time in his arms zipped inside his parka. His paws got too cold for him to stand on the ground. Not much in the way of shelter, the trees were too far from the tracks. Wind just blew all the time it seemed. JC shivered in his lack of preparation as the temperature continued to drop.

Ted came into his view hiking at a fast pace south along the tracks. He had a sizable backpack that reminded JC of military packs. It was fully stuffed with skis and snowshoes sticking out like antennae. He moved without seeming to notice the weight. The closer he got the bigger he appeared.

As he came closer Wrigley wiggled loose and went bounding toward him, a calliope of paws and wagging head. Ted slowed and the puppy hopped up and down, his paws pushing onto Ted's knees. Ted reached down and picked him up by the scruff of his neck. He held him up to get a better look. Wrigley lunged under Ted's chin and gave him a huge lick relishing the salty crust, knocking Ted's jaw with his big snout.

JC ran over to get Wrigley then realized he was looking up at Ted who said in a deep voice, "Handsome pup, how old is he?" Ted scratched behind his ears, patted Wrigley's head, and then held him out to JC who put him back inside his jacket. "Oh, I've only had him for a couple of days. I'm not sure before that. I got him by accident."

Ted looked at JC, the lack of winter gear, his pitiful backpack and said. "He's a good dog." Ted thought how vulnerable JC and this puppy were in their situation and how he regretted not being there when his now ex-girlfriend had been in need.

JC wasn't comfortable with Ted but welcomed another person in this remote spot and the distraction from the informative but sketchy train hoppers from earlier.

"Where are you going?" Ted inquired.

JC answered timidly. He studied the snow covering the railbed gravel at his feet, tracing a slow arc, and said "Bellingham."

"So, you train hopping?"

Wrigley squirmed around inside his parka. It took a minute for JC to realize he hadn't responded to Ted.

"Yeah." adding, "How about you?" He looked towards the snow-capped blue peaks.

Ted took his time answering as well. At last, he said, "Headed east to my cabin." After a couple minutes he continued with an undertone of ice, "Look up to those peaks; they were white for my whole childhood, now just the peaks. The name Glacier is a joke."

JC didn't hear any humor in Ted's voice. JC thought Ted must be six foot four and seemed solidly built. In the low light he couldn't see his face too clearly but appeared to have an olive complexion, black eyebrows, a wide forehead, and reminded JC of pictures of Sitting Bull he had seen. Ted was statuesque, he barely moved while they talked.

Ted continued, "You see the clouds up there? That's a storm moving in and it's going to be windy." He got his phone out, checking the date, "This is the only westbound track. Your train is coming, but not until tomorrow." he studied the snow sticking on the shiny rails, "That storm is coming first; tonight. I heard some thunder coming out of the woods. It will be a cold one too, you set for that?"

"You live out here?" JC was trying to imagine it.

"Have you called to get the internal tracking number for your train?" Ted asked pointedly.

"I couldn't get it before my cell phone ran out of juice." JC looked at the ground; dirty snow flecked gravel, "I should be fine."

Ted kept on, "Just twenty miles away, over at Browning, the temperature dropped a hundred degrees to minus fifty in under twenty-four hours. I don't think your pup is prepared for that sort of cold, do you?"

"He's a good dog, real strong. I think he'll be fine." JC felt a shiver down his spine.

Ted looked doubtful, "Have you got enough water?"

"No, but I'm going to get some." Wrigley whined and looked towards Ted.

"Tell you what: I can take you to my cabin about ten miles from here and you can fill up. If you want, you can spend the night. There's a siding where the trains slow before the bridge, you can hop on there." adding, "I have a bed you can put your sleeping bag on."

JC eyed the peaks and clouds, and looking at Ted, decided to trust him. "All right. Thanks, appreciate your help. How do we get there?"

"My snowmobile is just across the little bridge there and then about twenty minutes."

"OK, sure." Ted was already fifty feet ahead gaining speed as he walked across the tracks and over toward a break in the trees. JC had to scramble to catch up with him. They crossed a small bridge into a parking area. Ted pulled off the tarp of his snowmobile. He took off his pack and began adjusting the racks behind the seats.

He looked at JC and said, "Just keep your pack on. Be sure to zip up, it will be cold once we get moving." With that he secured his own pack and skis onto the frame, folded and stowed the tarp, and climbed on. He put on his helmet and driving gloves. He waved to JC to climb on behind and turned to say, "Keep hold of me and your pup." Then he switched on the headlight and at once sped off through the snow.

JC leaned into Ted to break the wind. It was much colder than he'd imagined. After the first minutes of flying with his ears in the wind Wrigley ducked down into JC's parka. They drove out along the highway and then cut across open fields for what seemed like a long time. The ground slowly began to rise toward a ravine above the tracks. JC was impressed how fast they were able to cross any terrain. Ted was a lead foot driver. They angled up and JC saw a small grove of trees in a protected hollow. Then he could make out roofs of buildings covered in snow at the center. Twilight was ending.

As they got closer, he saw a white metal clad garage building. The roof beam extended out over the front entrance from the high pitch roof with a hayloft door. A shed attached to the right side for the whole length. There were mature trees in front and behind. Farther up the hill there was a lone very impressive old tree, split by lightning but still alive. The garage door was huge, big enough to drive in a big truck, and the shed was fully enclosed with its own roll up door. They headed toward that one.

Ted killed the motor and hopped off. As he walked to the door flood lights came on washing the snowy scene. He flipped open a wall box and typed in a code to lift the roll door. It screeched and jerked, snow falling away at the bottom then smoothly raising up. All the exterior flood lights went off and the interior of the shed lit up.

JC stiffly climbed off the snowmobile and Wrigley jumped out from his jacket and began prancing around in the snow. Ted drove inside and parked the snowmobile. JC walked inside and saw that the garage went back a long way. On the right there were three bays each with its own connecting roll up door. Ted had driven through the first to park. It held the snowmobile and an ATV. The middle door had motorcycles; a BMW cruiser and a Kawasaki dirt, and three bicycles. The last bay was filled by an aged monster tow-truck with a plowing blade. He'd never seen an Oshkosh truck like that before, but it looked like all business.

Ted put his gear in place on the walls; everything had an exact location. He picked the skis off his pack and walked them down to a workbench. He checked the whole scene with a glance and walked out hitting the roll door switch on his way out. JC followed as the door closed and the lights went out.

Wrigley bounded up to Ted and they played 'who's the alpha' on the way up to the house, playing in the snow.

CHAPTER 6

JAN. 18, 2016
HENRY, POWDER RIVER BASIN, WYOMING

Henry drove to his shift in the Thunder Mine which began at midnight. He was not looking forward to the pitch-black monotony but it was a living. Like an airline pilot's job, hours of nothing then seconds to deal with a crisis. Crossing above four sets of railroad tracks on the Bill Montana overpass, he saw the brightly lit loading silo rising twenty stories above the railroad loading loop in the darkness of the Powder River Basin. Its feed conveyor angled over the tracks to it like a giant cypress root. Hundred car 'unit' trains snaked through the silo's loading tunnel: like tourists driving through a giant coast redwood on a busy weekend.

The black heart of the modern coal industry beats between Wyoming's Bighorn Mountains and the Black Hills of South Dakota. It pumps a million tons of coal per day on the rails of the Orin Subdivision between Donkey Creek Junction and Shawnee Junction making it the highest tonnage mainline railroad in the world. Romantically named mines like Caballo, Belle Ayr, Cordero Rojo, Coal Creek, and Black Thunder send one hundred miles of coal hoppers through this steel aorta every day. An endless possession of heavy coal trains delivers the carbon fuel of the pits to steam generation plants throughout the United States.

Henry was navigating between high tension power lines and rail track sidings, gradually descending as the road cut into the living earth. He glanced at waiting coal trains that foreshadowed the massive energy operations ahead. Into an epic diorama of geological time laid bare by engineering, men, and machines. He rolled up his windows against the dust and switched his AC to recirculate. Overburdened piles of sandstone and mudstone appeared as ghostly hills. Further down, cuts exposed the black seams of coal hundreds of feet thick. Formed by ancient sunlight sixty million years ago now dead and black.

The rise of the Black Hills uplift on the east and the Hartville on the southeast side of the basin bordered the present geologic formation, the Powder River Basin. Coal beds formed in the Tertiary eon by hydrocarbon layers in subtropical swamps inundated by ten feet of rain a year. Twenty-five million years of accumulated peat formed bogs instead of being washed to the sea. Periodically the layers of peat were weighted with sediments washed down from nearby mountains. Buried and compressed they formed coal. Over the last several million years overlying sediment washed away, leaving the coal seams near the surface.

In the pit well below the distant silo lights Henry pulled into the equipment yard and turned off the headlights of his pickup. In the quiet puddle of light inside his truck he collected his backpack and grabbed his 8000 lumen LED flashlight and lunchbox. He walked among massive machines: shovels, loaders, and monstrous earth movers silhouetted against the stars.

He picked out his assigned Cat 777G off road hauler. It could fill an entire rail hopper car with one load. In this pit his hauler was the money maker, connecting the drag line and mass excavators to the conveyors, silos, trains, steam boilers, electric generators, and finally to generating electricity.

Henry's hauler carried a hundred tons of ore at speed. It was like the giant C5 military transport compared to his pickup truck. Like an airline pilot he began a full inspection. As he shone his flashlight on each fill cap, sight gage, tank, filter, and axle fluid window he thought about what could go wrong with each system. Brakes, grease, fuel, every part of the truck needed to be checked out. He had seen lots of proof that things could go wrong in the pit. There was no stopping once he got on board. Craning his neck up to see the top of the tire he could tell it was new, usually a good sign.

He went to the front of the behemoth and swung his good leg up to the thick steel strap-step under the bumper bar and grabbed the cold handrails to pull himself up. His other boot found the square cutout in the bumper and then he climbed the seven steel treads to the railed catwalk around the cab. He opened the door, and it lit up. He set his flashlight on the seat, his thermos into the well next to it, and hung his pack on the hook. He sat and latched the door.

Turning the key in the ignition lock and checking the toggle switch bank on his left he looked at the main panel. It had a lighted 'check gauge, battery' sign and he looked over to the right to see things were geared for a full shift. Then he turned the key further and beeping began as the needles swung to indicate his battery, fuel, rpm, oil, and temperature. He turned the key fully to start up and the thousand horsepower engine rumbled to life beneath him. Checking his gauges all around and turning on his headlights, he engaged his dump bucket, raising the top of it to a full thirty feet above the mine floor and lowering it slowly back to rest. He put on his headphones, picked up the cb radio mic, and checked in for his shift.

He took the t-handle and pressed the lock button in to allow him to engage the drivetrain. Pressing on the accelerator it began moving forward ponderously. The pit boss came on his CB to let him know the route to his pick-up. The pit was like an airport with a myriad of runways, only without the lights or ground markings. Finding the correct road was important.

Ending up in the wrong place could be lethal. Some roads just ended over black cliffs, washouts, or into water.

Most of the dirt on top of the coal, the overburden, was scraped away but there was still some lighter earth at the beginning of his route. As he descended it tapered out leaving only the black wall of coal to show where he was. The easiest navigation was following the tracks of the trucks before him. Soon he had worked through all seven forward gears and was driving down the inky track descending ever deeper at forty-five mph. Down the ramp into the past.

Henry's childhood love of big machines all traced to a memory of Big Muskie, a two hundred twenty-foot-high machine with a three-hundred-foot boom that scooped three hundred tons and made the ground shake under his feet. Its scoop could hold two Greyhound buses side by side. It had moved twice the volume of earth as the Calabura Cut of the Panama Canal in its time. Henry had seen Big Muskie working on night shift in Chandlersville, Ohio and had been magic to him.

Years later he'd gone to see Big Muskie demolished in 1999. The dynamited boom crashed to the ground ending an era. The money was gone for high sulfur coal. Acid rain had killed forest life in downwind states, and they demanded scrubbers to take the sulfuric acid out of the sky. That was the death of Appalachian coal and the birth of the Powder River complex.

Strip mining required a handful of miners, and the low sulfur coal was just lying there, ready for drag lines to scoop up. The EPA had made coal companies remove abandoned equipment and Muskie was just that. In the Thunder Mine pit only one shovel was as big as Muskie, Ursa Major, or as his friend on the loader Wade called it, Ursula.

Approaching the enormous stockpile around the twenty-story high electric power shovel he was happy to hear Wade's familiar voice over his intercom. He loved hearing Wade's twang, "Yer next, bring 'er up ahead." and then "How's yer floozies? Still burning yer check on panties in town?"

"Yeah, I spent some time at the Purple Door in Deadwood, alright. Now I hook up online. Most of the old houses are tourist traps." Henry replied, "How'd you spend your time? Watching the game? Boring. Anyway, you got something for me?"

The shovel's horn sounded three seconds like a blast warning, "Here ye go...a nice big lump of coal for yer stockin'." and with that Wade opened the bottom of the bucket and dumped in fifty tons of coal, rocking Henry around his cab. Dust billowed past his windshield for a few seconds and as it cleared, he could see Wade's shovel turn on its revolving deck to face the coal. Like a pug's lower jaw, the bucket crowded the coal wall and scraped up the fractured face, filling as it went. Pulling back the boom it began its arc to deliver another load. He resettled in his seat and marveled at Wade's deft skill as he swung it back around toward him. Grateful too that the clearance above his hauler looked just right. Too high and the thunderous shower of coal could break it, too low and the fifty-ton bucket could knock him over like a Tonka toy.

"Here ye go, maybe one more dollop fer full measure?" Again, the hauler rocked as the load overflowed the hauler's bed. "Maybe not." Wade laughed, "Yer done! Alright, now git." The horn blasted again signaling his exit.

Henry rocked his hauler in reverse to shake loose Wade's comic overfill. Cascades of coal avalanched off the sides of the hauler leaving a ring around it to drive over. Then he moved out onto the darkened pit. Another hauler was awaiting a fill from Wade. With the coal aboard, his hauler handled differently, and it was an uphill climb to the off-loading shed. Getting to speed took time.

As he approached the crushing shed to dump, another hauler exited the near bay, still lowering its bucket down onto its chassis. Henry waited for him in the darkness to clear the area completely. The signal light told him to go, and he swung wide and backed into the shed carefully. Once fully at the brink, the light signaled stop. He began his dump routine. Too quick and his hauler could get squirrelly. Gravity pulled coal down the chute five stories into the crushers at the bottom. A conveyor removed crushed coal up two miles to the train loading silo he'd seen coming to work.

Load emptied, he dropped his bucket and waited for the exit light to go green. Once more he headed back to the stockpile and excavator. Another shift had begun, and he settled into the work, another night of monotony. His playlist was all set for keeping him awake; David Bowie's rock song *Rebel Rebel* played.

Henry was proud of the time he'd done as an ice road trucker building a pipeline across the Alaskan tundra. The money was great because of the risk. Ice road truckers prided themselves as the best. Ice was merciless as he'd found out. During an inspection of his rig, the machine had lost traction, slid, and injured his leg. It still ached on cold nights, and this was one of them. Being brave was only a small part of the job. Knowing what you're doing, that's what counts. Ice truckers must handle the harsher elements. It became more competitive as the permafrost melting meant fewer drivable days. His time in the frigid north didn't last and he'd gone back to Appalachia. Now he was here.

He'd put the hammer down on many of the runs in Appalachia. They would blow up a mountain and he'd haul sections of it out in his Mack Truck, driving fast along tight and narrow roads snaking through what was left of the mountains. Overloaded and under-maintained rigs had lots of problems, sometimes fatal. He spent a lot of time hoping the DOT and Highway Patrol would be somewhere else when he came through; winding along narrow roads with forty tons overloaded and always in a hurry. He got an extra run in each shift but became more concerned about living to tell the tale than making the additional money. He'd seen too many of his coworkers in wrecks. Unlucky cars pressed into the mountainside, flattened under the wheels, or shoved off the road. He'd lost a good friend who had driven their rig through a guardrail to save the other driver.

He felt the dry hot blast of air on his face and turned down the blower. It would be a long shift ahead. His mind wandered to whoring in Casper. There were plenty of girls and for a couple hundred dollars he'd be well cared for all weekend. Sometimes a john went to jail but not very often. Life in a truck is numb if things are going well. Hooking up for a weekend remained the high point. Wade's voice came over his headphones "You again, just a bad penny that keeps comin' back."

CHAPTER 7

JAN 18, 2016
DICK, LAS VEGAS, NEVADA

Dick Lockerby slouched arrogantly, studying the crisply uniformed sheriff working the prison release desk. The sheriff slid a basket with personal effects marked with his number across a putty gray countertop. Dick sorted for his watch and put it on, smiling inwardly as he felt the cold weight of the stainless steel on his wrist. His Rolex Air King came back to life when he put it on. Shifting only his eyes he checked the wall clock to reset the time, but it had remained precise. It felt like personal renewal. He would look up the price of Air King when he could spare a moment to see if it had appreciated while he was imprisoned. He checked his wallet and picked up his clothes to go change out of his prison issue.

Never one to show emotion with strangers and rarely with friends, jail time had hardened his already cold and stony presence. Dick's lips were just a thin line under his salt and pepper bristled copstache. Time in the yard had lightly tanned his usually pasty complexion. His droopy lizard eyes, dark like a slurry pond, gazed shiftily around the room. The security door buzzed open and he walked outside the prison walls for the first time in a year. The desert sun made him squint as he looked for his waiting limo. His chauffeur hopped out to open the door for him.

"Welcome back Mr. Lockerby." The chauffeur handed him a bag of hot egg McMuffins, his preferred comfort food, and pointed to chilled bottles of Moet Chandon to drink on the ride to his plane, which sat ready to take him to his condo on the Las Vegas Strip.

Settling into the leather seat he devoured them and threw the wrappers out the window. He cracked open his champagne. Smiling at the pop and watching the tiny bubbles rise he felt ready to fight anew.

He'd met so many inmates in prison who were, like himself, innocent victims of the law. Not the criminals like looters, but people in savings and finance, loans, or healthcare. Their careers were destroyed by scandals and wrongful convictions, just for doing their best work with all their might. It was the trivial people, the lazy and weak, who had brought the charges that had brought them down using those goddamn regulations.

Jail hadn't been so bad; the facility was clean and modern. The weather had been nicer than West Virginia's. The thing that hurt him most was the lack of gratitude paid to him by people who he'd employed in his mines. They would have been miserable and worthless without his company giving them honest work. There were few instances he felt they understood the privilege he offered them, of being on his team; but all too often they didn't. He'd make dealing with him a 'right to work' approach. His motto had always been 'do as I say.'

During his incarceration, President Karne had talked about removing regulations. Violating safety regulations had sent him to prison. Now heavy metals could go right into the water. A myriad of rules covered operations of a fortune 100 company and he resented each one of them. He felt like Gulliver on the beach pinned down by Lilliputian threads. They ate into his profit. Hell, that's why business existed in the first place. Making a profit and only making profit was honest work. All that crap about health and safety were impediments. President Karne was a dream come true.

Here was someone, just like him, who got the way things should be. If you weren't working on the bottom line, 'You're fired.' Nothing showed his management style more clearly than that. Numbers don't lie, they reveal performance. Those who perform deserve to rule and those who don't need to look out for themselves.

His driver pulled up to his private plane and exiting, Dick climbed the hot metal stairs into his Gulfstream. The flight attendant was a petite Vietnamese woman in her early twenties wearing a skintight skirt and lovely flowing blouse. She smiled warmly and welcomed him aboard. He brushed by without acknowledging her and went directly to his seat and stretched out for a nap. The champagne had gone to his head, so he spent the rest of the flight snoring, mouth agape.

Arriving at the private terminal in McCarran Airport, another limo picked him up and drove him to his condo on the Strip. Dick went directly to his suite on the fortieth floor. His secretary, who'd been hired as part of his severance package when he'd left the coal giant, introduced herself as Honey. She'd worked for Senator Carruthers and knew the coal business. She welcomed him and asked when he would like to have dinner at the SW Steak House in the Wynn. He answered 6:30 pm sharp, then went into the enormous bathroom to take a steam bath and freshen up from his trip. He emerged an hour and a half later in a white robe, looking like a cooked lobster wearing a snowman costume.

"Honey, take those clothes out and burn them, I never want to see them again."

"Yes of course. Anything else?" Honey took the doomed apparel and smiled sweetly.

"Look up the current value of my Sky King." He put his watch on the table for her, donning an alternative luxury timepiece for his meal.

At the SW Steakhouse a richly tanned maîtres'd' personally greeted Dick and seated him and his guests at Dick's favorite table near the fountain. Dining together were Dick, Honey, his former WV Supreme Court

Judge, a former scientist, and two ad agency people. Dick looked around the table expansively, "It's good to be here with you all. The funny thing is that the good people I met inside jail are better than the people in government who put them there." They all laughed on cue.

During cocktails and spirits, he pointedly asked how each of them was enjoying the hotel and spa treatments for their wives, or in the judge's case, the company of an escort. Without saying so, Dick wanted confirmation that the money he spent on them was accounted for. Satisfied, he then switched to his big news, he wanted them to be first to know. He pushed back from the table and stood. Looking around at his faithful team in this splendid restaurant, he took a moment and savored how far he'd come from his childhood. Growing up he had watched his mother's store and from the rooftop in the evening, witnessed miners coming out of the bar and bare knuckle brawling on weekends. His life was finally classy.

"I am running for Senator of West Virginia." he practiced smiling and looking around the table, "This is the way to get my life back. You have no idea how unfair it is to be in jail." he said in monotone, "I'm going to run the platform 'America First,' let them know I'm an 'American competitionist' and a champion of miners." The table burst into applause. People at other tables looked put out by their loud outburst but nobody at their table cared. He sat down again.

"You certainly deserve to be a senator. You were doing a fine job." Intoned his judge, an aging rotund hamster looking man, with a pointed nose and tiny eyes named Baron. Dick didn't have to follow the law so long as Baron was on the bench and in his pocket.

"Another thing I want is to get that liberal bastard senator who sent me away. Once I take his seat, I'll make him wish he'd never messed with me. He'll regret it, that's for damn sure. Maybe he can spend some time in jail. Perhaps I'll lock his whole fucking family up too. Him and those greeniac pain the asses going on about global warming."

Baron quickly agreed "He'll rue the day he crossed you, Dick. Just like all the others."

Dick continued looking around at his team, "So when I run they will throw up my past; those dead miners, the pollution, and mountaintops gone. We needed to play rough to get things done. Still, what do you think? How should we deal with it? Suggestions?"

A small, thin, PR man from the ad agency was at the table. He had sunken cheeks and a peculiar wisp of white hair alone above his forehead and was wearing a very expensive store-bought cowboy outfit including a string tie. He offered, "We change the debate away from you and towards the regulators, the government, and the lazy people on the dole. We can make people think regulators make it dangerous for mine operators to safely mine coal. We want to run against things your folks already hate. We've spent years building resentment and entitlement into their self-image. We can build off that and regulators are a start."

"That is a fact, I like that. So how do we use it, get that out?" Dick scanned the table.

Baron started a new line, "Isn't there something personal about our Senator we can go after? Hasn't he done, or not done, something we can exploit? Maybe the opioid crisis growing on his watch?"

Dick had settled back into his seat and held an elegant pistol grip steak knife in one hand and a fork poised in the other. The waiters placed his enormous steak in front of him and the group in unison. He nodded to Baron's comment then looked around and said "One group that's going to come after me are the environmentalists. They have a lot of support as people seem to get all excited for clean air and water. What do we do about them?"

The other flack chimed in, "We paint them as eco-terrorists attacking America's working families. After all, they are trying to stop mining coal. We say they are 'outsiders' who cause trouble and disrupt the livelihoods of hard-working folks."

Baron interrupted him, "Did you see Munky's wife smack that protester on the news? She just walked up to their leader, right through the marchers, like a Pit Bull, and attacked; smacked her across her face. That's some woman. They say bad things about her husband and smack! They got what they deserve." He looked at Dick for affirmation. Dick gave a rare laugh; Munky's wife reminded him of his mother. He'd seen her muscle people out of her store on many occasions 'no cash, no bread.' Not someone to trifle with. "Amen to that. I did a lot of that myself when I was getting started, and worse, breaking strikes and unions."

Baron followed up, "So now, with Karne getting sworn in as US President, coal is back. We'll see how much our donations bought us." He leered a conspiratorial chubby grin while chewing.

The PR man with the string tie added, "So back to your negatives, the mine explosion is still fresh in people's minds. We've got to have something to redirect. Don't ever answer a question about it, just switch topics immediately." he paused before offering his idea, "How about 'the regulators are supposed to make the mines safe but instead they are ginning up 'witch hunts' going after honest business.' That way we move the focus onto them."

Larry, the other flack, jumped in, "When it comes to the responsibility for the explosion you need to have 'acts of God' at the ready. Remember in Utah where they had some dead miners? Before they got the bodies out there was old Bob Munky himself at the media microphone repeating over and over that it was an earthquake. God did it! That's the message discipline we need for you."

String tie chimed, "That's right. Who can say for certain that this flood or that mudslide or the pollution of an aquifer is absolutely your fault. Even the buildup of methane before your explosion could be sent all the way upstairs to the Almighty. Nobody's going to criticize Him."

Baron added, "Don't forget the mission of coal, to bring power to the world's poor huddled masses. It is a mission of hope and light that will lift them from poverty and give them health and education." He couldn't help cracking his devious hamster smile.

Dick finished wolfing down his enormous meal while they fawned over his run for Senator. He was satisfied that his team was back in gear working for him, "Well alright. I'm running for Senate as a Republican in West Virginia. I'm in for half a million in already and I'll put in whatever it takes to win, I'm sure the party will help me out. Now let's enjoy dessert." The waiters lit their flaming Cherries Jubilee with drama and set them down in front of the expectant diners.

Larry noted, "So first thing is to win the primary, then we can get moving on our incumbent without delay. Maybe Karne will endorse you, he won big in West Virginia."

"Maybe he will, we are cut from the same timber." Dick considered himself and Karne as bonded in character. "Like George Washington, can't tell a lie."

After dessert Dick's young wife, Sherry, clicked over to the table in her Jimmy Choo's and sparkling gown. She leaned in sharing her newly enhanced cleavage to the table. She tousled his hair carefully with her elaborate scarlet fingernails to avoid displaying his bald spot and then flirted with them. "Sorry to take Dickie away but it has been a long time, if you know what I mean." She winked her eyelash extensions to emphasize the point.

Dick stood and excused himself, telling the party to continue at his expense with after dinner drinks. He whispered to Honey to record who had what and to put the bill on his account. Sherry grabbed his ass as they walked out to her waiting red Bentley. Dick slouched into the hot pink leather seat next to her. She drove them out of town to their grandiose home. Part hotel, part villa, an advertisement of their wealth and power. Trumped up, gaudy, and cancerously tacky it showcased all the class cash can buy.

CHAPTER 8

JAN 20, 2016
JC AND TED, GLACIER RANCH, MONTANA

JC and Ted went up to the house. As they entered a wood pellet stove roared to life creaking as the metal expanded. JC made a beeline to it and put his hands out to warm, he was freezing from the snowmobile ride.

The first room was large and served as living, dining, and kitchen with bookshelves lining all the walls. Ted opened a door and said "You can have this room, put your stuff over there. Over there is an outhouse. The water is off because it is winter, but I have plenty inside. Just find a tree if you need to pee." He looked around and said, "Roll out your bag on this bed."

The minimal kitchen only boasted a stove top and sink. Ted pulled out a bowl and set water on the floor for Wrigley, asking JC, "Do you have dog food?"

JC dug into his backpack "Yeah, here it is." He held out a nearly empty little bag of dry food. Ted took it and emptied it into another Pyrex bowl and set it on the floor and the puppy attacked it instantly as Ted refilled the water from a blue jug atop a stand.

There was a stocked propane refrigerator and freezer. Ted took a couple of big cans of chili off the shelf and pulled a block of cheddar cheese out of the freezer. He made two huge bowls and cut off hunks of cheddar which he put on top then microwaved each of them. He got out salsa and a bag of chips and chopped off chunks of a long dry salami. He put out a couple glasses of water and two spoons. "Let's eat."

JC was ravenously hungry and attacked his food. The stove in the other room stopped heating and the silence was only broken by the chewing and slurping. JC was warm for the first time in a week. He looked over toward Ted and behind him saw Wrigley happily sleeping near the pellet stove. Wrigley's feet were faintly running in the air, keeping time to some dream chase. He paused eating and said "Thanks."

"No problem." Ted was wolfing down another bowl full. "You clean up." Ted left and went out to the shop building.

JC cleaned up the dishes. This place was so nice and at the same time mysterious. He was curious, there were so many things he'd never seen. There were a lot of maps and some photos on the walls. Most interesting were some old Indian things. A feathered headdress and some painted leather pieces looked intriguing, but he didn't know what they might be. There was a pair of old Army snow goggles and a rucksack made of canvas. Behind it was a photo of Camp Hale, a rock festival called Tomorrowland, Sturgis motorcycles, and a poster of a painting of weird creatures in hell by Hieronymus Bosch. Next to that was a depiction of an Indian ceremony with braves hung from ropes by hooks in their flesh. JC shuddered at the thought. Moving to the living room he paged through a big format book, *Plundering Appalachia*, by Butler and saw photos by Wuerthner of moonscape looking mountaintops like the one at Grammys.

He peeked into Ted's bedroom. Spartan for the most part but some old, framed photos hanging on the walls. One was Ted in Marine dress, another a very pregnant native woman with her adoring husband Ted, and lastly a photo of a raven-haired beauty holding a protest sign 'Stop the Coal Train.' He quickly moved on, intimidated by the sparse intimacy.

On the door to his room was a photo of Ted Kaczynski in an orange jumpsuit on a billboard. The Unabomber was captioned saying 'I still believe in Global Warming. Do you?' On a small piece of paper taped below it read, 'According to the Heartland Institute's own press release the Unabomber image was only the first in a series to also feature Osama bin Laden, Charles Manson, Fidel Castro, and other global warming alarmists. The most prominent advocates of global warming aren't scientists. The leaders of the global warming movement have one thing in common: They are willing to use force and fraud to advance their fringe theory.'-Joseph Bast, Heartland President. Underneath the poster and clipping hung a USMC dress sword in its scabbard.

The last item on the door was a clipping titled 'Black Snow' with a photo showing the soot covered snow in a small town in Siberia downwind from coal generation. JC was creeped out and disgusted seeing snow blackened to where it looked like chocolate dip on a vanilla cone. The article stated the Siberians were seeking asylum in Canada as eco-refugees.

JC opened the door to go outside, thinking how out of place he was and immediately the cold air hit him. He gasped for breath and rushed back inside to get his inhaler. Wrigley shot out and bounded over to the shop building. Braced against the cold, JC went back out to a tree, inhaler in pocket, and relieved himself. He saw the paw prints leading to the door where Wrigley went into the shop.

Inside sturdy workbenches ran along both walls. Some floor mounted machines occupied special locations. Many of them were foreign to him but the metal saws, drill press, and big heavy-duty jacks and hoists he'd seen at the train yard. Above it all there was a crane that ran on rails along the side walls and could go anywhere in the space. Halfway down Ted had a ski in a vice and was sharpening its edge. Wrigley was hopping up on his leg again. "Sorry, I just went out to take a leak and then needed my inhaler.

Wrigley got out." nervously he added, "That tow truck looks really old." He noticed Ted's hand had a patch of boiled skin scaring the back of his wrist.

"Yeah, it was my father's Oshkosh, a rare beast, he loved that thing. It is impossible to get parts but I keep it running. That snowplow has saved a few folks too. He'd drag just about anything in here to work on it. He'd go down to Browning and his Blackfeet relatives would rope him into fixing some ancient pickups or pumps and it was easier just to bring them over here than try to fix them there."

JC felt like a kid in the candy store looking at all the cool stuff. Noticing the taxidermized head hanging on the wall he said, "Wow, that's a huge head!" Ted looked up from his filing, "That's Buffalo Bob, my great grandfather's trophy.

He had some balls; he was on foot when he shot Bob. He told us about how in times before the horse and rifle, braves and the Medicine Man would keep running after the buffalo like a pack of wolves and scare them to stampede," he looked at JC, "then they'd steer them off a cliff to their death. They called it a buffalo jump. There's a state park named for it south of here. Piles of bones ten feet deep at the bottom of the cliff."

Ted paused to open the vice and turn up the other edge of the ski, "My grandfather was scouting a path through the Rocky Mountains for the Great Northern Railroad. Blackfeet showed him their trail at the head-waters of the Marias River as a way through, like Sacajawea did for Lewis and Clark.

"He met my grandmother in the summer of 1890 near here at Two Medicine Lakes. He was fishing out on the lake. She was gathering herbs on the shore. One look and he was smitten. Her people were Bloods down from Canada for the Sun Dance." He paused his sharpening and gave Wrigley a pat on the head this pup's company helped him loosen up from his heavy decision to transform his life for a quest.

"It's huge." JC was still staring at the buffalo. Then realizing he was out of sync asked, "What's a Sun Dance?"

"It's an annual gathering of tribes and ceremony. Sometimes hosted at Two Medicine Lakes near the rail siding where you were waiting. Tribes come down from Canada to join in."

"Like a convention?"

"A lot is going on; trading and socializing between tribes and then there are rituals and important awards. There is dancing, singing, and drumming, all night sometimes. The main event happens around a lodge pole."

"Oh." JC had no idea what it was now. He felt overwhelmed, just being inside and away from the trains was a lot but this was all new to him.

Ted spotted a small nick in the side rail of his ski and got a coarser file off the wall "When my grandparents were first married, they lived in a tipi near the tribe. Later they moved here; it was a simple cabin with dirt floors and wood construction." He turned the other edge up and began to file it too, "He built this place when he finished working for the railroad. My father did more of the same, adding to it when he was home…" Ted trailed off, getting lost in a memory for a moment, then continued.

"I grew up in Bellingham in Washington state but spent half the year here. Dad worked in the boat yards of Anacortes. Out here he worked on cars, trucks, and farm equipment. He could weld almost anything too. People would come and find him when they had anything too difficult." He examined and adjusted the binding, "He loved gunsmithing, he could mill almost any part of a gun. He nodded to a far corner hosting an antique safe, "Inside that safe's a fine gun collection. He was a popular man."

"That's amazing." JC was impressed. This shop was so much bigger than anything he'd ever seen. His eye caught an antique miner's helmet with a metal 'Homestake' name plate riveted to it. "Cool helmet. I remember those from home."

Ted was finished with his skis and asked, "How did you end up here anyway?"

"I was in the railyard in Chicago and as I ran to catch a train the dust off a coal train started my asthma, so I missed it. The next train that came through going west came here." he paused, "What time is the train going west tomorrow?"

"It is scheduled to come by here at about nine in the morning. Charge your phone and keep it on airplane mode until you need it as they lose power fast searching for signals around here. You should get some sleep. Your ride to Bellingham is going to be tough. I'll get you out to the siding tomorrow."

JC yawned and noticed Wrigley was sleeping again. He slid his arms under him and carried the boneless body back to the cabin. His breath stung his lungs; he hadn't realized the shop was so much warmer. There were still so many fascinating objects to see but he was beat.

When he got back to his room, he organized his pack. Looking around he noticed odd books packed into shelves filling the bedroom. Books on chemical and civil engineering, trains, physics, politics, and books on climate. A whole wall had manuals on repair for snowmobiles, trucks, pumps, generators, and tools of all types. The closet was stuffed with climbing gear, down outerwear suits, motorcycle clothes, boots, and some sleeping bags hung like cocoons. JC had no energy to give more than a glance. He unrolled his sleeping bag and slid into a deep sleep hugging Wrigley. Ted, still at the workbench continued his sharpening.

Dull morning light came in and Wrigley jumped up and licked JC's face until he woke up. Ted yelled from the kitchen it was time to eat and get going. Ted gave him a gallon of water, Cliff bars, and a big can of Spam for Wrigley. JC could barely squeeze them into his backpack.

"It will be cold, take this to keep your pup from freezing." Ted zipped Wrigley into a puffy old orange down vest with a torn zipper and an ugly burn. Outside a foot of powder covered everything; white sky and mountains merged. Wrigley bounded around in the snow barely able to keep above it, filling the vest with snow.

Ted drove JC down to the tracks on his snowmobile. When JC and Wrigley got off Ted held out a business card with ALU on it and said, "If you need work in Bellingham here is how to reach me. I weld and we have some hourly jobs."

JC stuffed it in his pocket. "Thanks, I've got a cousin, well, sort of cousin, who lives there. She said they might have something for me where she works at a library. They need help moving books sometimes."

Intermittent sounds of a train echoed off the cliffs and drifted into their conversation. Ted patted Wrigley, "Take good care of this pup." then left. JC walked out toward the end of the loop that faced back toward the east. When he got to the intersection where the tracks and the siding loop joined, he looked around. The train's horn startled him, and the triple headlights were so bright they hurt his eyes. The earth shook with the rumble and roar of the oncoming behemoth.

His attention shifted to hopping on board without getting hurt. JC was pretty good at sprinting but if he worked too hard his asthma would kick in and that could be real trouble and now, he had Wrigley too. Luckily it was going slowly and shouldn't be a problem. After the engines went by JC found the spot he was looking for, an open boxcar with a tarped and chained machine in the center. He ran like hell holding Wrigley in his jacket, threw the water on, pushed Wrigley on, then his pack. He could feel an asthma attack coming as he ran to get a hold on the car. When he got into the car, he took several deep breaths. He hated having asthma. His deep breathing helped and he felt better now. Happy to be heading west again. Jamming his pack under the fat chains securing the load he relaxed and sat down. Wrigley came over and hopped into his lap.

He liked the front of the train, seeing ahead without a long line of cars blocking his view. The train was a mix of cars that stretched back endlessly. He despised the dust and grime that blew off the cars, it was hard to breathe if you got behind them. He felt lucky finding this flatcar.

JC zipped up Wrigley's funky vest, glad it hadn't fallen off. He laughed at how silly the pup looked with Wrigley's legs through the arm holes. He then fished his sleeping bag out of his pack. He tried adjusting his pack so he wouldn't be too visible at the crossings. As the train traced the southern edge of Glacier National Park the sun poked through and lit the upper ridges. He wondered how long it would be before he got into Bellingham.

Ted's card fell out 'ALU Allied Logistics Unlimited, Theodore Walton, Alumothermic Welding Specialist, Anacortes, Washington.' He remembered that his grandfather had talked about welding rails together that way. JC had seen them set a cauldron filled with aluminum and iron powder right on the rail joint and then a blinding whoosh, molten steel and the rails fused together. Then they chipped off the slag and used a grinder to smooth it out. It was amazing to watch, instant molten steel anywhere.

Ted parked his snowmobile and returned to his cabin. He mused about JC, so out of touch with nature in Glacier yet a solid young man. Wrigley, funny and strong, just like his childhood dog, Jack. He wondered if they would make it to Bellingham in the dead of winter.

He pondered the story of the mythical snakes eating all the gold. He was between the world of reason and spirit. His decision to heal the world, what his Jewish friend taught as tikkun olam, meaning 'world repair,' was made now. He needed to bring his whole self to the quest.

He went out to the shop and gathered a selection of tools. He threw them into his ATV and drove up through the snow to the lone tree. It had been hit by lightning after his father and grandfather were buried on high litter; where they were set free from this world to find the Sand Hills. Now was a time to put his spirit quest to the test.

He dug carefully between the roots through the snow and then down with pick and shovel through the hard ground for some time. Three feet down into the soil he found the metal bars he had been told of in child-hood. He dug fully around until he could lift them out. They were wedged tightly into the roots and covered in black pitch. He put them in his pack and returned to his workshop.

Ted scraped the brittle pitch away and then took them over to a de-gunking sink to clean the tar off them. Each solid gold bar shed their slimy black skin exposing 'Homestake' incised into the surface. Just as they'd said. He stacked them on a clean shop towel just under Buffalo Bob's furry head.

CHAPTER 9

JAN 20, 2016
PALMER AND MEL, TOPANGA CANYON, CALIFORNIA

Palmer, an imposing, athletic man with white hair combed back like a badger, strode out from his pool deck down the wide bluestone steps flowing under the arch of purple Wisteria blossoms into his pergola. Comfortable in his luxurious terry cloth robe and leather hand tooled flip flops he padded happily along in the tunnel it formed. Winter noon day sun dappled the rusticated granite walk. The only sound was the faint buzz of bees working in the blossoms collecting pollen from the trees laden with oranges. He walked along to a stone patio which opened at the end looking down on the sparkling Pacific Ocean. The sweep of coastal vista was breathtaking from atop his bluff.

Reaching in his monogrammed pocket for his minijet lighter he felt the technological marvel. From his other pocket he pulled out a Cuban Partagas Black cigar, unwrapped it and guillotined the end. He slid it beneath his nose and savored the aromas. Igniting his intense butane fire and applying it to fresh cut he put it to his thin lips and gently drew in, creating an orange glow and a wisp of smoke at the tip. His first puff of oily toothy carcinogenic smoke filled him with delight. What a perfect day he thought, admiring his private ocean.

His phone buzzed in his robe pocket, and he looked at the name displayed with some distaste but took the call anyway. "Palmer here." His expression hardened as he listened. After a minute he became agitated and walked back up, phone pasted to his ear while swinging his cigar with the other arm. The other end of the call went on and on. "Just a minute." Mounting the stairs to the deck, flicking his ash casually into the swimming pool, crossing the deck, he opened the heavy teak French doors into his study. Settling in his high-backed glove leather office chair he swiveled until he came around to where he could put his feet up on the desk. The voice on the other end paused.

"Well, goddam fix it! I don't want to have some jerk-off on the news yelling about our trillion-dollar coal reserves being worthless. What would you do if they said your 401K balance was zero?" He ended the call. His desk was appointed with his humidor and a couple of decanters with his favorite scotches. Grabbing a glass he opened the refrigerated ice bucket, threw a couple of perfectly clear frozen spheres in and covered them with single malt, Oban. Swirling his glass he thought to himself what incompetence... How does this sort of thing happen?

Don't they understand anything? Of course, you can't reason with people like that. All self-righteous, and now getting in our way. You need to be smarter, you need to be first, and you need to be effective. He'd always acted that way. It worked. The very idea of a tipi village camped on his project. Did they think this was a child's game?

He went back out to the pool where his secretary Mel, worked at a table in the shade on her iPad. She was dressed for summer in pale yellow culottes and a matching lacey sweater. Her hat had a broad brim and blocked the sun so she could work. Looking up at him over her sunglasses she queried "What can I do for you?"

As usual his mind raced into what he'd like to do but he put that aside and said "I need you to get our people on this terminal protest now." He thought it over for a bit and then dictated a letter to the men he expected to 'fix it.' Puffing and sipping his drink he said, "Call our attorneys general and let them know we need a lot of legal support. Now. If you need any help, call ALEC, the guys that ginned up the Tea Party. They will write up anything you need. You know our guy there. Get this out now." He paused looking back at the ocean considering a return to his reverie in his pergola but instead threw his cigar in the pool and went in to dress.

Mel gracefully stood up holding her iPad, slipped on her clogs and left the poolside. She went to Palmer's office and wrote to Jerry Moroney, the Attorney General she had been paired with the week before at the Republican Attorney General Association 'RAGA' meeting. She'd see just how much he was willing to do to fill his side of the bargain. They could get things done, like when they scuttled the Clean Power Plan.

She had a big ask; hiring police and private security to break up protests on public lands. Time to play hard ball instead of policy changes. She also began working on the notice to the Governor that this was going to be a priority for him. Her job was to bring them to heel and iron out the roles for each of them to do Palmer's bidding.

After she finished, she called their flack, Tracy Punch, to see what could be done. Tracy responded with the usual litany of ideas. "Hey, the activists are the bad guys here. But when we play hard it is easy for them to show themselves as victims. Remember, we are the victims, they are the eco-terrorists."

The conversation left Mel thinking Tracy wasn't very creative, offering only victim reversing and redirection. Jobs, jobs, and jobs. Saving poor people in the third world from energy poverty. So tired and such bullshit. She knew the numbers. More people are employed in pet food research than coal mining these days. Helping poor people was such hypocritical whitewash. Maybe it was time for a new PR agency.

She was surprised by a text reply from Moroney while she was working on her letter to the Governor. That's what I call good service, she thought to herself. She called him, "It was fun kayaking with you at the Greenbrier meeting. I had no idea you were such an outdoorsman."

"So, what can I do for you?" asked Moroney eagerly.

"Our coal in the PRB won't be worth much if we can't get to tidewater to serve new markets in Asia. We need your help getting the clearances for building the loading terminal at Cherry Point. I don't need to mention that now is the time. What we can't stand is delays and that's what these protests are causing us. We need you to give us cover to take off the gloves."

"Don't worry, I'm on it. I'll find some legal avenues and regulations so we can make these delays go away and justify extra security." After some description of the courses, he added "Tell Palmer I really appreciate our trip to St. Andrews. I love golf and that fulfilled my lifelong dream to play there."

She thought to herself what whores these guys were. She'd seen them just cut and paste letters and submit them for legislation or change their positions mid-sentence when Palmer pulled their leash. She wrapped up on the communications and returned to her spot by the pool.

Palmer came out dressed for work. "Give me a copy of my speech and listen while I run through."

She handed him the printout of his speech for the chamber presentation later that afternoon. Looking him over she assayed his attire at about five thousand dollars. Clothes make the man, she thought to herself.

"This is it so far." He straightened to his impressive height and fixed his gaze on Mel and read aloud, "Now is our time, we have a green light. Markets in India and China are where we can sell. They are the only countries building new plants and that is our demand. While they build electric coal burning plants, we need a tidewater connection. We need the Cherry Point and Millennium Terminals, and we need them now.

We need to sell in China and India if we are going to get the coal out and make some money. We are competing with major national players in these markets and their domestic production too. We can't be choked off from the efficient sea routes we need. This is the time for PRB like no other. We have the coal and the trains to get it to tidewater, but we need those terminals.

I don't need to tell you about the cost of rules and regulations. We now have a coal friendly administration and they have proclaimed our return to commerce. Things are going to be easier. We are open for business again.

Competition is heating up. Natural gas is killing us in domestic markets and wind too; even solar is rising. Because of the economy using less energy Powder River Basin Coal producers have seen our domestic markets decline. We don't have automatic sales anymore.

These terminals will drop our cost to supply Asia. We can make progress, but we need to invest heavily now while we can operate freely and get things done because nobody has a good tidewater terminal on the west coast. To tap these markets, we need terminals.

So, to close, tidewater is the prize. Time is money. This is our window while our coal is still close to the surface, and we have our boy in the White House."

Palmer finished and looked for her response, "Is it too long?"

"Just about right." Mel nodded her approval. She always felt dirty after giving him the go ahead. She didn't believe that coal expanding into new markets was a good idea; she just couldn't pass up the money.

Palmer's phone buzzed; the limo driver texted that he was outside. Palmer admired Mel for a moment, such talent, and a beautiful young woman too. Then he left for his conference.

CHAPTER 10
JAN 22, 2016
JULIA AND JC, BELLINGHAM, WASHINGTON

Julia was reading her book, nestled deep in the cushions of the over-stuffed chair in the clinic with a hot cup of herbal tea. Her coworker, Carol, continued filling out forms when the doorbell rang. She looked up and saw a huge silhouette made by a police car's flashing lights on the antique frosted glue chip pattern glass of the entry door. Carol put down her papers, rushed over, and opened it.

"Hi Joe, come on in." The county sheriff, tented in a reflectorized top-coat and hat, banged into the doorframe as he turned to get through with a young man slung like a big duffel bag over his shoulder. Puffing with effort, Joe set him down in the waiting room chair.

He straightened up, catching his breath. When he could speak, he said, "Hi Carol, I found him down by the tracks in the park, damn near froze to death. He can't talk. Take a look right now, will you? He's about half dead."

"Sure thing, Joe." Carol looked shocked and quickly moved to triage the unconscious man in the chair. She made sure he was still breathing, double checking because his breath was barely noticeable. She pushed back his hood and put her fingers on his carotid artery, he was icy to her touch. She pulled off his glove and his inhaler fell out and clattered across the waxed wood floor. Julia picked up the inhaler and raced to find another. Luckily, they had a couple in their supply cabinet.

After a bit Joe went out to his cruiser and reappeared with a big back-pack and set it down. "This is his, take a look when you can and see if you can help me figure out who we have here."

Carol and Julia ignored him and lifted the unconscious man into a wheelchair and rolled him into the bedroom that was the clinic's exam-ination room. Julia lifted his hand and gently placed one of the inhalers and closed his stiff fingers around it. She raised his arm up and put it to his mouth, she pressed the button, and he took a breath. He slowly opened his eyes and looked up into her face. His eyelids fluttered and he lost con-sciousness. Julia helped him take some more breaths. After a few minutes she decided he'd be able to breathe on his own.

Carol said, "You'll be ok, but stay with us tonight." JC was unrespon-sive. Turning around she continued, "Joe, come get him tomorrow." then to Julia, "Put him in the back room and let's thaw him out." Julia and Carol rolled him down the hall and into the back bedroom. It had a metal framed single bed made up, but the rest was cluttered with crutches, bedpans, some dressing supplies, and the cleaning closet. Julia and Carol managed to get him out of the wheelchair onto the bed. They stripped off his clothes and checked to see if he had other medical problems.

Carol left Julia to get him warmed up and returned to her station. Julia began to slow process of thawing him out using hot water bottles and an electric blanket. Placing the hot water bottle on his stomach, she held his cold hands to see if she could get any response.

Julia could hear the Sheriff and Carol talking in the other room as they went through his backpack. Carol asked quizzically, holding up a leash, "What the heck is he doing with this?"

Joe said, "I don't know, but there was a dog barking, that's why I got out to look. It was strange. I thought it was a person wearing a vest but then he kept barking! When I tried to catch him, he ran away down the tracks. Lucky for this guy or I'd have driven by." Joe scratched his head near his bald spot.

Joe chatted, "Did you hear about the South African who ended up in the morgue refrigerator for 21 hours?" He paused for effect." Turns out he wasn't dead! Started screaming bloody murder in the night when he realized where he was. It was so scary the nurses thought he was a ghost and wouldn't open his mortuary fridge! He just had a massive asthma attack, and his family couldn't find his heartbeat. They took him for dead and dropped him off. How scary would that be?"

Carol laughed darkly and interrupted "Yeah, you know the whole 'dead ringer' story I assume?"

Joe replied, "Putting bells in with the corpse so if they weren't actually dead, they could get some attention?"

Carol shot back. "How about Not Dead Fred? You know, he's 'not dead yet' when they throw him on the cart?" Joe smiled; Monty Python was his favorite growing up.

"That's a good one." They loved joking about old tv skits, it took the edge off some situations,

Carol offered. "How about some hot coffee?"

"Yes, but I'd better get back out there. Can I take one to go?"

They made small talk and Carol gave him his coffee in a big styrofoam cup with double sugar and cream. "Keep safe out there." Carol brought Julia the backpack.

Dr. Alice came out from her nap and checked JC over to make sure he would be ok. She reassured Julia who was still working to revive him that he would live. "It will take all night to get him back. Take it slow. Call me if he doesn't stabilize, anytime is fine." She said, yawning, on her way out the door, glad her shift was over.

Julia refilled the hot water bottle several times before any improvement began to show. The electric blanket he was laying on was a sharp contrast to his heatless form. She rubbed his hands and legs.

Julia caught herself looking at him and realized how handsome she thought he was. She looked through his stuffed backpack for another inhaler. There were none, instead she found a small old photo with him and maybe his sister wearing a track medal. She had her arm around him, and he was beaming.

Carol came in at four am and checked JC. She looked at Julia and gave her a thumbs up. She went back to the front desk and logged out from her shift. She got a cup full of coffee and came in for a last look, "Take good care of our mystery man. Joe said he'll come back and pick him up when we call. Good luck." She yawned, stretched, and grabbed her overcoat, leaving Julia alone in the clinic.

JC warmed up as the night wore on. Julia got out her autoharp and played some of her favorite bluegrass songs. It was a way to pass the time. She spent a lot of it looking at him wondering what his story was. JC drifted in and out of consciousness; sometimes he seemed to respond to a tune.

Finally near dawn JC seemed stable to Julia. She covered him carefully with the electric blanket and stroked his hair up past his forehead. He was warm to her touch and it made her feel good despite her exhaustion. She turned off the lights and went back to her chair to read. As often happened she fell asleep with the book in her lap in the quiet hours of early morning.

JC startled awake as he thought he heard Wrigley bark outside. He realized he was naked and had no idea where he was. His fingers and toes were throbbing painfully. He rubbed them and soon his pain diminished. He looked around and saw Julia sitting silently in the next room with her head back and her mouth slightly open. She had a book open across her knees and her autoharp on the floor beside her.

The clinic was quiet aside from the constant hiss of the steam register heating the room. He saw his clothes hanging up, rose quietly, and put them on. His whole body ached. He went around the clinic and collected his things and put them into his pack. He looked around again to see if anything was missing. It all seemed to be there, including his cash.

JC quietly made his exit from the clinic. Carefully closing the door to avoid ringing the little bells at the top. No way did he want to explain his circumstance to anyone. He wanted to get Wrigley, hoping he was ok.

The day nurse, a prim and cheerful woman with freckles, came in and set a tray of homemade chocolate chip cookies on the coffee stand. She looked at Julia asleep in her chair and waited to see if she would wake, then gently shook her shoulder. "Wake up sleepy head. You need to go home and get some rest." Julia moved to get up and her book fell to the floor. Picking it up she saw the empty bed.

"Thanks. Did you see the boy who was here as you came in?" Julia asked, pointing to the empty cot.

"No, nobody there."

Julia wondered if Sheriff Joe could have collected him while she was sleeping.

CHAPTER 11

FEB 10, 2016
TED AND PETER, ALU, ANACORTES, WASHINGTON

Ted had left his Glacier home and went to his job at ALU in Anacortes. It is the northern terminus of the US maritime industry. Along the water's edge across from Deadman Bay on Guemes Island is the ALU drydock and ship fitting yard. It is an unimaginative concrete pad ringed by buildings and a floating dry dock. It hosts repairs and construction for maritime customers. Well-lit chain link fencing encloses the entire property and a locked gate restricts access.

Ted worked double shifts sometimes into the night in a two-story steel shed, marked with a stenciled 'C' eight feet high in orange on a battered roll-up door. Inside, an enormous long cylindrical metal shaft ran diagonally across most of the available floor space in the center. Thick as an oil drum, it rests on blocking; wedged securely to a wooden framework.

Toward the end an oddly shaped refrigerator sized box is positioned on top. Several tall portable propane tanks stand safely off to the side, piping fuel to blue flames playing directly on the shaft. Work-stand lights flood into the box. Inside there is a large open tray with a couple of drains; one at the top, and one going out down below the shaft.

They are all in preparation for a thermite weld. Thermite is a simple mix of powdered iron and aluminum that chemically mix and melt together at a very high temperature and have been used for a century to weld railroad rails together. The train rails were tiny compared to this weld repairing a driveshaft from a big ship.

Ted was seated inside the overhead crane operators' box on the beam across the span, positioning a crucible above the shaft. He pulled down on the cue ball sized knob in his right hand and moved his left up to the console; then flipped the switch, locking it in place. He looked out through the glass into the shop under the arm of his crane at the hook on the bulky metal form suspended over the box on the enormous shaft. On the shop floor Peter, the shop foreman, was satisfied with its final position. He looked at Ted and signaled thumbs up.

Ted sat back against the cold vinyl seat. After a final study of the massive hook, he returned a thumbs up to Peter. He reached over and opened the door to the cab, climbed out, stretched for a minute, and clanged down the small ladder to the shop floor. He waved at Peter who now had begun his preparation to weld the crucible in place above the shaft.

To flow molten thermite into the break in the shaft, the pour must deliver a steady supply from top to bottom. Ted dragged a rolling ladder into place to take a look at the connection between the box and crucible still hanging from the crane atop the drive shaft. The whole monstrous thing looked like a fallen tree with a strange burl growing on top of it. He pointed a laser thermometer to check multiple points of metal for preheating results.

Flipping down the face shield attached to his hard hat, he climbed a rolling ladder and peered down into the tray to see the breakthrough the drain channel. The blast of heat from the industrial gas preheaters pushed against his face-shield and he could see both faces of the break in the shaft.

They were a quarter inch apart running clear through the shaft to the bottom. In his shadow from the upper light his silhouette was filled with dancing flames. He pulled back and turned on the laser alignment beams and checked the end targets to ensure nothing had moved.

"Come take a look. "Ted asked.

Peter came over and squeezed alongside Ted atop the ladder.

Ted turned to Peter. "It should work, if we wedge it right and it doesn't fall over when we fire it up."

Ted and Peter had spent many long nights working like this on outsized welds. Peter yelled over the heaters. "What's it take to break something like this?"

Ted answered. "Probably just the thrust bearing couldn't take the load." I think they had a normal run; this was a scheduled inspection discovery."

Peter said. "They want it soon, you think we can give it to them by Saturday next week?"

"Should be ready though shearing and grinding's going to take some time." Ted replied.

Peter smirked, "Glad I don't have to do it. Don't worry, we'll get the Grinder Bros on it. Aside from headbanging and obsession with belt sander races, they're good at these big chores."

"What's a belt sander race?" Ted asked.

Peter startled at Ted not knowing something. "You plug in a belt sander on a long extension cord, lock the trigger button on, and put it on the floor." he looked at Ted, "It's funny watching them skitter and bounce across the shop floor. When they reach the end of the extension cord it pulls out and they don't have any juice. Some crash into stuff but if they go straight the winner is the farthest to travel."

"Sounds like fun… just not near the heaters or my weld. Are you finished tacking the crucible into place?"

"It's good for now." Peter answered.

Ted left to go back to the crane again, lowering the hook so Peter could unhook the cables holding the crucible. Peter signaled thumbs up and Ted rolled the crane away from the work area and parked it. He climbed down from the cab and went off to get a forklift.

A while later Ted unlocked doors to a cargo container on the back wall. Inside it was piled high with palletized sacks. He drove over in the large forklift and pulled out a full pallet. When he came into the light, Peter could see they were marked 'Thermite.' He swung around next to the form and lowered it to the shop floor.

Peter looked up and said, "There's an hour or two ahead. Let's get some coffee?"

Ted cocked his head and stretched, rubbing his neck. Walking over, he rechecked Peter's welds, tacking the mold to the shaft enclosure. He took off his hardhat, setting it on the top of his enormous rolling toolbox near the door. "Sounds good."

Grabbing their jackets, they headed to the Brown Lantern Tavern under arrays of yellow lights. They were on poles so high above, they seemed to be floating untethered. They hustled across the windy, cold, and wet concrete yard. A couple of neon beer signs hung in the windows signaling the Tavern was still open.

Ted looked at the ships tied along the pier, some landing craft, tugs, and in the distance their project, an enormous tanker. It was quiet, late on a Wednesday, not much going on. Stepping inside they hung coats on the hooks at the entry and sat in a vinyl booth. Peter slid across to the other side. Ted sat in his usual spot where he could see the bar and front door. Molly, a plump woman in her fifties, came over.

Ted caught her eye and said, "Hi Molly, two coffees, thanks."

Peter added quickly, "How about apple pie a la mode for me?"

"Whoo hoo, big spenders! Anything else for you?"

"Just coffee, thanks." Ted replied.

"That's right Molly, you'll be rich." Peter laughed, "How's the lottery treating you?"

She softly smiled, "I'm a winner with or without it. So, are you and your motorcycles all set for the big rally in Sturgis this year?"

"Yep, bringing my big trailer. I'm taking most of August. I'll be driving south and picking up my sister's boy, Woodrow, in Twin Falls. We'll drive around the country to Jackson and Sylvan Pass before we head to Sturgis. We're hanging around until Sturgis and after, when we head back, we'll check out the eclipse in Casper on our way home."

"What eclipse?" asked Molly.

"It's a total eclipse where the moon gets in front of the sun. This one goes all across America for the first time since 1918." Ted explained.

"Oh. Sturgis's nice county. Hope you have a good time." Molly left to get their order.

After a minute Ted asked Peter, "I need to get my Bronco and BMW out that way, could you take them with you?"

"That German rocket you've been ridin'? I could fit you and your daddy's tow truck inside, no problemo. Maybe Woodrow would deadhead that old wreck for you too. Life hasn't been easy for him lately."

Peter looked sad for a moment but continued in his usual chipper cadence, "It's been hard to find a place in Sturgis since the 75th Anniversary. Huge. Almost 1 million riders came, more people than all the top ten cities in South Dakota combined. So, I've got a bed for you if you want it in Nemo. It's a ways out of town, the little cabin. It's not much but you could stay with us."

"I can't make Sturgis. I need to see my friend up in Lead, near the Homestake Mine. She's working at LUX, that crazy underground lab. She wanted me to drop it off. Could Woodrow drive my Bronco and drop it off in Deadwood? I've got some work. Then maybe I'll head over to Nemo."

Molly came back with the coffees and asked Peter, "Did you brew this year?"

"Just my regular awesome IPA. I'm tired of the goofy flavors brewers add these days."

Molly gave Peter his pie and topped up his coffee, planting her broad bottom on a stool. Things were so dull at night she was happy to hang around.

Ted asked Peter, "You still have the can sealer? The one with a flywheel?"

Peter, "Yep, gathering dust as we speak."

Ted, "I'd like to borrow it for a time. Do you need it next month?"

Peter dug into his pie, rubbed his belly, and grinned his gap tooth smile. "All yours. I love lending you stuff, it always works when I get it back."

Ted was satisfied that he would get the tool he needed.

Molly chimed in, to Ted, "Before you boys leave me, how about your mid-winter adventure? Looks like you survived your big mountain climb in Glacier. By the way, you look like a raccoon. You haven't said a word about it."

Ted answered, "I got lucky with the weather, but it was still cold in the wind. I love being out in that place, but it is hard to see the glaciers melting so quickly. I hate to see them go. Enough snow covered the ridges, which I liked on the downhills. Got out just in time ahead of a storm."

His serious expression became dark as he added, "I am fed up throwing more carbon crap into the sky. It causes the greenhouse that's killing the glaciers."

Molly and Peter felt an awkward moment. She headed back to the kitchen. Then Ted shifted back to a normal tone. "Peter, one thing, this kid came out and thought he could do some mindless work. Maybe he can help grinding with the Grinder brothers?"

"Sure! Why not? More hands, more help."

Ted pushed back from the table, leaving cash on the bill. They waved bye to Molly as they got their coats and left, making their way across the wet concrete, back to the shed. Peter finished tacking the refractory crucible in place above the shaft. Ted placed the thimble at the bottom of the cone inside. Then he climbed the ladder and emptied most of the bags of Thermite in to hold it in place within the refractory crucible.

They didn't finish until after midnight. Ted drove the ALU service truck to his WWII vintage one-story house near the yard. He was exhausted but pulled out his calculations for the weld tomorrow and focused his bedside lamp on them. He checked each equation and verified the estimates he'd made for flowing that much thermite. His father had always told him that before you cut, measure twice. He was happy they all checked out. He yawned, stretched, and went to brush his teeth.

The next day he set a crew to work with the rest of the bags of thermite filling the refractory crucible. He set his manganese ribbons into the mix and twisted them to a wick at the top, looking like a candle as the level grew higher. It took most of the morning and he directed them closely. People from other parts of the yard came in to see how it was going. An inspector from the ship and his boss came and by the time it was ready to light it up a crowd of fifteen stood around looking on.

Ted donned his protective foundry gear appearing as a spaceman from some 1960s sci-fi movie, wearing aluminized carbon fiber Kevlar coat sleeves and boots. He put his face shield down and sparked a propane torch, using it to light the magnesium ribbons sticking up out of the thermite. As the magnesium fire hit the thermite it reacted with blinding speed out from the center to the walls until the whole surface was ablaze and light filled the shed above it. Everyone except Ted took a step back. He pointed his laser thermometer around the forms, checking all the aspects of the flow.

The surface of the refractory crucible became brilliant white with sparks and orange gasses billowing in a solid column toward the open roof duct. Heat melted the air and the scene shimmered. The refractory crucible began to glow and then the first molten overflow welled up from the bottom catch basins and spewed out of the channels into the soft sand below. Altogether the pour took less than two minutes. Applause broke out as the smoke darkened and the reaction stopped, darkening the room.

Ted's boss bellowed, "Nice work." He was pleased and slapped Ted on the back. Ted felt he'd demonstrated there was no limit to his skills. Thinking of what was to come in applying them, he cracked a scarcely seen smile.

Still musing on his plans, Ted took the crane and dropped the hook to a loop handle on the side of the refractory crucible. Peter came over with a cutting torch and released it from the shaft. Ted raised and lifted it up and out of the way, setting it in a sand pile.

They assembled cutting rings on either side of the break and used three hydraulic power jacks to bring them together and shear off the excess red-hot steel from the perimeter of the shaft. As soon as this was done, they pulled the rings apart and took them away. The shaft had a cherry red line running through the whole diameter. Then they knocked off slag, leaving chunks of glowing steel on the sand. All that was left was the finish work.

Ted began to remove protective gear beginning with his helmet and face shield. Peter looked over and noticed his rare smile. "Bring on the Grinder Brothers!"

CHAPTER 12

FEB 14, 2016
PALMER, MEL, BEVERLY HILLS, CALIFORNIA

P almer threw his cigar in the shrubbery and climbed behind the wheel of his luxury electric SUV to go to the Valentine's Day dinner. It was his wife's favorite gala sponsored by the Coal Future Institute, of which he was president. Since powerful Senator Carruthers would be there, it was a command performance. More lavish and more boring every year. His wife was out of town visiting her family so he had invited Mel to join him. He was glad to have some arm candy and it was a bonus that she could engage anyone.

He pulled up in front of her apartment and honked to let her know he was outside. As Mel walked down toward him, she looked like a model on a fashion runway. Her white shawl over her silky and revealing red dress and the swing in her hips from the stiletto heels mesmerized him. He touched his car's control screen and the door opened automatically for her, "You clean up nice." He said, trying to make light of his leering.

For most of the half hour drive he droned on about how safe his car was as Mel smiled and listened politely. "The air filtration system, known as Bioweapon Defense Mode, is not a marketing statement, it's real. I'll literally survive a military grade bio attack by sitting in this car. Even the exhaust from the car is clean air! The World Health Organization considers air pollution the world's largest single environmental health risk and if you look at the air in some big cities, you can see why."

"I like the styling." She replied, lowered her window to feel the outside air with her hand, surprised by the smooth flow. "Nice car and quite a soft ride too. Have you decided what you're going to say tonight?"

"Nothing new. I'll just say that energy from coal is a positive good like air and water. We need it to live. Energy is not a luxury. We don't succeed in the United States despite energy consumption, we succeed in the United States because of energy consumption." he thought for a minute and added, "Any notion that the United States of America is going to back down from its energy consumption is just not right. And people that think otherwise don't understand the United States." he seemed satisfied but continued anyway, "We're going up! Instead of going down, we're going up. We're doing great with President Karne in the White House. The American economy is flourishing because of coal power. They can thank us."

Mel smiled and said, "Sounds good enough but be sure to thank Senator Carruthers for all his work with coal waste and removing regulations on toxic chemicals. There are a lot of costs he's helped us avoid. He loves to hear positive things about his work. Did anyone special from RAGA call you to say they are going to be here? We sent them all tickets."

"No, they'd tell you, not me. Try and make them feel important." Palmer smiled at her.

Mel thought to herself that was all she did, buttering up the fat cats, keeping them safe from regulation and embarrassment.

Palmer turned up the long, hand-set stone driveway to the house. Subdued lighting washed the shell patterned paving made it easy to navigate through the beautiful Dickinsonia fern grotto. At the top he joined a line of other luxury cars disgorging guests. He put the car in park and looked over at Mel; what a beauty he thought to himself. "We're here."

The doors opened themselves automatically for both of them. A valet came and took his key as he walked around to escort Mel into the party. Palmer enjoyed the envious looks from his old business associates. In the foyer he spotted the Senator and paraded her over to see him.

The Senator shook Mel's hand for a little too long and thanked her for all she did for coal. "Aren't you the lucky one tonight." the Senator proclaimed, looking at Palmer.

Mel excused herself and found her way to the bar for a cocktail. She had no lack of men to talk with and used their attention to advance Palmer's positions, as she'd done for years.

She met one of the utility leaders and asked about pending legislation to eliminate fossil fuels entirely for electric generation in California. He said, "Oh, don't worry, Governor Moonbeam is still on space patrol. We still have time to burn." he chuckled at his joke "We can always play the 'if it's not affordable, it's not sustainable' card on it." He continued talking given he enjoyed her attention, "It's a less affordable, less flexible approach to reducing emissions. You know, stuff like that makes it easy to stall the bill in committee. If we are really pressed we can build in some booby traps. You know, make the fee structures on anything new pay for retiring our infrastructure." Mel spied a handsomely dressed man standing apart and excused herself before he could restart.

"You're new here? I know most everyone." Mel smiled as she assessed the new player.

"Maksim, at your service." with an old-world charm, he bowed slightly and shook her hand, "I am so happy to support the charity tonight." He smiled.

Mel's smile widened as she quizzed him, "So, Maksim, aside from your generosity and philanthropic urges, what brings you here?"

"Coal. I have lots of it but it is hard to get out of Kuzbass, in Siberia. It's locked away in a remote basin, hundreds of miles from tidewater. Lots of coal but no workforce, no infrastructure, no power, no roads, no railways, no airport, so everything must be built from nothing. A very expensive additional cost that takes capital and knowledge we don't have; these people-" he looked around the room, "have found solutions to bring it to market from far inland. Your President Karne has extended a hand of friendship to help realize our mutual desire to see coal once again a preferred fuel."

"I had no idea." Mel's curiosity grew with each answer, "So did the Senator want to introduce you to anyone in particular or just develop your social connections?"

"He said I could learn a lot from the mine owners here. How to get things done."

"Well, you are in fat city, the room is crawling with that very talent." Mel smoothly steered him by the elbow over to an owner with an isolated coal field in Australia. "This is Maksim, from Russia; he'd like to know how to get his coal to market. I think your Galilee Basin is about as far away from tidewater as his Siberian coal, making you the most knowledgeable man in the room."

"Why thank you, Mel." The owner expressed, turning to Maksim, "I'd be happy to tell you what I know." He turned back to Mel, but she'd slipped off to the party. "Pretty one, isn't she?" He shrugged, continuing, "So what do you need from me?"

"I have no infrastructure, no electric power, no roads, no railways, no airport, and it is cold as hell. I must build the entire plan to mine my coal starting from sub-zero."

"Well, don't be too sad, Maxim, did I get that right? You can just burn coal to heat things up. You know back when they discovered anthracite in Pennsylvania, they had pipes under the streets to melt snow! Talk about too cheap to meter. The one good thing you have going is, I'm guessing, no regulations. Da?"

Mel worked her way through the ranks of friends of coal, listening to how they could help Palmer keep coal a viable fuel for as long as possible. Friends who were doing quite well riding their firms to bankruptcy. They were especially pleased by the new uptick in consumption and exports. She was headed back to the bar when a large brutish man with an enormous head and waistline bursting from his expensive tux, beelined over to her to introduce himself.

"I own a lot of coal." He stood ogling at her and flatly added, "Damn, you are hot tonight."

"Why thank you." Looking up above his crooked bow tie into his reptilian face, "Dick Lockerby, isn't it?" she replied.

"I didn't know I was famous." He was bolstered that she knew who he was.

"After your terrible earthquake disaster, with fifty dead miners, you made a lot of headlines."

"Well, they convicted me of not taking safety precautions. Can you believe it? I grew up in the mines. I lived in the mines, I worked waist deep in water and mud." he looked indignant, "None of the regulators ever had a shovel in their hands."

"You are a man apart. I heard you still have a hundred million in the bank for your efforts. Even after serving your sentence."

"Oh, why yes, I do. I earned every dollar. And I left just as coal prices fell. A very smart move." he perked up, "Now I'm speculating in real estate in Vegas. I'm going back home though, to run for Senate."

"It must've been hard, being in jail with all of your talent and energy?" Mel waited to see if he picked up her heavily laid sarcasm.

"Why it was; but I'm moving ahead with my life." he licked his lips spastically, "You know I organized the RAGA opportunity for our AGs to get together with industry leaders back at the Greenbrier."

"That was you? I had no idea." Mel was surprised he could be so connected and crude at the same time. "It is a brilliant strategy. We get a lot of things done, strong relationships, and the law is a powerful tool."

"It is. You bet we do important things with them. That's not all, I took out a Supreme Court Justice and I put mine in his seat on the bench, Baron. He decided to vote my troubles away! What a surprise that was to me." His thin lips curled at the corners and a light almost came on in his dull eyes, "Oh, I've been to the White House for my efforts. I got the judges I wanted too. They know who makes things happen in West Virginia."

Abruptly he asked, "Say, are you busy after this party winds up?"

"I'm sorry, you know how it is. I came with Palmer. I know he'd like me to be the designated driver tonight." She looked over and saw he could indeed use someone sober behind the wheel.

Dick was eager to continue so he pressed his business card into her hand, "Well here's my card. If you want to work on my campaign or anything I can do for you just give me a call. Anything." Unable to stop talking he licked his lips again and continued, "Yes, hot tonight."

Palmer was standing in a small group with his arm around the Senator drinking his third scotch. They were in an alcove off the enormous foyer decorated with spines of books from the nineteenth century which had been chopped off and pasted to closet doors. They were sharing a big laugh and as she approached, he delivered the punch line, "...now that money is speech, my money says fuck the environment!"

The Senator turned to Palmer in a new voice, "Excellent remarks about our work in Africa. I know my wife, Elsie, will be happy to help end energy poverty tonight." Everyone made room for her to enter the conversation.

"Tell me what the Chinese have up their sleeves in syngas." Palmer asked the Senator.

"Oh, it is exciting. They are looking to throw some cash into the extraction. I guess they think natural gas will go up in price and they will be supply side."

"It wouldn't be the first time for that." Palmer quipped. Mel discreetly asked him for the valet check. She saw the effect she was having on the Senator and decided to leave him alone with his thoughts and her tipsy boss.

As she walked away the Senator began, "I've proposed legislation that will trim tax benefits applicable to the wind and solar industries. That and cutting off research funding for batteries should slow their progress while we take our next steps. We also can keep the old nuclear and coal plants running as we squeeze the market opportunity for them. Sucking up all the electric demand is a way to starve the revolution. They can come back another day, after we've made our money." he smiled and she heard, "Welcome to the feast, oh sorry! We ate your lunch." Sparking raucous laughter.

Mel gave the valet her check and told him to get the car out front. She spotted her RAGA connection and made her way over to him. He was listening to a lobbyist pontificating "I don't worry about those polls. Not at all. I was here for the BTU tax, 1993. I mean, you'd have thought it was the Civil War revisited. And you know what they ended up with? Four cents a gallon of gas!" he laughed, "No, I don't worry about the polls. When people see that the United States government is getting ready to raise their energy prices, I promise you, they pay attention." he paused for dramatic effect.

Mel pulled the Attorney General away from his conversation, "Could I have a moment?" She took his arm and steered him over to a quiet spot. "We are so grateful you've agreed to intervene at the protest up in Cherry Point. Keeping law and order is so important to us."

"Well, I'm happy to help. We certainly can't have protests getting violent."

"No, that would be bad." She stood close to him and asked, "Do you think that the police are enough for this? Wouldn't it send a message if private security were there too, maybe Tiger Paw? They do such professional work."

He looked nervous. "Well, they were a little rough at the last one. People all have video cameras on their phones now. We don't want any news footage showing them acting like Turkish thugs across from the White House."

"Well, I know you will figure out a way to help us."

They went back to their conversation when a lobbyist began, "You know what's coming? We have an EPA that will choke the renewables before they take hold. Loading up on coal and nuclear stockpiles will keep demand for new energy low and voila! No growth in wind and solar."

Mel inquired, "Isn't that a short-term strategy?"

"Yes, but then we can take away tax equity finance and dry up the available funds for their projects. See, we don't have to fight them, just scare away their money. It doesn't matter if all our coal fire plants make money right now as long as they keep it away from renewables. People are using less energy too. That is a squeeze on the little guy. Count on Karne too, he's got tariffs for solar panels coming. Brilliant to use a 'buy USA' to keep the supply expensive and prevent jobs in solar from happening."

Mel followed a plate of Hawaiian prawns out of the conversation and asked Munky, another mine owner, if his political contributions were paying off. "Hell yes! I gave the president a three-page letter with my action plan and he's half way through in the first couple of months!" He grinned broadly, "Now that's what I call service." He began to elaborate, "We can dump waste into the streams, blow mercury and arsenic out our stacks, and the EPA will make sure nobody will get in our way, hell they are downright helpful!" He was on a tear, "The DOE is onboard too! It's like we just bought the whole federal government in one election. Kind of a 'going out of business' sale." as he got his wind up, Mel thanked him and headed off to another guest.

"Jerry, Jerry Whindam." He said, extending his massive hand to Mel. "You're with Palmer, aren't you. Tell him I'm so sorry, the regulators pulled the plug on our Kemper clean coal plant."

"You've got to do what's best for business." She struggled to recall who he was. "And where are you located?"

"Mississippi. We're the poster child for coal gasification and 'clean coal.' Our plant sits on top of our coal, no trains required." He felt overlooked because she didn't know.

"Oh, I heard. You've been through some tough times. Wasn't converting the coal you're sitting on into syngas the plan?"

"Yes, that's us. Regulators found a bunch of stuff and we never ran a full day so the public service commission pulled the plug on us."

"That's a big plug, aren't you into this for about seven billion?"

"It's awful, we're five billion over budget."

"Yes, I can see how you might be struggling with an overhang like that. Why did they decide to limit you?

"They say this is going to cost the ratepayers. The damn regulators won't give any more money for us to get there. There's a couple of years left in solving the syngas puzzle, they're just short-sighted."

"I'm sure you will find a way to make it work in the future."

"There is no future for our syngas unless natural gas prices go up. Way up. Cheap gas is what nailed our coffin shut."

Mel thought about how the game is played; first cheap products and plants converted to new fuel supply then any excuse to jack up prices. It would only be a matter of time before cheap gas would be cheap no more.

She went over and collected Palmer, who was now engaged in conversation with a very young female lobbyist, certainly not in any shape to drive this evening. They went out to the valet and Palmer patted his pocket for the claim check. She pointed to his car and said she'd drive. He flopped into the passenger seat.

She headed to his place, and he dozed off almost immediately. She liked driving his car; so quiet and it handled like a sports car. She rolled down the window and heated her seat. It was a beautiful evening along the coast, no need for biohazard mode. She wondered if her ambition had steered her too far off the path of a good life. Those guys at the party were such whores. Darkly she thought, it takes one to know one.

CHAPTER 13

MARCH 1, 2016
TED AND PETER, ANACORTES, WASHINGTON

Anacortes' waters sparkled under spring skies as Peter parked in front of Ted's modest bungalow. Looking at the rusting two tone Bronco parked in front, he wondered why Ted kept it. He opened the van's rear doors and lifted out a contraption with a big flywheel awkwardly attached to the side. Lopsided but not too heavy to carry, he made his way up to the front porch. Ted met him with an open door. He came in and set it on the speckled Formica table in the living room. He went back out and brought in a stack of soda can blanks still in the shipping boxes and a smaller box of pop top lids for them.

"Here you go. This is the can sealer; it should do a can a minute once you get the hang of it. There is a little stickiness sometimes on the lower rollers." he pointed to the pair of metal discs that crimped the side to the top of the can, "I drip mineral oil on to keep them going."

"Thanks, I will see if I can make it work." Ted was rolling the flywheel around and checking the sealing mechanism. Tracking each fold mentally through the complex crimping process to seal the cans.

"Did you talk to Woodrow about the deadhead for me?"

"Oh, yes. He's very excited to drive out for you. He wasn't looking forward to being in the truck with me. He's excited to go by himself and very excited to get to Sturgis. I brought some of my IPA. If you have a minute for a beer, I'll go out and get it."

"Thanks, I'd like that." Ted continued to study the can sealer and started to tinker with the set screws, rocking the heavy flywheel back and forth.

Peter came back with a couple of six packs of his homebrew. "This is my current crop. I've made a couple of styles like Longhammer Ale, and this one is more like Terminal. He popped the caps off, "Which would you like?"

Ted pointed to the Terminal style and nodded, "I heard they had some fifty handles going at Brewgrass last year. You have your work cut out for you."

"You know this is just for fun. If I win, I celebrate with a beer, and if I don't I console myself with a beer."

"How many brews are you making this year?"

"I think six should keep me busy." Peter estimated, popping the can open, "That was a hell of a pour. We really nailed that shaft repair. The inspector was very flattering when he checked out our weld on the shaft. It's the biggest project I've ever done."

"I'm happy that's behind us. It was a bear." Ted continued to fuss with the machine.

"I used that sealer for these IPAs. See if you think the can adds or takes anything away from the flavor. Or do you like bottles?"

Ted took a sip of the can and thought for a minute, "I don't think it makes any difference." Then, "Run me through this will you?" Ted handed Peter some empty can cylinders from the box and lid blanks. Peter set down his beer and inserted the empty aluminum can cylinder and placed the pop top blank in the holder above it.

"Just go easy at the start and make sure you don't crimp or bunch the wall and it'll do the job." Peter cranked the sealer through the cycle then pulled out a sealed empty can, handing it to Ted.

Ted rotated the can in front of his face taking in every little bump and flat spot. Then he squeezed it hard. It held. He dropped it and stomped it with his boot. The top stayed securely in place but the sidewall split.

"OK. I think it will work."

"What are you doing? Going to start a new line and cut in on my brews?" Peter joked.

"Nothing like that. I'll show you when I'm done."

"Seriously? Another big mystery?"

"Yes. I need to make sure it works before I show you what it is."

"Alright, won't be the first time you've surprised me."

"Not the last either!" Ted laughed and punched Peter in the shoulder. "I'll be sending a couple of containers overseas. I might need some help with the ship dates. I think I can do it but just a heads up."

"Whatever. I'm happy to help if I can." Peter thought about punching Ted and decided to give him a wink instead.

As they settled into enjoying the IPAs, Peter launched into a description of Sturgis. "Traffic, trash, and fun. *Hells Bells* singin', a giant inflated tiger, and booze bottles on the roofs of the bars. I liked the wheelie demo, some freak was spinning and burning his rear tire with the front brake on, clouds of burnt rubber smoking." he grinned.

"Sturgis can be fun."

"Remember the Junk Bike Bonfire of '93?" He looked at Ted, "What a hot mess that was. Junked motorcycles stacked up like BBQ ribs getting toasted by a fighter jet engine. Flames shooting out 150 feet."

Ted added, "Big Ed Beckley jumped his bike over the top of the smoldering scrap. I was impressed since he was so wasted when he did it."

They continued to talk about motorcycles. Ted fussed with the can sealer as they did and by the end of their conversation, he could spin the flywheel and seal a can in one single smooth motion.

Peter asked, "Was that the time you welded the roll-up door shut on those guys who hassled us for hours? What a bunch of assholes. They thought they were so tough. What a surprise when they realized they were locked in." Peter smiled at the memory.

"I think it was funny hearing them banging on the roll up, yelling help! help! Bullies to crybabies; didn't take long. Games of our youth." Ted smirked.

Peter noticed a bunch of new material on the kitchen counter.

"Is that ribbon made of magnesium? Bet it gets hot in a hurry."

"Good spotting. Yes, it is a good lighter for the thermite reaction."

"What's this going to be?"

"Arduino kits. They do anything you tell them to. There's a bunch of clocks and timers, some radio chips, and a battery. Nothing too complicated." Ted held up a couple of the pieces, explaining their functions.

"After you showed me the magnesite thimble, I began to think you are some kind of wizard when it comes to making things." Peter chuckled.

"This your drone?" Peter lifted it out of the hard case with fitted foam. "So light! Can we take it for a spin?"

"Sure, grab that case and I'll get my cell phone." Ted unplugged it from the charger, "Let's go outside where we can test it out. It flies almost by itself."

Ted set his cell phone into the controller and prepped his drone on the sidewalk. He commanded it to fly and up it went. He had it buzz Peter for fun then sent it to hover, high in the sky. They got in the Bronco and they drove along the city streets while it tailed dutifully along recording video as it flew.

"This is incredible! I feel like I'm having an out of body experience!" Peter was riveted by the cell phone screen showing them driving the Bronco. Ted made a U-turn and the drone automatically followed. "It's crazy smart this little drone of yours."

"They just keep getting better all the time." Ted pulled up and parked in front of his house. He hit the land command and the drone returned to where it had launched initially. He picked it up and began to stow it in the case while Peter talked about how cool it was.

Ted changed the topic. "Thanks for getting Woodrow to deadhead the old Bronco for me." He went over to a desk and pulled out an envelope handing it to Peter. "Here's some gas money, it gobbles. I put in some for a couple night's stay in a motel too, even a kid gets tired driving. The drop address for Deadwood is in there as well."

"Thanks, I'll give it to him. It'll be good for him to have something to do. After getting out of jail he's been driving his family crazy, just drifting. I don't know what he's going to end up with."

"Do you think he's turned a new page?"

"I do. He's kind of a refugee from all that weirdness fracking in Alberta with a scary neighbor. I'm not sure what Woodrow did with him but there were a bunch of charges around domestic terrorism when they sent him to prison. My sister was beside herself."

"What was that about?"

"Weibo was a religious man who moved his commune a town called Paradise out to the middle of nowhere and then when the fracking started leaking sour gas, his congregation had a bunch of health problems: miscarriages, rashes, and such.

He decided to blow up their fracking wells. At least they think he did. It got very nasty with private security and an agent provocateur bombing a well to show he was on their side. Woodrow was just in the wrong place at the wrong time as I see it."

Peter sighed and took a drink of his beer. "So, what about the containers you've been loading?"

"I need them for a couple of welding on some rail projects overseas; one in Siberia and one in Australia for China's Carmichael mine."

"Are you going over yourself or is this just supply?"

"I'm not sure but most likely I will go there at some point; these things don't weld themselves."

"If you need any help let me know, I'd love to see some kangaroos. Not so sure about Siberia."

"The Aussies need to build a new rail line to get coal to port facilities. South Korea is building about two hundred miles of rail for a hundred million tons of coal. They'll need to expand the port too. The banks are wary of big downside risks because it will destroy some of the Great Barrier Reef."

"What about Russia? You aren't working with Boris, are you? That guy gives me the creeps."

Ted paused and then said, "Oh about that kid I met in Glacier, I've given him a job at ALU."

"I'm for that. There's a bunch of little jobs I'd love to hand off at the shop. Does he have any welding experience?"

"I don't think so. He's a strong kid, willing to work and that's about all his qualifications. No obligation. You will like his dog."

"OK let's see how he does. What kind of dog?"

"Cane Corso, the Roman Legionaries' dog. Just a puppy still, but giant paws and an enormous head. He reminds me of Jack, my dog when I was a kid."

They stepped outside and the glorious day was still in progress. "Why do you keep this rust bucket anyway?" Peter pointed to the Bronco, "It's the most dangerous thing on wheels and looks like hell."

"Sentimental value, it was my dad's. I feel his spirit when I drive it. Also, with the extra fuel tanks it goes about five hundred miles."

"Suit yourself." Peter smiled and then got in his van and gave a wave as he drove off.

Ted waved back; he liked Peter. They'd been working together for a long time. He looked over the Bronco. The back window still had a cracked, faded Tenth Mountain Division decal stuck on it and Semper Fidelis round next to it. It was rusted out but just cosmetic damage. During high school he had been through some times with it. He popped the hood, checked the tire pressure, tread, suspension, and opened and closed all the doors before going back inside. 'Good old paint.' That's what his dad called it. He crushed his beer can studying how the metal compressed.

CHAPTER 14
APRIL 22, 2016
JULIA, TED, JC, FERNDALE, WASHINGTON

J ulia pulled into the rest home parking lot. A quaint one-story brick building with white trim at the top of the hill above Ferndale. She reached over and got the potted pink azalea and her autoharp from the passenger seat and went inside the Auburn Rest to see her mother, Betty. Nurses at the front desk waved to her as she headed down the shiny linoleum corridor to Betty's. Her door was decorated with an American flag taped to it by the stick. Julia knocked gently and then pushed it open. Betty was sitting fixated by Fox News on her television. She was startled to see Julia.

"Julia, you're such a dear to come see your old mother."

"I brought this to brighten up your room. It's Earth Day." Julia held up the azalea, "How are you feeling?"

Betty was riveted to the tv, "Just a minute, this is important. See" she pointed at the tv, "the president is keeping us safe. It is so good to see how strong a leader he is." She continued to watch until a commercial brought her back to Julia. "I do love to get the real story. None of the fake news that's out there."

Julia busied herself freshening the room, throwing out a dead flower arrangement sitting in slime and organizing some of Betty's clutter. She paused to look at the photo of her sister happily smiling.

Julia checked her daily pill dispenser to see if the pills were in order. "How are you? Are your medications working any better? Not so hard on your stomach?" She waited for her reply and realized that Betty was dressed in a fancy skirt and blouse with a matching jacket as if going to a party. Julia knew things like this were bound to happen more often.

"As good as can be expected at my age." She smiled and seemed very happy although she was shaking a bit.

"I brought my autoharp, would you like to hear me play some of your favorite songs?"

"Oh yes." She replied enthusiastically, the show resumed and she added, "but I need to finish watching this important news report first." She turned back to the show.

Julia was crestfallen. It was the beginning of the show and she knew it would be the same for the next half hour. "I'll play for you another time then. I have an event to go to today to help keep Cherry Point a clean and natural place. I'll come back soon."

"Good for you, it is such a beautiful spot. I loved going there when your father worked at the refinery." The TV flickered and she slipped back into focusing on the news. She looked up and said, "The coal loading terminal is just what we need, it will bring back jobs."

Julia had seen this before and knew there was little hope of recapturing her attention. "Well, be good. See you again soon. Bye Mom." Julia gave her a hug and quick kiss, picked up her autoharp, and left with a heavy ache in her heart.

Julia drove a couple of blocks down to the athletic field at the high school where volunteers were setting up. Behind the field were bleachers on one side and a driveway and some low storage buildings on the other.

Beyond the field was a chain link fence separating it from the railroad tracks with an opening to the crossing in the middle.

In center field there was a long flatbed trailer supported on jacks with portable stairs leading up from both ends. A couple of microphones on stands and a banner across the back made from a couple of bedsheets with giant black letters spelling out 'NO COAL TRAIN' suspended on poles. Prayer flags draped off to the side like car lot pendants. There was a makeshift loudspeaker bank, a couple of chairs, and a high stool.

Off to the side near the bleachers, a police van, fire department EMT, squad cars, and a black Hummer were parked. A half dozen policemen were talking in a casual group drinking coffee between the trailer and the railroad tracks. Julia spotted Sheriff Joe who had brought JC to the Belle Clinic. She waved, he raised his coffee cup and smiled.

Next to them was the ALU bus that had delivered the counter-protesters from the yard in Anacortes. A dozen guys had printed eighteen by twenty-four-inch signs stapled onto wooden sticks that read 'Join the pro-jobs majority', 'Build Coal Terminal Here' and 'Build Jobs Here.' Another van arrived from an engineering firm that was expecting to get work developing the terminal. Peter pulled up next to the ALU van and Wrigley bounded out. He and JC went over to get signs. Another ALU van pulled up alongside them. It was part of getting paid.

A few elderly people from town wearing festive hard hats and company vests, opposed to anything that might smack of environment over promises of jobs, carried identical printed signs in green with 'Power past the fear mongering' made their way over from their bus.

Some early protesters had blankets or folding chairs and were sitting eating lunch. Julia went over and talked with a group of her friends. She recognized from Audubon hikes they had been on together. They caught her up on all the local sightings. Some shared concerns they had about shifting timing for migrations.

She sat down on the edge of the stage to tune her autoharp and began quietly singing. One of the college students volunteering came over and held a mic for her, she smiled at him and went ahead and sang a warmup performance.

More people were arriving in cars, on bicycles, and in carpools. The Lummi first people drove up in a caravan. Thirty people of all ages, some wearing traditional dress, got out. A church group and some environmental groups gathered members in clusters. The field was gradually filling up.

A news van from the local station came in and parked by the ALU van. The cameraman and the tech got out and fixed the van's anchors and extended the telescoping broadcast antenna from the top of it. Cindy Sparks, a news reporter, sat in the passenger seat and put the finishing touches to her eye makeup using the visor mirror. Her cameraman set up a gold reflector and made light readings and scoped some backgrounds for her interviews. She looked out the window and spotted Cliff Jenner, a Lummi tribal leader. She knew him from an interview during the previous coal train protest. She finished quickly and went over to see him.

"Hi Cliff, how are things with you?"

"I'm good." he paused to look around, "Our war canoe team is getting really good. I hope we do well in the race this time."

"I remember last year it was a rough day on the water." Cindy was freezing when she covered it.

"Oh yes, it was a wet one, and cold with the spray."

"Would you give me an interview for tonight's news?"

"Sure Cindy. I'm happy to, it is always great to have our story heard beyond the reservation. We want people to join us, we are few, and the problems are many."

"Great, let's stand so Mt Baker, er Kulshan, is behind us." After getting the OK on sound levels and making the cameraman happy she got the go ahead. She adjusted her hair and held up the mic.

"I'm talking to Cliff of the Lummi Nation here at the protest of the Cherry Point coal terminal. So, Cliff, what do you hope to accomplish with this demonstration?"

Cliff spoke with a calm and resonant voice, "We are here to protect our fishing rights, our livelihood, and the earth for the next generations. And we are here to show the young people how to act, how to stand for their rights and their future. They need to act now to protect their future. It won't be healthy when they grow up."

"Do you think this protest will be effective?" she pointed the mic back to him.

"We are using all our tools to build our future. This is one. Our lawyers are working to keep our treaty rights strong and repel the attacks from the coal industry on our fishing grounds, our clean water, and our nation." he paused "Our people are networking and reaching out to everyone who loves this place and wants to help protect it from harm." he swept his arm to indicate that 'this place' was everything in sight.

"Global fossil fuel industries, coal, gas, oil, and now shale oil, have been waging war on our mother earth and father sky since they came to be. Often their worst pollution falls on our reservations, making our people sick. Their operations are destroying our livelihood, fishing. Now many tribes have come together around the world to fight back. The gathering at Standing Rock showed all tribes and people coming out to turn back the assault on the earth."

"But about this Cherry Point terminal…"

"Native peoples are active both here and across the border in Canada. Tribes are working to keep the coal away from our fishing grounds. Our rights over these waters are well established. The waters off Cherry Point are home to the crab, halibut, the salmon, and our livelihoods." Cliff pointed toward the terminal site.

"The giant terminal they want to build would use all the freshwater in the Nooksack and then some. How could we fish in a river that they have taken away the water to wash their coal? The land will be covered in mountains of coal for export. When their giant ships come in to load, they foul our fishing gear, they pollute the waters. Clouds of coal dust blow with the wind. There is no way they can operate without violation of our rights."

Cindy broke in, "The terminal is going to be a state-of-the-art facility, don't you think they have thought of the environment?"

"We are here to make sure they do no damage. All the plans they have shown destroy our livelihoods and our future. Eternal vigilance – the price for keeping our rights."

"Cliff, a Lummi Nation leader, thanks for your thoughts." Cindy signed off and shook his hand.

Cindy carefully picked her way across the grass in her high heels to interview someone from the counter protest. She spotted Wayne Henson, a personable local politician working the crowd. He'd spent a small fortune on yard signs for a local election. He was happy to see her and quickly agreed to an interview. Cindy and her tech set up and when he gave her a thumbs up, she began.

"I'm talking to Wayne Henson, running for county supervisor. You support the terminal construction, can you tell me why?"

"Whatcom County is a county where jobs are the biggest concern. My constituents want to have high paying secure jobs and the terminal would bring in construction and operational positions for hundreds."

Cindy countered "Jobs don't always come with construction or stay in the community. There are large contractors who hire extra workers, but they have their own skilled people. How can you assure that the jobs will go to local people who need them?"

"I'll be working personally with the terminal developers to make sure that these issues are addressed. This new road to Cherry Point was my work, and it created a lot of jobs."

"What do you say to the Lummi and the fishing community about how their jobs and livelihoods will be impacted by the construction and operations of the planned terminal? The rail connections for coal trains, the loading terminal itself, the pier, miles of conveyors, and the bulker ships that will need to dock and load?"

Wayne no longer saw her as pretty. "Look, I'm a local myself, I have studied this terminal development for some years and can say that this will create highly paid jobs for local people, it will bring tax revenues to Whatcom County, and it will be done to the highest environmental standards of any project I've ever seen." With that he extended his hand to shake goodbye.

Cindy held off. "The jobs that come with insulation of homes and renewable energy are growing all over. Are you investing your energy in making our sustainable workforce grow as well?

"Of course, I'm a green advocate. I've always said that energy jobs are important. Thanks, I've really got to get going."

"Wayne Henson, running for your local representative. This is Cindy Sparks for Whatcom News." Wrigley bounded over and barked at Wayne and then bounded off with JC chasing behind.

Cindy laughed at Wayne shrinking from the dog. Wrigley looped back and nuzzled her arm and petted his massive head carefully to avoid getting slobber on her outfit. "Who's a good boy, are you a good boy?"

JC came up to them. She asked, "Is this your dog?" JC bashfully replied it was. He was impressed how poised Cindy was.

Ted arrived on his motorcycle and parked near the police. He smiled when he noticed Wrigley prancing about Cindy and JC ready to collar him. As he walked past the uniformed police to see Peter, Ted noticed a man wearing all black who was standing at ease pointing out people for a pho-tographer next to him to shoot. They were in front of a black Hummer with 'Tiger Claw' written on the side and a paw with claws extended above it. There was something about that guy that Ted knew from his time as a Marine, trouble. He took a 'jobs' sign and thought how ironic it was to be paid for holding it, given his work on defeating the coal train last time.

CHAPTER 15

APRIL 22, 2016
JULIA, FERNDALE, WASHINGTON

The sound system squealed and some put fingers to their ears. Larry the organizer took the mic "Welcome to our Earth Day everyone, that means you too" he said waving to the counter-protesters and police.

A couple of them waved back.

"We're all here because we care about this place and how to make a future that will work for everyone." He looked around "The Lummi tribe is here as they have been for several millennia and the rest of us newcomers, folks from town and from businesses, and a lot of neighbors." He got out a little notebook "I hope you will enjoy our lineup of speakers. You most likely know some of them. So let's start with an elder of the Lummi people. Here is Cliff Jenner."

Cliff had put his ceremonial robe on. "Welcome to Xwe'chie Xen, our Lummi name for this place called Cherry Point. Here in the shadow of Kulshan, that's Mt Baker to you, we have fished the abundance for one hundred seventy generations. Now that's what I call sustainable fishing!

We love our home and are happy to care for it. Much of our heritage is gone. The big cedars that would grow down to the water's edge are gone for lumber, the abundant bird and waterfowl that darkened the skies are diminished, and our fishing grounds suffer from marine traffic. Our sacred ancestral lands are covered by aluminum smelting and oil refining operations.

Now the coal developers say they want to bring a mountain of it to the water's edge. A huge terminal for their trains with coal from the Powder River in far off Wyoming to ship to Asia. It will destroy this place. This coal loading terminal would end our livelihood, our ability to fish, and gather crab. More than that, it would end our ability to be good stewards of the land.

The trains to bring the coal and the ships to take it away would be deadly too. Every train would be a mile long slice through the heart of our homes. Like Pig Pen from the old Peanuts cartoons, they would dust our people with coal as they rumble through.

The propellers of gigantic ships already cut up our fishing gear and pollute fishing grounds, and with this terminal the ships would be even bigger and more damaging. Together the new coal trains and ships for this terminal will repeat the horrors of the first railroads.

When they crossed our plains, they brought death to the buffalo herds and starvation to our Blackfoot brothers and sisters.

We are here to heal the earth to fight for a clean future for everyone. And we are here to support your rights to this beautiful place to live. We made binding treaties with the USA. They guarantee our right to fish. Nothing legal will destroy that right. "

Lummi elders, youngsters, some wearing the woven basket hats and traditional costume came up onto the stage and joined him. Cliff announced, "Hear the songs of our people." Cindy had her cameraman take footage as they performed drumming and singing. Each beat sent a public message that their fishing grounds were not for sale.

When they finished Cliff said, "We are here to protect and defend, not to get paid to look away." They unrolled a mock-up of a check from the terminal developers. He fired a propane torch along the bottom to set it on fire, throwing the ends to the wet grass. The crowd cheered as the tribe left the stage and joined the people.

Larry took the mic and a tall, fit, older man dressed in khaki pants and plaid shirt, and Panama hat was introduced. "Professor of Sustainability from Evergreen University, one of our most popular professors."

"Thanks, Larry. I'm here to ask you to think for yourselves and decide if this coal terminal is something you want or not." He got out his notes.

"College isn't a daycare to keep young people out of the workforce. It's where we have the chance to learn for ourselves the difference between truth and lies. Yes, there are lies and the people who tell them have motives.

We're being played by developers from outside our community who want this terminal. Think for yourselves, be critical of slick messages and appealing propaganda. The coal people who've done this think that we can't learn to think for ourselves, we can't be educated, and our judgment doesn't matter.

They know that if they can make this confusing or just 'he said, she said' we can be bamboozled. Imprinting our consciousness with their endless slogans of 'clean coal', 'human energy', 'beyond petroleum', 'war on coal', 'natural gas' and 'you deserve a break today'. All that noise beats on us night and day.

Some of the news has become a funhouse mirror where photoshopped actors offer their opinions as they perform the news. Performers who have no ideas of their own and who will say anything that they see on the teleprompter. This garbage that they spew at us comes ever denser and faster and it is dumbing us down. We fall prey to the loudest and most persistent, not the most truthful. Our only hope is to think ourselves out of this mess. I'm a teacher so here's a pop quiz.

Do you like breathing coal dust?

Do you believe that mercury and arsenic aren't a health problem?

Do you want your sky to be their toilet?

Do the fossil fuel industries care about anything but profit?

Do you want them to continue to buy your representatives?

Our fossil fuels dependance is a terrible master. As President W Bush said, 'We are addicted to oil.' Do we want to be addicts? The adoption of clean sources and capture is sustainable and healthy. We must choose, as serving two masters is a waste of our lives. It's time for each of us to wake up, and act! Now, together, we can make this coal train terminal history. Thank you."

Larry "Thank you Professor. Next is Gloria from the Navajo Nation near Black Mesa. She has lived downwind of a coal burning electric generation plant. She is here to share her story." He welcomed her to the stage, adjusted the mic for her, and showed how to keep her mouth close to the mic. Larry remained close behind her on stage. She was a plump young woman with beautiful black hair in a traditional braid down her back and she wore a native cloth poncho over her western clothes.

Gloria looked around nervously and took a deep breath. "Hi everybody." she took another breath and began "Growing up on the res, everyone knew everybody. We had a little park down the road. There was a swing set, slide, the little bendable horses. It was fun. We had trails in the hills. You just walked around. No technology, nothing like we have now, where everybody just stays inside. They were building the Navajo Generating Station in our backyard. This was big, like the coal terminal will be.

They finished the plant and started burning coal. Then, when I was ten I started having to use an inhaler. I'm an adult now and I still use it. A month ago, I went to Oregon and didn't use my inhaler at all. But as soon as I got back to our area, I was sucking on it again.

My boy has the same problems. He has an inhaler, and at least once a month he must use a nebulizer to open up his lungs. If I forget, he must go on steroids. If we don't do it, then it can turn into pneumonia or bronchitis.

These people who come in and haul away the fly ash from the plant say it's not harmful. But I ask, 'If it's not harmful, why does your wife have to check you to make sure you didn't bring any into the house? Why does the paint peel off your pickup after you've been out there on a rainy day?'

Sometimes I wonder, Where did my son's autism come from? I grew up on the hill above the tribal building, and I always wonder if it started there, with his development, because that's where I was living when I was pregnant with him. The dust from the plant would come through the valley and then come up to us. We lived there for ten years, and then my parents were dead so I inherited their house, closer to the plant." She stopped and cleared her throat and took a drink of water.

"It's a miracle when my people reach age landmarks here. Fifty is a miracle. I left last week for a business meeting and came home to two elders, two brothers, were in the hospital. The driver who picked us up is like, 'Alex and Ronny are in the hospital.' For those two brothers to be in the hospital at the same time, how do you deal with that? They have another brother, Tommy, and in one fell swoop there could be just the one brother left.

We have a small cemetery with little family plots, and ours is filling up. It's kind of warped, because we're like we might have to move our family plot to accommodate all the people who are dying.

I hope to be buried there, but I don't see it in the near future – at least I hope not. I have a son to look out for. My lungs, you know, if they don't hold up … or what if it moves to where my heart doesn't work? It makes a deep impact because I want to be here for my son." She stopped and hung her head, then she got a tissue and dabbed her eyes.

"I tell him when he sees me sad, 'It's OK, sweetie. Mommy's just crying because she's happy, OK?' He's a little bleeding heart. When he hears his mom cry, he gets a little teary-eyed himself." she looked out to the crowd. "It is hard to think he will have the struggle his whole life.

We think of moving, but that is our home, where our people are." She looked up above to the sky. "You all live in a paradise, don't trade it so they can unload their coal." She clasped her hands and looked down.

Larry came over and put his arm around her "How about a round of applause and appreciation for our sister, Gloria?" and walked her across the stage. Julia met her as she came off stage and gave her a warm hug.

Larry introduced Julia "One of our strongest supporters and some-one you know from the Belle Clinic, Julia will now share her music." People applauded and Julia took the stool over to the mic. She played a few bars on her autoharp and then clear and strong she sang a hopeful song, Cat Stevens' 'Peace Train.'

> *"Now I've been happy lately. Thinking about the good things to come.*
> *And I believe it could be. Something good has begun.*
> *Oh, I've been smiling lately. Dreaming about the world as one.*
> *And I believe it could be. Someday it's going to come…"*

She finished playing and while people clapped, she began her remarks. "I'm here to demand an end to this unnecessary damage to our earth, ourselves, and our children's futures. No terminal, no coal trains, yes one hundred percent renewable clean energy." The crowd clapped and some whistled and cheered.

"Mining coal, we harm the earth then we burn it and harm the sky. When we send it to China or India the pollution travels back to us on the wind and in turn we breathe in the pollution and harm ourselves. I'm a nurse and see patients suffering respiratory damage. My father died from exposure to toxic chemicals because the owners didn't care to protect him as much as they loved their money.

We are all connected. Coal-powered energy is a poison to all living things, and like most poison the more you take the worse the effects.

We love this place. This place… right here… right now. Look at Mt. Baker, our mountain, our streams, our rivers, our forests, our bay. It is so beautiful, it is heaven on earth. We can't be silent and let it be destroyed. Speak out with me to keep our home safe and clean. This is our Garden of Eden. We are growing a future. Let's make it even more beautiful than the one we've inherited." She looked into the crowd and saw interested faces.

"This is from the Bible, 'Nature is not mocked, not susceptible to compromise, to regrets. It's inexorable, it's absolute.' She drew another breath, 'Whatsoever a man soweth that shall he also reap.' She exhaled "We are about to harvest the effects of a trillion tons of CO_2 and other greenhouse gasses. Now we breathe it in from the smoke from Canada's wildfires. We see it when the sky is orange. We are reaping the harvest of heat, too much heat.

We can't renew our relationship with nature without a renewal of knowledge, will, freedom, and responsibility. All need to be recognized and valued. All people, not just the few coal mine owners and Wall Street energy speculators, are valued. Joy, peace, political love, mutual care, are part of civic renewal. It makes itself felt in every action that seeks to build a better world. Together we need to share our joy, we need to let nature inspire us with awe. We need to teach the path to a healthy future.

This coal train full of rocks to burn is a ride in the wrong direction, to a barren planet, where we harm the earth. We need to get on the peace train where clean energy is the only energy. Peace with our planet, peace with ourselves, and peace with each other. Peace." People were quiet and then they applauded and Julia left the stage.

Larry gave her a high five.

Ted clapped from his motorcycle. He thought to himself that she was still jousting at windmills.

CHAPTER 16

APRIL 22, 2016
TIGER PAW, FERNDALE, WASHINGTON

Larry took the mic. "Next, we have Bob Bonnington from the energy group at Stelle Ventures. They finance community choice projects in PV solar. Bob took the mic from him and strode to the center stage. For a business type, he was gangly with a black shock of hair, parted perfectly. He was dressed in an LL Bean ensemble for the occasion.

"My name is Bob Bonnington and I'm a rich guy — really rich. I'm a venture capitalist who got lucky, PV solar is good business. Now I own a bank here in Bellingham.

Look, if you're happy giving coal mine owners power over your every decision, operating their dirty energy game from afar, don't do anything. They are content to keep making the money and they are AOK with their terminal in your neighborhood.

If you like giving them tax subsidies, don't speak out because that's your money propping up their zombie business.

Coal stopped being the economic choice a while ago. These guys took out their money when many folks lost their shirts. They got rich running it into the ground. So, if you think they care about you, and your job, keep that in mind.

Coal is a finite resource that is getting ever harder to get, more fuss and more mess for less. The business is ever more centralized in fewer and fewer hands. The kind of person who is attracted to this part of the game isn't the innovator. They are the carrion feeders, devouring the kill. And when they've gorged themselves, they will be long gone leaving the rotting carcass, spoiled land and water, for us.

If you see a brighter future in owning your own power, PV solar or wind, that you control and you profit from, then listen up. The sun shines all across the globe. Wind and waves flow from the energy it delivers. A solar powered future is abundant and equally available and open to decentralized models. The half century of PV solar development is bearing fruit, luscious ripe fruit. We can own our personal energy farms and harvest wind or sunlight. Once you set it up the fuel is free!

Wind turbines are awesome technological marvels to make energy from wind anywhere the wind blows on earth. Shifting from the centralized coal fired economy will disrupt the industry. That's why they are fighting so hard to keep things unchanged.

They love to say they are 'helping the poor get energy'. What they want is to centralize big coal burning plants. That is the opposite of local renewables. Think how cell phones grew in places that never even had landlines. Think about digital image takers like your smartphone replacing film cameras. Innovation makes life better and better.

The future is better than the past and it belongs to the young and those who embrace it. So when coal investors lie, cheat, and steal to keep solar and renewables from you, it isn't that they aren't aware that those energy sources are better. It is *because* solar and renewables are better. If they could figure out a way to charge you for the sun or wind, they'd change today.

Their favorite argument for coal is jobs. Jobs in coal. How stupid is that? There are already more workers in clean tech than fossils. New things make new jobs. Old jobs are the first to be automated out of existence.

When big coal left Appalachia for the Powder River, the miners were expendable so out they went. Then when coal came back in Appalachia, they didn't need many miners, because instead of mines they just blew off the mountaintops and used their mega – machines to take the coal. No miners, no unions, no worries. Now they are working to get autonomous machines so they can fire the few guys left working the coalfields.

Rather than investing in a clean future, the coal industry invests in politicians. Tilting the scales gives them leverage over the game. If they can block development of renewables, they can keep fleecing us at the pump and the receptacles. They are working hard to stick us with the clean-up costs too. That's why they invest in political power. It pays off.

We need to shift the cost back to the coal industry for cleaning the overburden in streams, slurry in mines, and greenhouse gas in the sky. You've seen prison gangs in orange collecting trash on the highway. How about the coal industry suits up? Why should we clean up after their dirty business, as the old saying goes 'they took the gold we got the shaft'?

It is important that people demand their governments push now to collect the cost of carbon from people who make it. So, like I said, if you like what is going on, just do nothing. Coal companies are happy with the status quo. Do something and stop this terminal."

Larry came out and shook Bob's hand and Bob waved a friendly wave and strode off stage. Larry smiled and to the crowd, "Reverend Doctor Earth will hold church next! Give him a warm welcome." The Doctor took the stage dressed in black with a priest collar and approached the – mic with a flourish of his cape.

"The doctor is in the house! Today we will diagnose the patient, our dear old Mother Earth. She came into my office covered in soot, coughing up coal ash and mercury. It was obvious to me that she is afflicted with a deadly disease, Coaltrainitis. Awful case of it, open sores where the coal was taken, her rivers poisoned by coal dust blowing off trains, and she was choking on greenhouse gas, rising ocean acidification, and a fever. A very serious fever and rising. A case of Coaltrainitis.

To heal her we will follow the Hippocratic oath." he paused "First, do no harm. Can you say it with me? Do no harm." he chanted on "Do no harm! Do no harm! Do no harm!" Some of the crowd began to warm to him. As if on cue the blast of a train horn blew and he pointed toward it. "That! Hear that? That's the problem." The train blasted its horn again. He yelled into the mic talking over the train as it rumbled past.

"When you rip the earth, dig the coal, and destroy the land-" he paused for effect.

"That is harm!

Then you load a hundred tons into a hopper, string a hundred together and make a sixteen-thousand-ton train, run that train fifteen hundred miles, unload it, load it onto a ship, and sail across the ocean.

That is harm!

Then unload the ship, put it back on the train, unload the train, and burn it and poison the sky with soot.

That is harm!

And the carbon combines with twice its weight of oxygen and flies to the atmosphere to cook our planet.

That is harm!

And some falls into the ocean and acidifies its chemistry.

That is harm!

And some combines with the calcium starving our smallest life forms or material for their shells.

That is harm!

Then you take the money you made and buy yourself a politician or two.

That is harm!

Then you go bankrupt, you abandon your mines and the miners, leave the mess, just take the money, and run. That. Is. Harm. So, to heal dear Mother Earth of her coaltrainitis we need to stop the spread of the disease. Then we need to remove the malignant tumors and replace them with clean sustainable energy sources.

But, Reverend, that sounds so hard you say! It sounds hard but it really isn't. All you need to do is let King Coal go. If we don't feed him, he will fade away. Thanks for coming to my doctor's office."

With that, and another flourish of his cape, he walked offstage with his arms up fingers making 'V' peace signs like disgraced President Nixon. The train gave another long blast on its horn.

On the infield, Wrigley's ears perked up hearing it and he bolted toward the tracks, his leash trailing like a silly boa. JC scrambled to his feet and started after him. Wrigley bounded across the field. JC sprinted after him. His asthma kicked in and he doubled over. He fumbled to get his inhaler out of his pocket. He watched Wrigley crossing home plate, heading past the police vans and counter-protest vans.

Julia had just finished putting her autoharp in her car. The coal train was making such a racket. She saw Wrigley running toward her and worried he might head to the train and hurried to cut him off. JC was running again and he was passing the line of police. He saw Julia running fast and gracefully, closing in on Wrigley. Wrigley pranced away from her and the others in pursuit and sped up, enjoying the game of chase. As JC ran past the Tiger Paw Hummer the man in black stuck out his boot sending him flying. He landed, his head snapping hard onto the asphalt. Wrigley continued racing toward the train.

Ted had been watching the chase. He kicked his bike into gear and sped out, cutting Wrigley off from the tracks. "Whoa, Wrigley, you can't stop a train like that." He let Wrigley jump up on him and grabbed him, scratching behind his ears. Wrigley responded, wagging his tail. Ted added, "Takes more than your big bark to stop this coal train."

Julia saw that Ted had Wrigley and was relieved that he was safe. She felt a twinge of nostalgia for their past romance. Then she saw the EMT's put JC on a stretcher and roll him into their ambulance. One of them was wiping away blood on his face. She recognized him as her patient from the Belle Clinic. She ran back to her car and drove after the ambulance.

CHAPTER 17
APRIL 23, 2016
JC, JULIA'S CABIN, MT BAKER, WASHINGTON

The hospital wouldn't release JC alone given his head injury and asked if Julia could keep an eye on him for a day. Peter came to the hospital. He said he'd keep Wrigley. She checked JC out and they decided to go to her cabin.

It was past midnight when they got there, and she helped him out of her car and inside. JC went to the couch and steadied himself as he sat. She beelined to her wood stove, squeaked opened the door, and began to lay the twigs and splinters into a teepee inside. She lit it with a single match and as it flared, went over and put her phone on to play John Hall's old song from the anti-nuke protests in the 1970s.

"*Just give me the warm power of the sun*
Give me the steady flow of a waterfall…"

The fire popped and she deftly placed split wood inside and closed the door with dull clang.

The song played on "*Just give me the restless power of the wind*
The comforting glow of a wood fire…"

JC tried to seem unconcerned, "Thanks for meeting me at the hospital. You're sure this is OK for me to be here?"

"Probably not," she joked, "I'm a nurse and you were pretty loopy for a while." She smiled and sat down in her reading chair. "Your friend's got your dog. The guy on the motorcycle who got him is my old boyfriend, Ted."

JC was a little hazy and asked if this was the same Ted, he worked for then added. "He's the reason I made it here. Small world, I guess. Peter has Wrigley, that's good, Wrigley likes him. He's so fast, and my asthma always seems to kick in at the wrong time." He thought for a minute and added, "But I think my asthma is getting better, living here."

"About that. You never thanked for me thawing you out. I knew it was you when I saw you running and then getting your inhaler." JC flushed and he fidgeted with his hands remembering he had to find his clothes when he woke up at the Belle Clinic. She asked. "So, why did you leave the clinic that morning?"

"I wanted to find Wrigley. I had no idea if he was still OK." He smiled sheepishly, "And I didn't want to go to jail."

"I don't think losing a dog or freezing to death is a crime. Joe, our Sheriff, is really a big teddy bear. He was happy you didn't freeze, and that he saved your life. Did you notice him at the protest? He asked if you were OK, before he asked where you had gone."

JC looked around the cabin and spied two bedrooms. "This is cool, you live here alone. It's about the same size as the house I grew up in. Only we had my brother, sister, and sometimes cousins too."

"Yes, I love the stillness here on the mountain. I'm guessing with all your family living together you didn't have much space."

The cabin slowly warmed and Julia took off her coat and hat. She pulled the white paper pharmacy bag with JC's prescription from her pocket and set it down. The bandage on his forehead stood out as a white blob and she gave a critical eye to it.

JC changed the subject and said "Thanks for going after Wrigley. He's getting harder to catch."

Julia paused before speaking, "I'm happy Ted caught him. I know this is awful to say, but that guy from Tiger something stuck his foot out as you ran past him."

"Oh that's what happened! The first thing I remember is when the EMTs got me on the stretcher looking up and seeing the creepy smile of the Tiger Paw guy."

"Seriously, that's awful. Well, anyway, can't do anything about it now." Julia sighed, "Thanks for letting me bring you here. They wouldn't release you on your own." she smiled "Where did you grow up?"

"West Virginia, above Myra. It's where Chuck Yeager, the famous test pilot, was born, on the Mud River. You know that old song, Country Roads? I lived on one. 'All my memories gather round her.'" JC quoted the song.

The playing song ended. Julia scrolled for a moment then clicked onto John Denver's folk song Country Roads.

As it began, JC said, "I always wondered what 'miner's lady, stranger to blue water' meant. I must have listened to this song a thousand times."

JC looked in a mirror across the room and was shocked to see himself with a head bandage.

Seeing him looking Julia remembered how bad it was after her car crash in high school. She had the same giant white turban on her head. Healing had seemed like forever.

"I know how bad head injuries can be. You can't see it most of the time butI got it when I busted through the windshield." JC was surprised. She leaned her forehead closer to JC, pulled her hair back, and took his hand, guiding his fingers across a long ridge of scar tissue under her hairline.

"I was hanging out with a fast crowd at school but my parents didn't care. I got wild too. One night we were out at The Spot and I got drunk. Driving home I hit some ice and skidded through a stop sign. The other car was going through so fast they couldn't stop. I totaled our car. My friends got hurt badly but luckily, they survived."

"That's sad, sorry to hear it, but you... wild? Seriously? I can't see it." JC looked up at her.

"My parents had no control over me and there was no love at home for me. One day I was the Rose Queen and the next ended up sleeping over with friends most nights. I just went along and soon was just drifting through life. Anything exciting or fun, I was ready for it. Yes, I was wild."

Turning the conversation back to his roots she asked, "What was it like growing up there?"

JC thought about the good times when he was growing up before the mountaintop was blown off. "In summer, the trees were too thick to see anything much. Our creek across the road settled into a little pond. Below that, there was a spring house where water welled up. Inside was so cool and nice. Every rock had a salamander or two, and the occasional black snake. On hot days we'd try and sit in the water for just a minute but no one could. It was way too cold. Then we'd run out to the sun. We'd catch frogs and turtles.

Every day, we'd go over and it was always something to do. We'd wade up our creek. There were a lot of animals; sometimes deer would come down to drink. Possum and skunks drove our hound dog, Buddy, nuts. I even saw flying squirrels. When it rained hard, we'd go swimming at a lake, catch bullfrogs and fireflies, and pick flowers, or push on puff balls to see the 'smoke' shoot out. In fall we'd go to see Grammy. My cousins would be there too. We picked apples in the orchard and ate so much pie. Her house was on top of everything. I'd run all around that place with my twin sister, Lo. She ran like the wind, when we raced she always won. ``

JC went over to warm himself at the woodstove stretching his fingers out above the firebox. He tilted his head up and examined the roof. The round beams still had their bark on for the most part. It was a simple elegant design, kind of like Grammys but fresh and cleaner. He still felt a little out of it because of the drugs they gave him for the stitches.

"That sounds beautiful. I love this mountain, it is my home and it feeds me. The trees give a green bath every time I'm outside, except for winter, when it's white." Julia saw her feather in the alligator clip and brought it over to show JC.

JC said, "Wow, that's amazing. So delicate." He moved it around to watch it flutter. "The bay was so blue today. It was amazing seeing it with your snowy white mountain here sticking up behind. I never saw so open a view. Back home, the mountains and forests were close in, except at Grammys. There you could see out across the ridges.

Things used to be so beautiful. We lived on a bend in the road that went around both ways and the hill behind us went up into the rocks to a cliff. We'd climb up and look across to the creek looking like a white horseshoe when it was cold enough to freeze.

I loved the ice storms that came through and coated all the trees. They looked like glass or rock candy to me... and the hard ice shell over puddles were fun to stomp when it would freeze. We'd smash them with our boots and they sounded like breaking glass. Once I stepped through and water underneath poured over the top of my boot onto my foot. That was a cold walk home."

Julia laughed. "I know cold."

"It was beautiful...until the coal company came for our mountaintop. I was eight when they came by and said we should move, just sell our home and leave. Daddy said no. Then the surveyors came – a couple of guys in a shiny new pickup truck. I remember one guy had a beautiful green canoe strapped on top. He tramped all over the place. We'd see him in town but he never seemed to see us.

My dog, Buddy, started barking at him. The man didn't seem upset and asked if he could pet him. I said yes and we talked a bit. He asked if he was a good hound. I said he was the best. The guy was excited about fly fishing. He told me about some places where he went in his canoe, how big the rivers got and such. He took a map out of his glove compartment. It was shaded with the mountains and valleys and he showed me where we were. I'd never seen a map like that before. I never thought about home that way. Anyway, he had a nice job. Before leaving he gave me the map.

Then one day, big trucks brought in the dozers. They came and mowed down the trees, all of them. Hickory, birch, walnut they didn't care. Cleared the whole forest off the mountaintop like nothing. Every bird nest, burrow and den gone. Giant tractors came and scraped the broken mess into piles and burned it with diesel fuel. They were rough men, like the mine bosses. For a while, the animals were all running around confused. One day a black bear came charging down the creek, scared me shitless.

That bunch moved on after a while. Then the bulldozers pushed the topsoil off into our creek way up high. They buried the whole stream in rock after that. Road crews came in to make roads for the heavy stuff, they changed our country road into a coal road. From there on out, things kept getting uglier.

A dozen men would drill deep down into the rock every fifty feet or so and fill it with the stuff that Timothy McVeigh used to blow up the Fed building in Oklahoma. They'd set off a long line of charges across the whole face. Smoke billows up and the rock face blows off. The ground would shake and then the sky would darken. Sometimes it turned orange. So creepy in the middle of the day. Then they just put our mountaintop into trucks. Two years later the coal ran out and they were gone."

"To see your childhood memories destroyed before your eyes." Julia felt the anger she was dealing with over Cherry Point rise. "That sounds awful. It must have been terrible."

"When we were little, a car coming on our road was something special. We'd stop to watch as it drove through. Then the coal company made it into their freeway. The equipment just kept growing bigger and dirtier and faster."

JC came back from the fire and sat down on the couch. "Most folks took the money the coal company offered for their houses. We stayed. There weren't enough people left for the church or the school, so we had to drive to them if we wanted to go. My mother loved our little church before we changed. I remember she would sing really loud and when services were over, she'd stay and talk for hours. She had a hard time moving to the new church. She still saw some of the same folks, but it was different, just not the same. She just got sad. She drifted around the house most days like some ghost."

JC felt sadness over his mother's suffering and he tensed. Julia went over to where he was sitting and asked him "What's your tattoo, over your heart? I saw it when we were checking you at the clinic."

JC looked at her, hiding his hurt. She extended her arm and touched the spot on his jacket softly with her finger. "There."

He looked into her eyes and said "That's for my twin sister, Loretta. Lo died."

"I'm sorry. Was that the photo of you two in your backpack?"

The cabin filled with awkward silence. Julia adjusted the vent to the stove and came back. She asked JC if he'd like to go get some rest. Instead, he continued his story.

"Lo was so sweet and kind. We all thought she looked like Loretta Lynn, the famous country singer who sang 'Coal Miner's Daughter' with her long dark hair and bright fiery eyes. She grew up early and seemed older. We were just kids but she really watched over me. We were only thirteen when she died."

After a long pause, JC uttered, "Sometimes life sucks."

Julia patted his heart and then moved back. "That must have been awful. I know how it feels to lose a sister. Seems like we have some tragedies in common. Mine died when I was eight. She had cancer that just swept through her. No time to prepare or say much. We were at the hospital day and night. My family began to fall apart right there. It was just too much for us.

After she died, I went to stay with my aunt for a summer. She was harsh. I never felt she missed my sister much. I did. My grief never gets better, it just fades with time. What happened to Lo?"

JC took a long breath and exhaled slowly, "It was a late afternoon and the sun was going down. We were playing tag in the field across the road near the creek when I had an attack. Lo ran home to get my inhaler. I just lay down. It was so bad.

When she was coming back across the road a coal truck came down from the pit. A pickup came out from behind to pass. An empty coal truck coming the other way hit the pickup and it flipped over toward our house. The empty coal truck swerved across the other lane and onto the shoulder. That's where it hit her.

Lo was running across fast but it hit her anyway. I saw her flying like a rag doll in slow motion until she landed against a big oak tree near me. She just fell straight down onto its roots and the grass. She didn't move and it was weird, her body just crumpled to the ground."

Julia leaned toward JC.

"I couldn't scream because of my asthma. People stopped to get the family out of the pickup because it was leaking gas. They didn't see us; I couldn't call to them. Then Katy, our neighbor, came shrieking out of her cabin. She drove her pickup right into the field where we were. She was tough, no nonsense. She backed right up to us and flipped down the tailgate. She picked Lo up and put her into the bed then helped me in too. I was scared how fast she drove to the hospital.

Lo was lying next to me, covered in an old wool blanket, and black dust from the truck bed kept blowing around. I looked down and blood was soaking through it from her leg and where she hit the tree with her shoulder. Her eyes were closed, unconscious, but I thought she was still breathing. When we pulled up to the hospital emergency door Katy ran in screaming bloody murder.

Two of the hospital men in blue came out running with a stretcher with its wheels chattering and Katy huffing to keep up. They pulled off the blanket and I could see blood from her wounds, I started to cry but I still couldn't breathe right. They gently picked her up and then once she was on it, they raced her inside. Katy said, 'Don't bother with him, he's fine.' I wasn't. It felt like an elephant sitting on my chest.

I was still lying in the truck bed and I felt so cold. I waited, it seemed like forever. This mom with her kids left the ER and one of them saw me lying there. She pointed and her mom came over and asked if I was OK. She didn't wait for an answer, she just told the kids to stay and ran back inside to tell them. Katy came out with a nurse and got me. Once we were inside, they figured out I needed an inhaler. Finally, I could breathe. Afterward, they cleaned all the coal dust off me from the ride in the truck."

Julia listened and fought back her tears.

"I was in the bed next to Lo that night with not much light to see by. She didn't make a sound but I saw her move her eyes, and look at me, like, 'It's OK.' She was like that, always taking care of me. She was holding on to life by a thread.

It was an hour before an old doctor came from another hospital. He hurried in to examine her. Just as he looked into her eyes she died. Just like that. I saw him shake, he could hardly stand. He turned and walked past me, looking so sad. The nurse put her arm around him and helped him out. She came back in and pulled the white sheet over Lo's face. That was the last time I saw it. She was so young and beautiful. The nurse pushed my hair back with her hand and stroked my head for a minute. 'Your sister has gone.' She was crying, and she turned away so I wouldn't see. She put her hand on my shoulder and then pulled the curtain between us and left."

Julia slowly came over and sat on the wide arm of the couch to give him a hug around his shoulders. He sat stiffly recalling the painful event and continued.

"The truck that hit her just kept driving. I watched it go around the bend while I was on the grass. Then it was just the sounds of the people over at the pickup truck in pain. The police said they thought they found the truck driver at another hospital. They charged him with leaving the scene of an accident, and failure to render aid, and operating a motor vehicle on a suspended driver's license. They figured it was the same one who killed Lo, but they didn't press charges. They let him go." JC felt his emotions running away with him.

Julia gently dropped her head onto his and tightened her hug and they sat like that for a few minutes.

"Before she was killed Daddy couldn't stop telling everyone that was his Loretta. 'That's my pride, my angel.' He'd point her out and say 'that's my girl' to total strangers. He even got all cleaned up and drove out to see her run at the county track meet one time. Everybody agreed with him, she ran so beautifully, gracefully. She made it look easy even at the end of the race. I'd watch her in awe.

Daddy treated me like I killed her. I was only thirteen. He was so hard on my mom and little brother too. She finally gave up and left him. He was drunk all the time and got laid off at the mine. He found a new job and slowly just went bad after that. All he did was work in the mines. He volunteered for extra shifts and the most dangerous jobs. Anything wet or muddy, the high-risk stuff. When Lo died, all the joy left my family."

JC's head was on Julia's arm, and he crumpled. Julia stroked his hair back from his bandage and held him. JC looked up at her and slid his arm around her waist and drew her to him. She pulled him close, careful to avoid his bandage.

CHAPTER 18

JUNE 17, 2016
JULIA, LONGVIEW, WASHINGTON

Julia reveled in the lush and evergreen carpeted mountainsides on her drive south from Bellingham to a protest near Portland on the Columbia River. Waterfalls spilled hurriedly, pouring over the rock streambeds into culverts along the mountain flanks as she passed by the lake. She rolled down her window and enjoyed the doppler approach sounds and the finishes of the splash as she whooshed by.

She spotted a pair of eagles soaring along the ridge by the clearcut high above the sun, lighting up their white tail feathers. She felt a thrill at how effortlessly they ascended the thermals. She was sad to see how slowly the scarred, bald ridge was regrowing. Only the trees propagating along the edges seemed to live. It had been twenty years since the loggers came and cut it clean. Their feeble replanting had been wasted effort. Would she live to see it whole again or would erosion cut the topsoil away?

Julia had rearranged her schedule with the Belle Clinic and was driving to Portland to protest the proposed coal terminal near Longview on the Columbia. Carol had been grumpy about taking a shift for her but Ginny offered so it was easy after all.

Julia had stopped in to see her mother briefly before driving south. She never knew how Betty would be, but this visit she seemed to be doing well. Julia was happy she'd had a chance to spend the afternoon with her. Having time to sing and play left her feeling content and close to her.

She spent the night in Seattle with friends and continued in the early morning. They suggested Julia call her old Portland high school friend, Kathy. She hadn't spoken with her for years. The car crash changed everything but Julia decided it had been too long. She called and asked, "Hey Kathy, it's Julia. Any chance you're in town this weekend? I'm coming down for the Millennium protest."

Kathy answered, "Hey Jul, a voice from the past! Good to hear from you. Yes, I'm paddling Saturday in the Mosquito Fleet. Want a boat?"

"I was planning to be on shore and haven't been out for a while… but yes please. It is always such fun to be on the water. Sure, that would be great. I'm sitting in Friday Tacoma traffic and I'll be there in a couple of hours. Would it work to meet?"

"Let's go somewhere in the Pearl and get some coffee." Kathy looked at the time, "I can meet you at ten if that works?"

"Sure, I'd like to stop in at Powell's after. We could meet at Ken's on 21st?"

Parking was awful, one driveway had a voodoo warning against parking, but she found a perfect spot a couple of blocks from Ken's Bakery. Walking down the steep streets took her back to her high school years walking to school. She spied Kathy waving at her, like a raven flapping a wing. She had gages in her ears, the size of silver dollars, a wispy tattoo flowing out from her armpit to her elbow, and luster in her dark eyes.

Kathy and Julia hugged. Her boyfriend, a climbing guide from Boulder, was with her and they went into Ken's, got in line, and began studying the pastry case. Such temptation! They sat at a common table made of thick slabs of ash about ten feet long with the other customers. Kathy began "So good to see you. It seems like forever...and yesterday."

Julia smiled and said, "It does." Looking at Kathy she remembered the wild young woman, so proud, defiant, and pretty that conversation dropped when she walked into a room.

"So, you're here to stop the Millennium?" asked the boyfriend. Julia thought he looked like a Viking with his wiry red beard and broad shoulders. Kathy smiled ear to ear as her boyfriend began to talk.

Julia replied, "That's about it. This administration has reopened the crypt to let out coal demons. The poisonous ones we've worked for years to contain. What a coincidence the coal guys have opened their wallets to Karne. But they need a tidewater terminal to sell their coal."

"Well, you came to the right place for protests, 'Little Beirut' is alive and well." Kathy slid over on the bench so a desiccated man with white bristling beard could sit down. He looked like he'd stepped out of a Degas painting in his black overcoat and beret.

Julia exclaimed, "I saw you on the news! You stopped Shell Oil's icebreaker from heading to the arctic. So, tell me what it was like under the Saint Johns Bridge."

Kathy's boyfriend replied, "I loved hanging out under the bridge. It was beautiful with our banners blowing. We were a tight team and each of us was linked together with arcing ropes.

Dozens of kayaks and canoes pinched the river channel. We turned their icebreaker around. It couldn't squeeze past us the first day. We held it up for a day.

But in the end, they sent it through with a Coast Guard ship leading them. Tough to see them knocking over kayaks and pulling them out of the water on their zodiacs." He took a sip of his chai.

Kathy continued, "Shell couldn't even keep their drill platforms off the rocks. I get so tired of these greedy bastards. They have unlimited money to screw up. Seventy degrees north! That's where they want to drill. What could possibly go wrong?" She let her face mock shock, "They didn't learn anything after their drilling rig Kulluk ran aground on Sitkalidak Island five years ago." She was animated and went on, "I know a Coast Guard heli pilot who had to rescue the crew when it cut loose. It was eighty miles out at sea. He said it was exciting. What he meant was it was a shit-storm, fierce winds, fifty-foot swells. Then there was the Nobel Discoverer, a five-hundred-seventy-foot boat aground in Dutch Harbor. Oops!" she drummed her hands on the table as she spoke.

Kathy's boyfriend added, "They spent billions looking for oil so they could drill and then came up dry. All that treasure could have been put toward making renewables work." He was taking all this personally.

Julia chimed, "Well, if drilling in the arctic is bad, the idea of export-ing coal is just as bad. They want to ship Powder River coal to China and India. Lots of it. Or they can't even make money. Why can't people see Karne's insanity?"

"Where's the Powder River?" Kathy asked, "I've never heard of it."

"East Wyoming. Nobody has. It is a coal field the size of Connecticut with dozens of mines. A bunch of mechanical monsters ripping the earth open. Like the Death Star in scale." Julia continued, "The worst is that after they rip it out, they put it on trains that follow river routes. Not just a little lump of coal, but they plan sixteen miles of trains daily. Then sixteen miles of empty cars back."

"That's a lot of trains." Kathy was appalled, she lived near a rail line and spent time waiting at the crossing, "They go slowly through the city. If you waited for all thirty miles of the train, it would take three hours." She sighed.

"What are you going to do if you need a hospital on the other side?" Julia asked exasperatedly.

"It's madness. The fossil industry isn't playing defense in a war on coal; they are offensive. Knowingly waging war on humanity, poisoning the sky. What hubris and arrogance they live by." Kathy put down her coffee, "We tell ourselves it isn't happening. Maybe we deserve what we get." She got up and stretched, like a dancer, and asked Julia, "Want to get on the water and see if you float?"

"Oh, I float all right." Julia laughed. Kathy never seemed to age, "Hopefully right side up."

"OK let's get on the water. Meet me at two. Remember where we put in, near the bridge?"

"Sure, you have a paddle, spray skirt, and PFD for me too?"

"If you insist." Kathy smiled.

"Great. I'd love to."

"See you there." Kathy gave Julia a hug, and she and her Viking headed off. Julia went to visit Powell's Books, one of her favorite places. She wondered if she could ever leave once inside. It was a magical place where you could forget about all the pollution and problems and let your imagination play.

Ready to go kayaking, Julia pulled into a lumber yard on the southeast side of the Lewis and Clark Bridge over the mighty Columbia River. She rummaged in her bag to get her sweater. Not ideal but warm. She put her windbreaker over the top and went down to the sandy strip along the Columbia under the bridge. Kathy was standing next to two polypropylene single sea kayaks with stickers covering the decks. Julia took a spray skirt and PFD from a little pile of gear, pulled her hair back, and put on her cap.

Kathy was staring at the scar revealed under Julia's hairline. "It doesn't look too bad." she said reassuringly.

"I guess I'm good at using my head." Julia smiled sheepishly.

"Let's paddle down to Walker Island and take a look. You can see how your muscles work on the way home."

They adjusted the foot pegs for Julia and she dragged the boat over the sand to the water's edge. Julia slipped into the seat and adjusted her back support. Then she sealed the cockpit with her spray skirt. She picked up her paddle and gave a thumbs up to Kathy who launched her into the river with a hoot.

Kathy slipped into her boat, and with a heave forward followed her into the current, and they headed down the Columbia toward the Pacific Ocean. The river was a half mile wide and upstream there were huge ships docked along the bank on the Washington side. The water was cold and a deep green color. They ferried across a quarter mile to the middle of the river to get into the main channel.

Julia caught up on years of Kathy's life and loves in Portland as they paddled downstream out in the middle of the channel. As they passed the Millennium terminal site, riprap stones armored the shore and it was fenced. "Imagine this all blowing coal dust and PET coke with giant bulkers tied up to miles of loading conveyors." Julia visualized the noise and the dirty mess around the shoreline. Even as it was, they were using the riverbank as a dump. "Nobody wants this terminal except the coal mine owners."

"Did you join the Women's March?" Kathy asked.

"Didn't everyone? It was such fun. Like a self-medication to inoculate us against the venom in Karne's White House. Everyone I knew joined. All across the country and all around the world. It was epic. Millions of nasty uppity women wearing pussy hats. We called out President Karne and showed him what democracy looks like." Julia remembered the fun she had being with so many women and men who needed to get out and demonstrate.

Kathy asked, "What did women who voted for him expect? Did they want the world he is making? It is beyond me. Maybe they just vote like their husbands tell them. How could they vote for someone who is so obviously afraid of women and needs to dominate them? Maybe they think he is going to buy them furniture?" Kathy spat in the water.

Julia let herself enjoy watching a cormorant fishing, instead of piling on.

To get to Walker Island, they ferried back across the main flow and cut into a big eddy spiraling along shore. Bumping over the turbulent water 'fence' separating the currents, they settled into the upstream flow. They sat quietly for a moment and then paddled into the slough of Walker Island. The island is a wooded haven amid the industrial corridor. Waterfowl watched warily and splashing their webbed feet to launch flying indignantly to another spot.

Kathy and Julia beached their boats on the fine sand, popped out and walked up a way onto a grassy bank. Kathy unfolded a thin ground cloth made with high tech bubbles. Behind them a low thicket of bushes made it their own private island. Perfect spot for enjoying some fruit and a roasted eggplant sandwich for a snack. The sun broke through the clouds.

They spent the next hour exploring a decade of memories. Kathy shared her feeling of grief and loss with Julia. "Sometimes I just feel so sad to see destruction of these natural places. It breaks my heart. We were so lucky to grow up in a time with promise and abundance. I feel guilty, like we failed to protect it."

"So do I. Before we were born Jimmy Carter made it very plain in simple English. We didn't listen and instead decided to 'embrace wasteful and wanton burning of fossil fuels' rather than conserve and look for better ways to keep the lights on."

"I guess they are our Frankensteins, these fossil fuel barons. Dwight Eisenhower called them a bunch of stupid oil men. Maybe they were then, but looks like they've bought some smarts, and now they have the cash to say otherwise. Money from fossil fuels says we don't care if you die using our fuel. Just keep burning it, because we want more money and if it stays in the ground, we don't get any. Thank you for burning."

Julia replied, "Coal pollution is poison. It makes a lot of people sick and kills millions each year. Lancet Medical Journal's new study from over a hundred countries shows global pollution kills three times more people each year than HIV/AIDS, tuberculosis and malaria combined. They reported nine million dead worldwide. We just keep treating the symptoms without going after the cause."

Kathy said. "Let's make a start and see if we can keep the coal terminal off this river tomorrow. It may not be the only cause, but it sure isn't going to make anyone healthy." Then she laid back to relax and take in the beauty.

They got back in the kayaks and paddled upstream against the current. After a while Julia recovered her paddle stroke making it easier to keep up with Kathy.

Kathy exhaled then said, "I have something to ask but I feel it isn't fair to bring it up after all these years."

"You're wondering about what happened after the crash in high school? It has been a long time." Kathy nodded. Julia looked away to the water flowing along and said, "What happened after the crash? I just vanished. Everyone was impossible to me, even you. I lost touch with all our friends, even lost myself." She felt sad recalling the losses she suffered.

Kathy began to cry softly. "We were close friends but I let you down. I'm sorry it was an accident. You know that. I know that." Kathy reassured her.

"But I was the one driving. I-"

Kathy cut her off., "I'm so sorry for all the hate directed at you. We were all a little jealous of you. You were too perfect, Rose Queen and all the boys. We just didn't know any better." She struggled for words. "It hurts me to think I wasn't a good friend when you needed one. I wish I could take that back. I'm sorry."

"It was awful. I'll never know if there was something I could have done. Any way or anything I could have done to avoid the crash." The memory of headlights and the instant of impact jolted Julia as a physical shock. "We were going too fast but so were they." She fell silent. They continued paddling in silence together back to the put in. Kathy gave Julia a long hug once they were out of the boats.

Kathy said. "I'm so sorry." Julia felt years of grief and shame melting away and savored the friendship renewal.

The next day was a beautiful sunny Northwest day for the protest. The Mosquito Fleet was a colorful floating kayak protest/party. Some brought signs and faced the site. People streamed into the riverbank from up and downstream for the assembly. Julia and Kathy had a good time together on the water, happy to have shared their intimate moments the day before. Out together with scores of other boats, Julia pulled alongside Kathy and smiled a conspiratorial smile. "I've got some news."

"Do tell!"

"I met someone. He's younger but I think we have a good relationship." She blushed. "He's a little rough around the edges, but his heart is open."

"How did you meet?"

"It's a funny story. Sheriff brought him, frozen, stiff as a board. He looked otherworldly. I was a regular Pygmalion bringing my frozen statue to life, but I didn't get to talk with him. Then he reappeared a couple months later at a protest." Julia blushed.

"Talking's overrated. I'm so happy for you! That's wonderful." Kathy reached over and gave her a hug, tilting both boats toward capsizing.

"There's more. We were at the Ferndale protest and his dog got loose. He was chasing him and this asshole intentionally tripped him. He slammed into the sidewalk and got a terrible cut on his forehead.

They rushed him to the hospital and I followed. When they were ready to release him, they wanted someone to make sure he didn't have a brain injury. He didn't have anyone, so I took him to my cabin. That's when we got to know each other."

"Is that all? You sound like you did more than that." Kathy raised her eyebrows smiling.

"OK... we kissed and then spent the night together. I think I'm smitten. We've been seeing each other for the last two months." Julia felt happy and a little scared of her feelings. "I don't know if this is going anywhere, but I'm going to give it a go. I feel safe with him."

"So, tell me more."

Julia said. "We share some loss and some loves. He is kind, maybe a little young. We have fun together."

When the protest ended and they were ashore, Julia took her phone out of the dry bag and saw she had missed a call from her mother's rest home. The voicemail played "You better get up here as soon as you can." There was a pause, "Betty's in the ICU."

Julia shuddered, "I've got to go. I'll call you." She stripped off her gear and ran to her car.

The bottom had dropped out of her life, she was in freefall. After driving for several hours in a zombie state she called JC. "Can you meet me at the Good Angel Hospital? My mother, Betty, is in the ICU. I don't think I can go alone this time." She began sobbing, "I don't want to lose her."

"Of course. Let me know what time you'll be here." JC put his hand to his head and then went to see Peter to tell him he would be out for the day and to ask if he'd take Wrigley.

CHAPTER 19

JULY 10, 2017
TED AND WOODROW, CHICAGO, ILLINOIS

A year later Ted's plans were in a new phase and he was energized. Woodrow was in a whole new world, his uncle Peter helped him find a room to rent, and he'd been able to feel positive about his future living in Bellingham. He'd never flown before and O'Hare International was a huge airport, even bigger than Seattle, where he already felt overwhelmed. Woodrow wondered why Ted wanted to meet him in Chicago. Working with Ted was like that. He just told you what to do without explanation.

Woodrow marveled at the tunnel ahead. Soft reflecting tones of undulating glass walls, lit to create a ceiling of coral colors framing the center neon excitement mirrored from above. All covering the moving sidewalks. Like one of the color assortments displays in a paint store with value and hues in endless progression. The brightly polished terrazzo floor amplified depth and dimension to the tunnel connecting Concourses B and C of Terminal 1 at O'Hare International.

Ascending via escalator, daylight poured into the lobby and Woodrow missed seeing the dinosaur at the top entirely. A Brachiosaurus skeleton standing four-stories high, and seventy feet long and Woodrow was oblivious to it. He only saw the gate number Ted had given him, took a seat, and waited.

When Ted arrived, Woodrow barely recognized him. He was wearing a stylish smooth black leather jacket, a dress shirt, and slacks. Ted pointed up and Woodrow followed his direction until he noticed the massive dinosaur saying, "Did you see Jurassic Park? The T-Rex is about this size but has a different diet." Woodrow tilted his head back and looked up at the distant skull atop the narrowed neck, poking against the brightly lit arched gray steel roof girders. It was so out of place. Down on the concourse the legs were surrounded by rolling bags and hustling passengers. Weirdly out of scale.

Ted asked Woodrow, "What would you do if this dinosaur was threatening your life? How would you stop it? What would you do? Seriously, this one was more than fifty tons. You are just standing here, what would you do?"

Woodrow was surprised by the question. It wasn't a scary dinosaur. He was confused why he'd want to kill it. Certainly, this one wasn't built for speed so he'd have a minute or two. Even if he could get up there to attack the head, he would be afraid of being that far off the floor. Looking at the massive leg bones he saw they were as big as he was. "I don't know. I never thought about anything this big."

"Hard to imagine it alive and dangerous, isn't it?" Ted paused, "Suppose you had to go after one of these giants? Where would you start?"

Woodrow looked at all the people in the terminal going by, oblivious to his mental task, and finally offered "I'd get a rocket and shoot it, or maybe a fighter jet?"

Ted looked amused, "Like in monster movies! It's funny, when Godzilla first walked out of Tokyo Bay, he was only about fifty feet high. Now he's over three hundred fifty. You'll need a bigger rocket." Ted continued, "Where would you get one?"

"I don't know. Maybe instead I'd tie the legs together like the AT-ST walkers in Star Wars with a strong rope or a cable."

Ted paused, considering, then replied, "I like that. A tripping point for this monster. Might work, assuming you could get away once it fell. It would just be lying in front of you hogtied and wondering what happened. It likely wouldn't even notice you."

"I had no idea they were this big." Woodrow said slowly, still scanning the skeleton floor to ceiling.

"Coal monsters are bigger. I call them 'geosaurs.' They're far more terrible to the earth than these lizards." Ted led Woodrow out of the terminal to find a taxi.

Ted continued once in transit, "In Germany's coal fields, they have a dragline. It is a thirty-story high building, with two football field sized areas where the bucket scoops up coal and dumps it onto conveyors. They are mile-long ribbons running from behind to the train yard. They load the coal trains and off it goes. A small moveable city on top of a crawler, with a seventy-foot diameter buzzsaw at one end. It weighs two hundred thousand tons."

"That's big." Woodrow was still thinking about the dinosaur.

"When the coal owners say they make jobs, think about this: it takes only five men to run the German monster as it gobbles coal day and night."

Woodrow tried to understand these big numbers. They meant nothing to him. Ted was hard to understand most of the time. He got the part about only five men to run the monsters.

Walking outside, the summer heat and humidity wrapped around them. In the taxi, it was cold. Ted went on about the 'geosaurs', "We will be the hunters going to bring down the monster."

"We will what?" Woodrow wasn't following.

"Draglines. Hard to believe but that is the scale of these draglines, geosaur monsters." Ted was exasperated and looked to see if Woodrow was with him, "We will hunt it like wolves. We stay on the target. The game tires and slows, but we don't. That's the way my grandfather hunted Buffalo Bob and was able to kill him." Woodrow had no idea what Ted was talking about.

The taxi drove through ever more sketchy neighborhoods, abandoned for decades on the South Side of Chicago. They turned onto South Commercial Avenue, in an area called 'Slag Alley,' because so many lots were covered in abandoned coal and coke. Far in the distance the Sears Tower appeared tiny. The driver stopped in front of a dilapidated brick garage with huge swing out doors, and a domed roof. Old, cracked wire-glass windows were all painted out. Vacant lots defined by rusty chain link fences adjoined the building. A sofa with its guts out was facing the street.

Hanging on a lag bolt, suspended by a coat hanger, a small, air-brushed fiberboard sign read 'Chop Shop' in fancy shaded letters. It was the only visible marker aside from the street number, which was carelessly spray-painted about two feet high in bright yellow.

Woodrow was still thinking about the Brachiosaurus skeleton when the taxi driver said, "This is the address you gave me." He paused, "You sure?" Ted paid in cash without answering. The driver was so eager to be heading out of the neighborhood, he almost drove off before they unloaded. Ted quickly smacked his trunk so they could grab their duffel and backpacks. The sweaty day made their clothing stick immediately.

Ted pushed open a man door cut into the fifteen-foot-high swing double doors and entered the industrial brick building. On their right was a box shaped office building with a flat roof and an air conditioning on top. The center was open to the back of the building, and a giant spray booth to their left, with lots of air handling equipment and an exhaust stack up through the roof.

Gray primer dust covered everything. Industrial lights hung down from pipes with cages over the dusty white reflectors. A loud staccato 'vuv-vtvuuuuvt' of pneumatic tools echoed around the cavernous space. The back of the main floor was filled by six hydraulic lift bays and a heavy-duty frame-straightener at the far end, bolted down to the cement. Limo parts and frames hung from the arched wooden rafters like Christmas ornaments.

A couple of wrecked limos were cut in half ready to be recombined. Motorcycles were parked next to the office at the front, and two brand new black Lincoln Town Cars parked next to them. There was also a cherry red Chevy van. Stepping inside the office it was quieter, but just as chaotic. At least the air was clean. Woodrow was surprised to see a couple of huge computer monitors displaying complex schematic mechanical drawings.

Ted crossed to the desk where a middle-aged man with greasy jet-black hair with a white streak sat. He swiveled around from his work. His beer gut looked out of place on his solid body. He stood and came over to greet Ted with a bear hug. "How is the thermite king?"

Ted smiled and replied, "Boris, you know I'm a respectable ship-wright? Right?" Boris looked surprised and then laughed, with a bit of a snicker.

"Of course you are. Quite the artist with that stuff." Staring at Woodrow, he demanded, "Who are you?" While Woodrow stammered, Boris looked back to Ted, "Where's Fabrice?"

"This is Woodrow, he's going to be my driver today."

Boris looked at Woodrow, "So you are going to drive." Then sharing a wry smirk with Ted, "The company you keep… really." He stared for a bit longer, then turned back to Ted. Woodrow was relieved when Boris wasn't studying him.

"The van's all set for you. Your dispenser racks just barely fit, good specs. We lined them up and tested them with some cans of Dr Pepper. They work just like t-shirt cannons! Good range too." He laughed, "Some of our neighbors weren't expecting the showers." He added, "The other two sets shipped to Anacortes as you requested. All the VINs are gone on the vans, they are clean."

Ted held out a small duffle to Boris, "Thanks, I know you know clean." While Boris took the bag, looked inside, pushing the bundles of cash around, Ted added, "Fabrice died doing aluminothermic connections undersea on the pipeline supports under one of the platform legs. Something went wrong and it crumpled, pinning him about eighty feet down. It was a horrible scene. They couldn't get him air and couldn't get him up in time. Later the whole rig collapsed all because the company ignored their engineers."

"Dangerous work in a dangerous place. Sorry to hear." Shaking his head, "I liked him. He was a funny man, and like you, an artiste!" He gave Ted a shoulder hug and fake uppercut punch. "Da?" He took the van keys out of a small safe and handed them to Ted. Woodrow noticed a couple of Glock semi-automatic pistols in the safe before Boris closed it.

Ted looked directly at Boris, "It would be good for you to make sure none of the plans ever existed. If it gets hot it will be thermite level heat, and it's going to get hot, guaranteed."

Boris laughed, "Good luck." He glanced at Woodrow, then back to Ted, "Sorry about Fabrice. He was a good man." He leaned back in his swivel chair, "See you in church."

Ted laughed and said, "Give Tatiana my best. Dasvidaniya."

Woodrow started to say goodbye, but Boris was back at his monitors.

Ted handed Woodrow the keys and said, "You drive."

Woodrow finally understood his purpose. He unlocked the driver door to the red Chevy van and climbed in. Ted sat in the passenger seat. Woodrow started the van and carefully backed out onto the street. In daylight, he blinked at the red. It was like a fire engine. Not a typical Chevy van, no radio, glove compartment, insulation or door covers for starters. It looked normal from the exterior but inside was skeletal. Bare metal everywhere and the contraption bolted to the floor in back, no mats, no ceiling cover, nothing. Woodrow had trouble hearing Ted, even when he yelled to give him directions out onto the highway.

When they got onto Interstate 70, Ted had Woodrow pull into a rest stop. Ted handed him a roll of cash and some documents, "Here are the papers and registration for this van. Don't get pulled over. Meet you at my ranch in East Glacier." Woodrow took the money and waited for more explanation. Ted gave him a thumbs up, climbed out, and walked away. Woodrow looked at the bills, a lot for gas money. There was no air conditioner. The van was going to be a miserable ride.

CHAPTER 20

JULY 12, 2017
JC AND JULIA, ANACORTES, WASHINGTON

Peter, from ALU, lived near work in a big house. He had turned half his detached garage into a living space. He'd done a good job insulating it so the electric wall heater was adequate. His shop and motorcycles were in the other half of the garage and he parked his big trailer on the driveway.

JC's room that he rented from Peter had a bathroom and main room. JC got an inflatable queen-sized bed with a built-in electric pump that kept it filled, and his sleeping bag spread across it. On one side of his bed, he had a plastic milk crate for his lamp and clock. There was a mini fridge, kitchen sink, hot plate, toaster oven, and electric hot water kettle. His backpack was empty and stored in the closet. Wrigley had his own set up too. Dog bowls for food and water, a dispenser for large bags of food, and in a high cupboard, some leathery treats to shred. He slept on a Mammoth floor bed, filling it completely. It took up most of the available floor space.

JC and Julia had been sharing time between her cabin on Mt Baker and JC's room. They were enjoying the Northwest life together. Skiing or snowshoeing in winter, hiking, and mountain biking in spring, and now they were trying out sea kayaking too. She outfitted him with most of the stuff he needed through her friends who had extra gear.

Julia loved how easily JC had taken to outdoor life. She liked to pick a destination and name the way to enjoy it. They had been out almost every weekend for the last couple of months.

It was a warm night and still light when they came back from biking around Lopez Island on the ferry. Peter came out and met them, "How'd you like to try my homebrew tonight?" He had already set the outdoor table on the lawn with some snacks and mugs and a collection of his IPAs in a cooler.

JC, "Sounds great. Let us put our stuff away first." He looked at Julia and added, "Maybe an hour, so we can take showers."

Wrigley bounded over and put his big head on Peter hoping for attention. He sat and put his paw up and Peter fell right into his plan, petting his short stiff fur. "How's our little bodyguard?" Julia was glad to see the training they had sent him to was paying off for him. He had been such a wild puppy and now everyone commented what bearing he had. Wrigley sauntered over to the pile of firewood and picked out a small log and began to shred it into pieces.

When they came back Julia's long hair was still wet and shiny from the shower.

Julia and JC came out and sat with Peter, "What do you recommend?" Julia asked.

"Oh, definitely my Welderman IPA." he said." and added "A little hazy but powerful." Pouring each of them a mug.

Wrigley was sleeping at JC's feet, "I've been looking forward to testing your beer craft."

They drank for a bit and recounted their island adventure. Julia was thrilled that they'd seen a family of Orcas from the ferry. She talked about how they were playing and breeching and how the baby Orca followed his mom.

Peter poured another round of beers and talked to them about his nephew, Woodrow. "He's going to need a place to live. He is starting at the bottom the way you did. Cleaning up, organizing the materials, and working the late shift. He's a kid who's had some tough times. When he was up north, he was accused of damaging some fracking wells. I asked him, and he said he wasn't doing anything but living there. He said they needed a scapegoat because they couldn't catch this crazy man, Wiebo.

I don't know if I believe him, or maybe he was involved. He is a good kid, though. I guess not a kid but your age." Peter scratched the back of his neck and added, "I'm thinking that you might be earning enough lately to find a better spot so he could take this place you are using now."

JC nodded, "Woodrow seems like a good guy from what I've seen. Julia and I have been talking about finding a place closer to Julia's work. Something in Bellingham or Fairhaven. I don't mind commuting and it would be closer to her cabin."

Peter sighed in relief, "I'll wait for you to find something. Let me know as soon as you do. This is good news on timing! Glad you two lovebirds can migrate closer together."

They enjoyed the sun outside and decided to get some pizza to go with their beer. "Have you heard anything from Ted recently?" JC asked Peter, "I haven't seen him at work."

"I was going to ask you the same thing. There isn't much at ALU that we need him for these days. Most of the time we can farm the work out among ourselves. I guess he decided to go out to his place in Glacier. He doesn't always say what he's up to. I heard he asked Woodrow to meet him in Chicago, but he didn't say anything more about it."

CHAPTER 21
JULY 15, 2017
TED, EAST GLACIER, MONTANA

Ted climbed out of his Bronco and intense heat from the asphalt parking lot waved over him. He reached across and grabbed a briefcase from the passenger seat. His feet roasted on the short walk to the Blackfoot Casino. The casino was located between the rez and the pale blue silhouettes of Glacier's peaks. Ted noticed that even the highest peaks had barely any snow.

Entering the Casino, the temperature dropped forty degrees. A cacophony of bells, jarring alarms, and lights assaulted him. He made his way quickly through the maze of machines to the elevators and punched the top button for the Eagle Suite. He exhaled slowly and his feet cooled off.

Arriving at the Eagle Suite the elevator doors opened and Lenny, the manager at the casino, caught his arm and steered him into an empty room. Wearing Ariat boots and a tailored suit with a heavy gold bracelet, he said. "Welcome Ted, I don't know what you are up to, but your weights were spot on. You will find your credit is very good across the border."

He kept hold of Ted's arm, "As you asked, there isn't any paperwork. When you get to Medicine Hat, text Sun Chief. He is a good man and remembers you from your childhood visits. Here is his number. This is a lot of money. Sometimes things like this can get messy, call me if you need anything. Sun Chief will take care of you. Whatever you need, just let him know." Ted was relieved to hear his financial plan was complete.

Ted faced him and shook his hand, "I appreciate your help on this. There is nobody else who could do it for me." They walked through the vestibule into the meeting area. Lenny pushed the down button to go back into the casino and Ted walked into the elegant conference room.

Ted was excited and nervous as he saw the familiar faces of the elders, the dozen old men of his mother's family, seated around the big glass tabletop carved with salmon and eagles. Ted greeted each of them, and then went to the head of the table. They sat, open to hearing his story. He took a couple of deep breaths and began.

"Thank you for coming, I know you want to be with the people and prepare to celebrate at the Sun Dance." He paused and took another deep breath, "I was on top of the Backbone of the World in the dead of this past winter and I had a vision, it was like the glaciers were alive but dying in front of me. As I came out of the wilderness, just up here at Two Medicine Lakes, thunder of the mountains spoke to me. Now I am leaving here to go on my spirit journey."

"Are you sick?" one of his uncles asked.

Ted laughed a relieved, deep laugh. "No, I am hoping to have a long, slow trip to the Sand Hills. I have deeded my land, my buildings, and my tools, to our Community College. I hope our young people will learn to make things and build a future with them. There are many needs to be met in our community. I am giving a small donation of money to staff the start-up for this program too."

Running Rabbit nodded slowly and then asked, "Is this your vision? To help the young people?"

"That is part of it. My vision is to bring glaciers back to the mountains. To do this is to dispossess the coal industry of its ability to take coal from the earth. Coal is a major cause of the heat that kills glaciers and people. I know this won't bring them back today but they must come back or the mountains will just be lifeless rock." He felt his words were inadequate but went on talking.

"You all know me as a mechanic with welding skills who has served the tribe and a Marine who has served our country. I asked you here to witness my decision to dispossess myself of all the material things of my life. I will give up my home, real estate, and place of work. In its place, I'll take up my quest to preserve the sacred in this world. For me that is our glaciers." He hesitated and continued, "The US president is giving coal a new life with his support. I can't wait any longer. I will stop them from taking more coal from the Powder River mines, at least for a time. Their mining causes great harm to us, our next generations, and all the living creatures of our mother earth.

"They claim to be rich and powerful because they know where to dig for coal and how to get legal rights on public lands leased for pittances from the federal government. They use their money as a weapon against us. They use the money talk as a tool to tilt the table so they can continue to take money out while leaving pollution and destruction to all of us. They know the impact of their schemes but lie and corrupt the process to suit themselves."

Ted continued, "Dispossession is not an American virtue. It is a crime. So are the lies they tell to keep selling their dirty fuels, the poison, grief, and ashes they leave for us."

The elders looked at each other around the table. This was a heavy message from someone they saw occasionally in the summers and who mostly helped with fixing machines.

"Are you in trouble?" Running Rabbit, his mother's brother, was concerned for Ted. She had been so proud of him when she was alive.

"No, not now. But I know some who will be angry with me soon. I want you to know my intent is to heal. I want to stop the glaciers from disappearing forever." He looked at each of them in turn. "Tell anyone who asks that I've gone to the Sand Hills. I gave all my things away. I had a vision and left to follow it. Nothing else matters to me."

White Cloud Gathering spoke in his measured tone. "The Sand Hills are a magical place. You need to die to enter. Are you wishing to leave this earth?"

Ted was surprised. "No, I'm working very hard to stay and help it heal. To prepare myself I will join the braves in Oh-Kee-Pah tomorrow. Today I give my land and gifts of my ancestors to the tribe. I will take nothing with me."

I have lived in two worlds for too long. Now I am He-Mah-Ta-Ya-Latkake – Thunder Rolling From the Mountains, the name my grandfather gave me as a baby."

White Cloud Gathering spoke, "Your grandfather was a great man and he named many. He was my friend."

Ted opened the briefcase he'd brought. "Here are the deeds and all the keys to open my fences, my workshop, and to my cabin. I've spoken with Dam Beaver. He knows all of my secrets of my house, property, and workshop." He handed Dam Beaver the keys, and White Cloud Gathering the deed, and shook their hands. Finished with his speech, Ted sat down.

There was a long silence after which White Cloud Gathering spoke, "We hear your vision and we share your suffering. You bring honor to your parents and to us all. We welcome your gifts. You are generous. Thank you."

The others added their thanks and appreciation talking about the work ahead and the generous gifts. There was a lot of concern for Ted as well.

A catered lunch arrived and Ted sat with White Cloud Gathering. They talked about the Sun Dance and honoring his great grandfather and mother. White Cloud Gathering's family had been at Carlisle Indian School to represent the Blackfoot Nation in 1910 for the ceremony giving up lands to become Glacier National Park. Like Buffalo Bill's actors they were paraded in Washington D.C for Teddy Roosevelt in their finest attire.

They talked about his family camping in the lobby of the Glacier Park Hotel to show native ways to the guests. This was sadly while they were kept out of the hunting grounds in the park. White Cloud Gathering told many stories of his family and funny things that happened. It was late afternoon when they left to go home and prepare for the potlatch. The sun was still high in the sky and the parking lot was even hotter as Ted crossed back to his Bronco. He felt a great weight lifted from his shoulders. He felt free to begin his quest.

The next day, tribes cut and carried a tree for the center pole of a lodge. For the Sun Dance ceremony in the field near Two Medicine Lake. Ted enjoyed his part in raising the structure. Once it was erected, people came from far and wide to be together for the Sun Dance. Hundreds of willow poles held up the center and many sacred bundles were fixed to respect the old ways. When all was complete, they retired and came back later that night to sing and dance. The next morning the potlatch ceremony would begin.

Ted wore native clothing for the ceremony. Medicine Woman came forward holding the Pipe Bundle and spoke to the gathering. "The man you know as Ted gives us all his worldly goods today. He is our beloved and we honor his gifts. We wish him our strong spirit to succeed in his quest to heal the earth." She walked him around in front of the assembly. "Now we will know him as He-Mah-Ta-Ya-Latkake – Thunder Rolling from the Mountains. Let the people know through all the tribes of the plains that he is our beloved brother."

Ted stood in the center near the pole with Medicine Woman, "I am Thunder Rolling from the Mountains, He-Mah-Ta-Ya-Latkake, the name my grandfather gave me at birth. Today I am here with courage and sadness. Courage to fight the coal owners for our glaciers, the headwaters of our land. Those who rape the land and burn the sky with their greed. I will take my courage from our ancestors. I am here with sadness for the Backbone of the World. Our beautiful glaciers are melting, and it will be many generations before they are once again whole. They feed all life below them and we need to help their return. I ask you to help to heal this world.

My journey will be away from my home. Today I am giving all my things, my many tools, my land, my house to you so that I can be free. It is a blessing to give them to the people. I hope you will use them as you see fit and that they will help the tribe."

Medicine Woman and White Cloud Gathering stood with him and welcomed his potlatch on behalf of the tribe.

Ted went into preparation for the next part of the ceremony. He knelt with the other braves who were going to participate and freed his mind. He took off his ceremonial buckskin shirt and walked to the center pole of the lodge. It was a sturdy tree trunk the size of a telephone pole set for the Oh-kee-pah ceremony. He took two of the hooks dangling at the end of long lines from near the ground and poured alcohol over them before piercing them into his flesh above his chest muscles to anchor them. He walked slowly away from the center pole and the lines tensioned. Leaning back against the pain he began a long-suffering dance with the other braves.

He stood with the other braves in mystical ritual time until the hooks cut through his flesh and freed him. He collapsed on the ground. When he woke, he was in a tipi with several other braves. A woman with a long black braid and perfect molasses color skin was tending his wounds. She smiled and looked into his eyes and caressed his face. He passed out again.

Semi-trucks far away in Anacortes picked up Ted's containers at ALU yard and drove them to the container dock for shipment – one bound to Vladivostok and on to Siberia, the other to Tynes Container Yard in Brisbane, Australia for China's new Galilee Basin coal mine.

CHAPTER 22

AUGUST 21, 2017
TED, POWDER RIVER BASIN, WYOMING

Ted finished his shower and went through his checklist again. He prepared for an intense day ahead. He finished his breakfast in the spacious dining hall of the modern style Wright Motel, the closest one to the Black Thunder mine in the Powder River Basin. A group of executives with their families were excitedly talking about the eclipse at the table next to him. They had jackets and shirts with embroidered logos, swag from Black Thunder, Rawhide, and Antelope Mines. Their little kids were chasing each other around the hall. The adults were reverently passing around a special telescope with filters on it to use for observation one of their friends had brought. Ted mused about their gift to their heirs – a lot of money and a planet on fire.

He checked out and went outside but when he came to his ALU truck a Land Rover was blocking it. He felt a rare moment of panic and went back into the dining room. He asked if the group knew whose car it might be.

One of the dads fumbled in his pocket as he got up. "Sorry, I thought, with the eclipse and all, that you wouldn't be needing that truck."

Ted forced a casual smile and followed him out to the ALU crane truck he'd borrowed back in Anacortes. The ten miles to the overpass flew by quickly as he headed to the mine complex. It was a sunny cloudless day for the eclipse and he was back on time to meet it.

Going across the overpass above the four mainline tracks he was relieved to see that Woodrow, Peter's nephew, had already parked the bright red van. The magnetic Coca Cola decals looked like the real thing. When JC had refused to help Ted, he had been in a spot. Luckily, Woodrow deadheaded the Bronco, and then helped him get the van.

Woodrow had set up all four of the launchers – the ones Boris had fabricated in Chicago to dispense the cans into the hopper cars and one above each of the main tracks of the Orin. Next to them was a stack of boxes with the cans he had made in Anacortes. Everything looked as it should.

Ted parked and Woodrow came over holding a clipboard with Ted's diagram and checklist. Every step was detailed exactly with checkboxes. It looked silly, but he was just there to help. Woodrow was uncomfortable to trust Ted blindly and Ted felt the same. Uncle Peter had given him confidence that Ted was doing something big, something important.

"I think I've got all your numbers on the checklist and the stuff set up as you asked me to. So, what's all this?"

"As I told Peter, it is best for all of us if you don't know. You will see soon enough." Woodrow shrugged and went back to his chores.

Ted got into the ALU truck bed and clipped a hook onto a couple of straps with the crane. He helped Woodrow up into the truck bed, and together they muscled two oxygen canisters into the bucket of the cherry picker using the circular stainless-steel rails around their tops to maneuver them. Ted strapped them down.

"Big day! It is going to be exciting around here for the eclipse!" Ted slapped Woodrow on the back and they climbed out of the truck bed.

Woodrow looked around and saw only vast open prairie and a couple of train tracks, nothing exciting to see at all.

Ted went over to each one of the can launchers, the ones Boris had packed into the red van. He checked the compressed air tanks and the loading mechanism over to see if they were in good working order. He launched a couple of Mountain Dew cans onto the tracks from each of them to satisfy himself. He watched them splatter dead center between the rails. His cans filled with thermite were tougher and would hold together as they hit the coal.

"Looks good, thanks for all your help getting them ready. Any coal-filled train that comes under is ours. Go ahead and fire a can into each car. I'll be back for the eclipse." He checked his watch. "Be sure to wear your glasses when you look at the sun. It should be exciting to see!" He hoped Woodrow would stay steady with his task.

With that, Ted got back in the ALU truck and headed to Wally's twenty-story loading silo. He pulled into the parking lot next to the industrial propane tank a hundred feet long. He fixed a pack with red painted cans to the thick exit pipe where it joined the enormous manifold.

CHAPTER 23
AUG 21, 2017
TED, POWDER RIVER BASIN, MONTANA

Wally, a slight and thoughtful young man, was driving his aged Kia to the coal loading silo to start his shift. He exited the cloverleaf off the main road from Wright. As he came up to his turn, he noticed a bright red Coca Cola van parked on the shoulder of the overpass over the tracks. Curiously, he didn't see anyone with it. He turned north toward work at the twenty-story high concrete double silo a half-mile down the road. He parked close to the silo entry door and waved to the guys leaving their shift. He took off his dark glasses and put them carefully in his glovebox and put on his inside pair. Climbing up the dusty concrete stairs to his office and hanging his coat, he checked around the small boxy room and took his seat at the controls to load coal into the hopper cars. He gave the clear signal to the waiting empty train.

The train horn sounded and three bright headlights of the train engine shone from the loop track outside and lit up the pitch-dark loading dock below him. Diesel exhaust fouled the air as the engine rumbled into position. The two glistening steel rails were all that stood out in a floor of black dust below. The sphincter of the coal loading operation above it was a mass of black-on-black shapes. Orange BNSF train engines passed by his window and his first empty car came up. He moved the small joystick to drop the fill chute slightly into the car. Pushing the red button next to it, he released a hundred tons of coal, evenly showering into the hopper. For the rest of his shift the view would always be the same, a never-ending line of empty rail hoppers. Another day had begun.

He pulled a magazine from his collection and opened it to the story he'd been reading about the eclipse. Above him, he could feel and hear the coal thunder out of the surge bin into the apron feeder. Then a deep rumble as it flowed through the slide gate and down onto the shuttle conveyor. After that it hammered onto the undercut gate in front of him. Just like clockwork, this vast machine twenty stories high sifted coal evenly into hopper cars leaving a classic bread loaf shape in each.

Sometimes there was a glitch. The coal could build an arch inside the silo and then thunderously collapse. Or a rathole could form in the coal supply cutting down flow to a small tunnel inside the silo. Usually it was the same old, same old all day long. Train engines pulled the car under this rock fall of material for less than a minute, and he raised the cut gate slightly to clear the car's back wall and the front of the next. Then he dropped the cut gate into the empty car and hit the red fill button.

The filled hoppers rolled out of the silo into the light of day. His loading silo ran at high speed and computer scales made sure every car filled to capacity. Sometimes a customer would send in a guy to try and catch the scales reading inaccurately but that hadn't happened as far back as he could remember. In just over an hour, he could fill an entire unit train of a hundred cars. Things weren't as hurried as they had been a few years ago before the natural gas boom. Loading moved steadily under his watchful control. He went back to the article.

Wally noticed the ALU truck pulled up near the propane tank on one of his video monitors. His surveillance monitors helped him to feel less claustrophobic – a TV window to the outside. The truck was only there for a minute, and then it sped out of the lot and bumped across the tracks to the support tower of the conveyor. Maybe this was the electrician he'd heard would be coming.

It parked next to the feed conveyor support towers across the tracks. The guy in the cherry picker lifted a big backpack and hung it around one of the supporting legs of the tower. Then in sequence he took packs out for all the other steel beams and braces. He positioned the dozen packs on the steel at funny angles and climbed down. He brought the bucket back into the truck bed.

He unrolled and taped up an orange paper banner that said "Get the hell out of here. NOW" Then he went back and blew the truck's horn three short, then three long, then three short blasts, S-O-S before he sped away. The eclipse began to slowly tint the sky.

Ted drove away from the silo area, conveyor tower, and propane tank down toward the mine entrance.

CHAPTER 24
AUG 21, 2017
TED, POWDER RIVER BASIN, MONTANA

Ted waved to Woodrow as he drove the ALU truck across the overpass and down the main road into the mine between coal trains and a two-mile-long white covered conveyor. Halfway down he bumped off onto the prairie on an unused dirt road. Five hundred feet further, he arrived at a small electric substation. Ted crashed the chain link gate with his bumper, turned around and backed over it, and parked close to the poles supporting the transformers.

Four square metal poles suspended two transformer decks about twenty feet above him. Aside from the hum and buzz, it was dead quiet. Above them, high tension wires branched out in all four directions. He duct taped a blue bandolier of cans onto each of the poles fifteen feet above ground and secured them with long nylon zip ties.

Bouncing back out onto the road, Ted drove down along the conveyor for half a mile, and then turned down the road that led down to the bottom of the five-story loading shed. Henry was in a queue of giant haulers waiting to dump their loads in at the top floor. He was eager for his turn to dump a last load to end his shift. He looked down and saw Ted arrive at the bottom of the crushing and sizing building in his ALU truck.

Ted could see the crushed coal pouring out of the fill chute at the bottom of the building and onto the eight-foot-wide rubber belt. He backed his truck up as close as he could to the spot just before the steel canopy enclosed the entire conveyor belt. His ears were throbbing from the thunderous sound. Ted investigated the giant steel tube carrying its river of coal up to the silo.

Making sure his yellow painted soda cans were tight atop the oxygen cylinders he squeezed into the bucket with them. Using his joystick on the crane controls, he lifted them over the fast-moving river of coal on the conveyor belt. Lowering as close as he could before opening the cherry picker door he unstrapped and pushed the heavy oxygen cylinders out onto the belt. He was relieved that they didn't explode. They joined the coal and were out of sight in a second.

Replacing the cherry picker, he drove up onto the main road headed back up toward the overpass. He checked his watch. The oxygen containers would arrive at the silo end in twelve minutes, synchronized with the eclipse totality. Then he drove out onto the main road once more and up to Woodrow and parked.

Woodrow was wearing his eclipse glasses and he gave Ted a thumbs up as the launcher put a can in each car of the trains moving slowly beneath them. Ted noticed a new train coming underneath the overpass.

In the cab of the lead locomotive, the engineer driving underneath them, looked up and saw Woodrow watching. Turning to his fireman he said "Lookie here! We got a 'foamer.' Take a good look, he don't have a camera but he's got a mess of stuff up there! Suppose it's to look at the eclipse? Looks like he works for Coca Cola."

The fireman put down his porn magazine and started laughing. 'Foamers' was slang for train fans who took pictures and videos of them going past. "Hope he don't cream his jeans with our big bad unit. Go on, give him a toot." The engineer put down his book and pulled a blast on the horn as they went under the overpass. Directly above them, Woodrow went weak at his knees at the intensity of the sound. The train kept moving ponderously below and the launcher began lobing cans into the cars as it passed beneath them.

The sky darkened as total eclipse neared.

At the substation the thermite ignited. Cutting through the steel support structure with white hot showers and orange melted metal, transformers and the overhead wires ripped free of the transmission lines sending sparks everywhere throughout the substation. Fires started as downed wires writhed on the grass. Breakers and relays popped and shut down the entire electric grid for the mine.

Wally was hoping to finish loading the train and go outside for a look at the eclipse. He had a handful of cars left to load. The power went out, totally, on all his systems. This was new. The emergency lights went on in his control room and on the chute outside but none of the heavy machinery was live. He tried to raise the cut gate but it wouldn't respond. The car's rear wall came up onto it and smashed into it with enormous force making a terrible racket. He tried to call the command center, but his radio wasn't connecting. He got on his cell phone and saw he had no connection.

The hopper cars out his window passed by, unfilled and banging on the damaged cut gate. Then the silo rocked with the explosion of the propane tank outside. Wally bolted from his chair and fled down the stairs bursting outside in time to see the debris field of the propane tank explosion. A section of the tank had flown across the yard into his Kia smashing the passenger doors in and popping his windshield out. The fences were flattened by the explosion. The train was still moving under a huge smoke cloud working its way skyward above the pad. The sky was blackening and stars were coming out. What the fuck?

He didn't know what to do after the explosion so he began walking toward the towers to take the stupid sign down. As he was walking across the four sets of tracks, all the packs on the conveyor support columns flashed brilliant white light showering orange sparks around. The steel looked like lava and then the supports each sheared away diagonally along bright orange lines of molten steel. The weight of the conveyor pressed down on the sliced legs, twisting them, and then crashing down ten feet to the foundation pad.

High above him, in slow rotation, the conveyor began to sway. Its anchors to the silo pulling free, it began scraping down the concrete silo wall. Finally, it fell away spewing coal like a rogue garden hose. Coal showered onto the ground and the conveyer whipped wildly as the belt and rollers separated. It dropped across the four rail tracks where Wally stood, slack jawed.

Twenty stories above where the conveyor had been connected, a large tear in the wall of the cylindrical silo opened. A flash of orange fire burst out of the gaping hole and a firefall of coal showered down the torn wall. Wally began running toward the train engines for cover. He had no idea what was going on but it was clearly not worth risking his life to find out. Running breathlessly alongside the tracks toward the orange train engines pulling away from the silo. He caught up with the engines. Screaming at the engineers to get the train moving and out of there, he hopped onto the running board.

The train's engineers were already in a panic to pull the train out of the loading tower. As the silo fell apart, the rest of the loading gate tore loose and came down atop the cars still exiting pulling a giant piece of equipment along until it hit the exit opening. This pulled it out through the silo wall and a split ran up the concrete walls of the cylinder. Weight of the coal falling inside the silo onto the end cars was more than the train's couplers could stand, popping them open and sending the train lurching ahead, slamming the engineers into the walls of the cab. Wally was barely able to keep hanging on squeezing the handrail on the steps outside of the cab.

Looking back, he saw the silo splitting both directions; from the conveyor connection down and the train exit up. It was macabre. He couldn't believe he was seeing this but the fire had overwhelmed the upper floors and was spilling through the torn conveyor connection and the whole structure was coming apart. The ruptured cylinder of the silo looked like some kid's ceramics project on a potter's splitting open. Only this was showering burning coal as it collapsed.

Ignoring the drama down the road from the overpass, Ted took his drone out of the case. He put his phone into the control dock and then took another cell phone from the drone case and connected it. As the train rolled under them, he threw the phone onto the pushing engine as it passed. He started up the drone, sending it soaring high into the sky, turning it to look back at the destruction of the conveyor and silo. He put the drone into chase mode and it flew down to five hundred feet and then began following along, tracking the phone in the train moving south.

CHAPTER 25
AUGUST 21, 2017
TED, POWDER RIVER BASIN, MONTANA

Orbiting a quarter million miles above them, the moon completed its eclipse of the sun. Four coal trains, each a mile long, thundered ponderously delivering their loads of coal, oblivious to the celestial machinations above them. Two headed north and two south away from the overpass in Bill, Wyoming.

This day, tens of millions of Americans had come to the centerline of totality, like a continental scale cellular mitosis. All along the centerline for the hour and a half of its passage, astrological pilgrims came in automobiles, trains, and planes to bear witness. Adventurers on bicycles and afoot joined the throng.

Crowds confounded traffic patterns and caused traffic jams on little roads to remote view spots. Like the appearance of Haley's Comet, it was singular. A rare moment of celestial focus when all eyes across America turned toward the heavens. Millions looked up wearing darkened sunglasses and stepped completely out of their routine. For a few minutes their lives coupled to celestial motion as the moon crossed and then blotted out the mid-morning sun.

Ted watched as, in total darkness, in each coal hopper car, tiny points of brilliant white blazed atop the black coal.

Away from the trains eclipse spectators applauded, cheered, and were awestruck as they observed celestial alignment. Strangers hugged and some wept. Ted zoomed in his drone video to show the progression of the light in the coal spreading to become orange fire throughout the hoppers. Prairie air breathed onto it like bellows, fanning flames throughout the carloads.

Heat of the fire touched the aluminum walls of the hopper cars and began to consume their structure. Each car became a hundred-ton barbeque burning ever more completely. Then, as fire softened the aluminum hopper walls, they stretched under the pull of the engines and gave way, shearing in two. Massive iron trucks twisted off the undercarriage and cartwheeled explosively off the rails.

Leading sections of the first train pulled ahead. Couplers pried open and lost their connections, and the cars went haywire ripping the entire train apart. Breaching into the sky they crashed calamitously back to the ground. The wrecked cars tilted down at the break, digging into the rails, gouging the crossties vaulting the rear into the air. The following cars piled into a mangled inferno screeching along the tracks. Dozens of careening cars compressed against the wreckage. In howling disorder, they jackknifed, slid, spilled and twisted into ever more elaborate pretzels engulfed in expanding coal fire.

The front half of the train continued to blaze ahead, spewing fire as it went. Fire and chaos widened out onto the prairie and the line of forward burning cars obliviously distanced itself. Each burning car disintegrating with heat; train whistles screaming a discordant chorus on the prairie.

Engineers uncoupled their engines from the train as heat threatened their safety and the diesel engines. Autonomous braking kicked on in the following segments. They radioed their situation to the control center while they stared wide-eyed at the disaster outside their cabs.

Engines and cars in isolated train segments came to a stop in the Orin rail spur connected by lines of fire. The enormous conflagration burned the cars, the track, and the prairie. Four hundred cars burned, while others contorted in compression, heat, and stress in the jumbled wreckage spewed over miles of the Orin. This massive fire was a tiny dot in the vast coal fields of Eastern Wyoming under newly sunlit skies.

Ted had changed and left the ALU truck. Now he sat calmly on his BMW motorcycle in a full leather suit in the newly returned sunlight. The wounds from the Oh-Kee-Pah ceremony were still painful. He motioned to Woodrow to climb behind him on his motorcycle. He rocked off the kickstand, hit the starter, and eased out the clutch to follow the drone.

Half a minute later the van exploded in a gasoline fireball, and when that burned off, he could see the remaining chassis alight with white thermite reactions. Within minutes the totality finished and as the sun reemerged the sky quickly returned to brilliant midday. All that remained of the van was a smoking, charred hulk with a pool of molten metal at its center. Down a little further was a crane truck with "ALU" on the side.

As Ted and Woodrow rode slowly down off the overpass onto the road beside the railroad tracks Woodrow was amazed at the live drone images, he could see over Ted's shoulder on the controller screen. Like an unreal news show, smoke billowing into the sky and disaster tangled below it. Woodrow held Ted's shoulder in a vice grip, watching the fires consume the train. Fear overcame Woodrow as he realized his part in this assault. He felt lightheaded, his heartbeat chaotic, and his skin became clammy. He felt nauseous, but held on, and tucked his head, no longer wanting to see more of the unfolding disaster. What had Peter gotten him into? One thing for certain, he didn't want to go back to jail.

The roar of fire consuming the coal dissipated in the stillness of the vast prairie. Ted pulled over and swept the drone around the entire scene from higher altitude. Satisfied with his video record, he landed the drone near the motorcycle. When he parked, Woodrow anxiously threw up, barely missing the bike.

Ted walked over to the drone and pulled the SIM card that held the video record of the events from its slot and zipped it carefully into his jacket. He walked back to his bike; abandoning the drone where it landed. Woodrow was standing, frozen in place. Ted reached around his massive shoulders and gently collected him. "Time to go." As Woodrow inhaled, he caught the sick burnt oily smell of the fires and threw up again. In a daze, Woodrow held on as they sped away from the Orin. The wind began to howl as they raced down the highway as fast as the pavement would allow.

Satellite infrared readings spiked and were automatically relayed to the data center for Homeland Security and the Fire Control Center in Wyoming. Orders went out to dispatch local fire response teams from Casper and Gillette. NASA planes tracking the totality filmed the wreckage as part of their overflight of the eclipse. The rail system overseer at his station in Houston noticed bizarre signals relayed by satellite microwave uplinks on his display coming in from Orin. The national train network status, displayed in real time on huge monitors lining the wall in front of him, showed everything else still normal. He scratched his head for a bit and then smacked the side of his desk console to see if a little help would get the network running right. No change in the bizarre reports showing four trains stopped dead on the Orin.

Ted had severed the aorta of the coalfields, a heart attack for the mines. Bankrupt companies gorging themselves on coal would soon feel the shock. He thought of his vision of writhing snakes and wondered if this was fulfilling it. Racing down the highway he added up the damage in dollars. The cost of coal cargo was the least of it, a million dollars at most. The rail hoppers were fifty thousand dollars each and five hundred of them totaled twenty-three million plus damage to the engines. Then there was the cost of the repairs to the track and down time out of the market. At Black Thunder mine, a concrete train loading silo had just collapsed dropping the feed conveyor belt across the tracks adding another million or two. Real money to coal operations in bankruptcy with a bleak future.

Coal companies waged war on humanity for the last fifty years knowing the damage they caused. Now he had just fired what he intended to be a 'shot heard round the world.' Now there were two sides engaged in combat. No longer would the coal industry foul the air and heat the planet unchallenged. He was exhilarated. His plan had worked and his drone had recorded the results.

Ted wondered if the rest of his plan would go as smoothly.

CHAPTER 26
AUGUST 21, 2017
TED, LEAD, SOUTH DAKOTA

While Ted drove fast along the road away from the Orin he mentally edited his drone video of the calamity he had just caused. Woodrow felt untethered from reality as he drifted deeper into a shocked trance of denial.

An hour and a half later they pulled into the parking lot of Chubby Chipmunk Hand Dipped Chocolates in Deadwood. Woodrow ran inside to find a bathroom while Ted locked his motorcycle and walked around the block and found Peter inside his RV watching a video. Ted was happy to see his Bronco parked behind Peter's RV.

"Good to see you. I'll bring Woodrow here in a minute after he gets changed. He did a great job. Give this to him when he decides what he's going to do." Ted handed Peter an envelope filled with cash.

Peter took the envelope. He reached down on the floor of the passenger side for a bag with clothes in it. As he handed it to Ted he thought how odd Ted was sometimes. "Thanks, I'll give it to him." They shook hands. "Where are you going?"

Ted looked past Peter and said, "The Sand Hills. It's hard to find on a map. I'll tell you all about it when I see you next." With that, Ted went back and handed Woodrow the bag of clothes. "Just put the clothes you are wearing in the bag. I'll take care of them."

When Woodrow came out Ted told him where to find Peter. "Thanks for everything. I hope you can find a good life ahead, your uncle is a good man." They walked outside.

"So that's it? What have I just done?" Woodrow started panicking, "What the fuck is going on here? Those trains and the drone...I could do hard time! I am not going back to jail. What did you drag me into?"

"You have done a job and that is all. But now you have a choice. I can tell you all the details and you can come with me to the Sand Hills or you can go back to your life in Bellingham."

"Go where? I deserve to know. What was that with the trains and drone and-"

"All you need to do is choose." Ted said curtly, "Either you really want to know everything or you are out. Just choose."

Woodrow stared wide-eyed at this insane suggestion. He realized that Ted was crazy and he wanted nothing to do with him. He'd never thought about what he had gotten into, and now he was terrified to spend another minute with him. "I'm out. I never want to see you again as long as I live."

"I am grateful to you. Peter will give you what I've asked him to when you get back home. I wish you well." Ted nodded slightly and left.

Ted walked over to his BMW motorcycle, strapped down the bag of Woodrow's clothes, and drove off. Woodrow ran to the RV where Peter was waiting for him and started yelling, raging against Ted. Peter told him to calm down and tell him what was going on.

Ted rode his motorcycle up the mountain to the town of Lead, he felt free. At the summit was the site of the historic Homestake Mine. He remembered stories his grandfather told of the old gold operations. How when it finally stopped mining it changed the mountain into an underground research complex. Scientists decided it was a perfect place for hunting neutrinos. He thought about the summer he'd spent there, welding and exploring the labyrinth of tunnels deep in the ground beneath the mountain.

The sun reflected off the sleek metal clad design of the Sanford Homestake Visitor Center as he drove by and turned up Summit Avenue. At the security gate, he chatted about the eclipse and showed the guard his contract for the conference room. The guard waved him through and he drove up to the top. The curious building that housed the shaft elevator looked like a grain silo or a barn with exaggerated vertical dimensions. No one was around; nobody wanted to be underground during the eclipse. Schedules were out of whack, so he went outside and rolled his motorcycle across the lobby into the cage of the shaft elevator, put down the kickstand, and closed the doors.

He held down the button titled 'LUX Large Underground Xenon Level' and talked to the hoist operators over the intercom who engaged the hoist and dropped him to 4800' depth. He rolled out of the cage and followed the path to the closed off shaft that goes to the drill room. In front of him was a drill hole that went down another mile and a half.

He had to push some barriers aside but after that there were no warnings. He locked his helmet and outerwear onto the frame, opened the gas tank, and deflated the tires. Then he rolled his motorcycle into the open shaft, giving it a final shove. It was a good friend all these years and it hurt him to let it go. Strange; he'd given up everything and this one hit him hard. He listened for several seconds before he heard the splash. It would take some time to settle a half mile through the water to the bottom. This labyrinth was beyond description.

Ted walked back to the tunnels that made up the LUX laboratory. Sited underground to protect it from cosmic radiation at the surface that could drown out dark matter signals. Years ago, he'd welded some of the specialized scientific apparatuses. It had grown since then and things were fancier. The work he'd done welding them into place in the deep rock formations of the laboratory was now covered over behind well-lit wall sections.

He spotted signage to the main tunnel connecting to the other shaft about a quarter mile away. Ted found the shaft elevator and waited for it. When it came down, a tour group of a dozen Asian physicists stepped out and he stepped in. They exchanged curious glances. Then he pushed the lobby button on the panel and again the hoist operators brought him up. The door clanged shut and squeaked as it rocked side to side as it began to ascend. Lighter warm air flooded in as the car ascended.

Pulling back the heavy wire cage door, he entered a new world. The modern exhibit lobby was spotless. On his way to the reception desk, he passed the model depicting all the myriad tunnels and levels of the labyrinth of the complex. It looked like modern art more than an engineering model. Every tunnel was represented by a polished stainless tube about as thick as a finger. It stood nine feet high and had hundreds of horizontal and dozens of vertical sections held up by wires to the ceiling.

Along the walls backlit diagrams of mine and deep earth science studies on astrophysics and neutrinos lined the walls. The public main floor installations showed the old mining operations pulling gold out of the mine.

Outside was the epic open pit of the gold mine. A small green mat served as a golf tee so visitors could smack a golf ball out into the depths, adding a thousand-foot drop to their drive.

He went outside and picked up the red painted bicycle he'd rented when he booked the conference room. He wheeled it to the receptionist's desk, checked in, and collected the FedEx package he'd sent himself. The prim young man at reception signaled a paunchy security guard to show him into the empty Visitors Center conference room. He parked his bicycle in the conference room's projection booth and opened the FedEx with his laptop on the counter. He plugged the SIM card from the drone into a slot and uploaded the train wreck video.

The next half hour he edited his drone footage into his video presentation. The intro video showed Ted appearing on the screen, facing the camera wearing Blackfoot war paint and a traditional vertical eagle feather bonnet, saying, "I am Thunder Rolling from the Mountains fulfilling my vision to restore the glaciers. My actions are my way of telling this story so you will listen. I've used thermite to ignite the unit trains rolling through the Orin rail lines and to bring down one of the many loading towers in the mines. Watch this video from my drone." The devastation from the thermite explosions and the silo's dramatic collapse filled the frame like a Michael Bay movie. Shots of the beauty of Glacier Park followed.

"When Glacier Park was established, it was to protect nature and wilderness. We have failed. I know this won't restore them today. I hope this heart attack to their delivery system will give pause to the owners and executives of this morally bankrupt coal industry." Photos of dirty coal miners and Blackfoot Indians filled the screen. "Using the victims of this kind of business as props, and making them into symbols, instead of treating them with respect as humans, is a crime." In a dramatic end, he had a shot of thermite burning. "Look for me in the Sand Hills." Altogether it was about ten minutes.

He pulled out a bag of thumb drives labeled with the names of reporters and major news agencies. He began copying the finished video file onto them. He stowed his laptop in his backpack and left it with his bike.

Ted knew his attack meant nothing if it was a private act. He wanted the world to see what he saw as the connection between burning coal and melting his beloved glaciers. He went into the tech booth and set his video clip to automatically play on the center's projector in fifteen minutes.

He walked out into the room and greeted a few of the news people he'd invited personally to the site. In the conference room he got on stage and said, "My video will show you my love of the glaciers, my deep concern that they are vanishing, and impacts of that disappearance on the ecosystem in Glacier National Park."

Then, as the lights dimmed and his presentation began, he quietly walked to the back of the room, collected his bicycle from the booth and slipped out. He took the elevator down the shaft from the lobby. He rode the rental bike back, deep into the mine, a mile through raw rock faces and muddy sections of the mine to the other shaft. Decades different from the LUX tunnels, these looked like it had been years since they were used. He made his way through the tunnels which got smaller and older. When he finally got to the end, he could see daylight around the edges of a steel door, locked closed.

"Shit." Ted looked around for something to use to open it. He couldn't spread the jamb, so he began to work the rock away from the frame with a small piece of rebar the installation crew left. It was slow going. He couldn't believe they had put this in. Such a remote tunnel seemed like it should have gone ignored, but here he was chipping away. Finally, a small rock chipped off and he pushed the latch bolt in with his knife and popped open the latch. Pushing on the door, it was stuck. He levered the rebar in between the frame and slowly it screeched open.

His eyes took a moment to adjust to the outdoors. He was below the summit in a neglected part of the compound. Just a parking lot and some weathered buildings. A sharp contrast to the polished features of the science and public facing spaces. This was how he remembered it when he had worked there, years ago.

He kicked the door shut and mounted the bicycle. At the bottom of the ravine was the Mickelson trail, a well-maintained bicycle track. The wind whipped his hair as he descended. Soon he could see the town of Deadwood below him. Before long, he was back at the Chipmunk parking lot where Peter had left his aging Bronco. Ted put the bicycle inside and took out his small bag with clothes and everything he needed to travel.

He walked over and checked into the Deadwood Social Club, pre-paying with cash and a fake ID. He took a relaxing shower in his room and went out to the barber shop for a cut and shave. He put on a cowboy hat, which was now a little loose, and returned to the hotel for a fine steak dinner. When he got into his room, he collapsed in his bed, feeling his wounds from the Oh-Kee-Pah throbbing.

CHAPTER 27
AUGUST 21, 2017
FBI, HOUSTON, TEXAS

Cheryl Valen, a tall brunette with a lanky frame and one of the top FBI agents at the Houston Texas Office, looked over her report and headed into the copier room to bind it. She stacked the edges on the desk and bound the file, cleared off all her notes, and locked her file drawer. Everything needed to be just perfect. Whoever this was who attacked a coal company had crossed into her jurisdiction, essential infrastructure protection. Coal explosions were usually investigated by Mine Safety as safety violations, they were not attacks. This was a targeted attack on vital infrastructure – something new.

She walked it upstairs to her supervisor, Rich Samson. He was a sixty-year-old who paid constant attention to his appearance, his hair unnaturally black given his age. He looked through the glass wall at her and casually waved at her to come into his office. He was talking on the phone when she got there, so she stood and waited patiently until he hung up. Handing him the file, she said, "I've just got off the phone with our satellite office about this attack. They're putting a trace together."

"Good, give me the bottom line."

She recounted the damage to the mine infrastructure and railroad. Then added, "What he's done is creative but technically simple. Why kick a hornet's nest? That's what I don't get."

Samson paged through the file and asked, "What do we know about this guy? Is he connected to anyone we are watching on coal? The Sierra Club? Earthjustice? Greenpeace? I don't think they have a very active local chapter in Casper or Gillette. Any connection to the KXL Pipeline, Standing Rock suspects or Dakota Access? There are a bunch of them."

Cheryl responded, "He seems to be accompanied by one other person, no ID on him yet. So far it is just the two of them, as hard as that may be to believe. We have a clear track for him through the attack and then exiting the scene of destruction. From there we have him traveling to Lead, South Dakota." She handed him a photo of Ted.

Samson shook his head. "You sure this is our man?"

"Yes, I am. Theodore Walton. Caucasian male, Blackfoot mother, age 36, black hair, sometimes with beard, six foot three, large burn scar on back of his right hand. Marine, worked as a Seabee in Underwater Construction. Father was an Army Ranger. Employed full time at ALU – Allied Logistics Unlimited as a marine outfitter and aluminothermic welding specialist. He has a high level of security clearance there as they work on military nautical craft. He is an outdoorsman and mountaineer.

No living immediate family.

Several recent financial sales transactions: sold house in Anacortes and transferred title to a ranch in East Glacier, Montana. No open credit card or bank accounts. Transferred six registered vehicles – Subaru Impreza in Anacortes, Ford Bronco 1998, 1948 Oshkosh tow truck, BMW motorcycle, Kawasaki dirt bike, snowmobile, and a small fishing boat.

Here's what I think we should do next. I've got the requests for time on the satellites and staffing. I'm ready to move on it, now." She leaned toward him.

Samson didn't seem to notice and continued with his own thoughts. "What is he thinking, what's going on in his head?"

Cheryl dutifully responded to his question "It seems to me that he answered that himself when he sent a live feed out to a bunch of news organizations from Sanford Underground Lab complex in Lead using their videoconferencing link. Like the Pentagon Papers, he sent it everywhere. He sent it out, in person, from the conference room, which he booked well in advance."

"Holy shit. Did it work? Did it go out to all the news agencies on this list?" He looked surprised. "Do you have it?" She nodded. "Let's see it."

Cheryl took a thumb drive and stuck it into the USB port on his screen. After the FBI identification of the file the video played. Ted appeared on the screen facing the camera wearing Blackfoot war paint and the traditional vertical eagle feather bonnet "I am Thunder Rolling from the Mountains fulfilling my vision to restore the glaciers. My actions are my way of telling this story so you will listen. I've used thermite to ignite the unit trains rolling through the Orin rail lines and to bring down one of the many loading towers in the mines. Watch this video from my drone."

"His drone video? Oh no. This is going to be bad." Samson looked shocked, the first time Cheryl had seen him lose his calm demeanor.

"Where the hell is Lead, and what is this Stanford lab? I thought that was in Silicon Valley." Sampson became impatient.

"You are correct, Leland Stanford Jr. University is in Palo Alto, CA. This is Sanford, with no 'T in the Black Hills near Deadwood, South Dakota. It is a deep underground research facility. The lab includes top US DOE and Livermore Labs projects and supports international research."

Samson put his head in his hands. "This is bad." he slowly looked back up "Who was on the feed again?" Samson continued to grow more agitated.

"All the environmental groups active in energy, major newspapers, many individual reporters, and foreign media."

"What's our next move?" he asked rhetorically. Cheryl waited for him to answer his own question as he never really wanted input.

After a few minutes of saying nothing, Samson looked back up and said "I'll call you. For now, do your best to counter this with something else as news. Should be possible to do something with the eclipse. I don't want a big mystery report, like 'eclipse UFO burns train' just create something convincing about a load of self-igniting coal. And set up a no-fly zone. Get his Wanted info out to all the agency offices and local law enforcement, anywhere he might show his face." He continued looking through Cheryl's file.

When Cheryl left and his door closed he picked up his phone again and buzzed his secretary. "Get me security at the Coal Institute on the line. No, get me Palmer." As he looked over Cheryl's file on Ted, he thought to himself, why would anyone pull this kind of shit? Doesn't he know this is game over?

His secretary buzzed and Samson picked up the call, "Palmer? This is Samson at the FBI."

Samson began, "We have a serious problem. Four unit coal trains and a loading tower were destroyed. Keeping this quiet is going to be hard because the guy broadcast the whole thing. The agency doesn't want another Esquire Magazine article on the big bad FBI being in bed with you and spying on activists. Seriously, an FBI office acting as a private security force for an energy giant is fodder for these guys. They made us sound like a bunch of retired cops working a guard shack." Samsons jaw clenched, "Of course I'll keep you posted as we move ahead." Samson looked around the room, "Yes, be sure to keep me informed as things develop on your side too." Samson hung up and buzzed his secretary, "Get Cheryl back in here. Now."

As soon as Cheryl was through the door, Samson interrogated, "Did the video broadcast or was it limited to the conference room?"

"He emailed video files as mp4 and pdf for the documents broadly. They were received and downloaded by some at least. I don't see keeping this off the news. Luckily the eclipse has filled the media cycles."

"Oh, this is bad." Samson put his head back in his hands. "Get someone on this to make some fog and a counter-narrative." Then he pounded the desk, "And bring him in now."

"We can see his progress from the mine to the Sanford facility but then he is tough to track. He went into the facility."

"Either he is in there, or he has come out. How hard can it be to find where he went in and if he came out?" Samson demanded.

"I'm not sure. There aren't that many people to track around there but the eclipse introduces a random quality that makes it challenging. The mountain is like Swiss cheese. There are three hundred miles of tunnels on eight thousand feet of mine covering seventy-seven hundred acres underground and a quarter million square feet of surface floor area above ground." She sighed, "Because of some flooding below four thousand feet, they haven't updated surveillance for a decade, outside the scientific experiment areas. They've been digging for a hundred and twenty years, so there are lots of unused tunnels."

"OK, I get it. Do the best you can. I want people out there now. You are funded. Call me if there is something you need." He thought about it and stopped her on her way out. "Get his normal Marine picture out as wanted for questioning."

CHAPTER 28
AUGUST 21, 2017
JC AND JULIA, BELLINGHAM, WASHINGTON

JC and Julia were relaxing on their Ikea futon couch in JC's rented room. It was in a Victorian style home near Fairhaven, close to Interstate 5, convenient for his commute to ALU and for Julia to navigate between the Belle Clinic and her cabin. He had a garage too to keep outdoor gear. Wrigley was asleep on his dog bed, running an imaginary race, his feet gently twitching.

JC got a call from Peter out in Deadwood. "Turn on channel 5. You need to look at this news story." He sounded frantic. "Ted took credit for blowing up some coal operations in Wyoming. They're saying he's an eco-terrorist and are looking for him."

JC got up and turned on the TV news and caught the end of the piece. There was a still photo of Ted in Blackfoot ceremonial dress and video of coal trains catching fire, going off the rails behind the commentator saying Ted had made a video of this and claimed to be doing the damage to protect the environment. There was a notice at the end to send any information to the FBI in Houston.

Julia was horrified and shocked by the image of her former lover on the screen. After a minute or two she said "I don't want to but I can believe it. Ted and I broke up because he said that sometimes violence is the only way forward. He has that intensity and all those skills to execute a plan." She sighed. "I told him violence never solves problems, only makes them more intense."

JC's jaw dropped, "I had no idea. This is a wild story. It was just a couple of hours ago, right? During the eclipse." His mind raced through his encounters to try and explain this. He forgot he was holding the phone until Peter spoke.

Peter said "Yeah, just during the total eclipse. I can't believe my eyes. Ted looked scary." He remembered Ted had been a Marine. "He knows how to do something like that alright. Earlier in the story they said it was thermite that lit the coal train on fire. No doubt he could do anything he wanted with that stuff." Peter sounded concerned. He thought about timing and Woodrow's helping him. He wondered if he should call the FBI and tell them what he knew.

JC hung up and turned to Julia. They sat in disbelief for a while and turned off the tv. Finally, Julia gave JC a hug. "Are you hungry? I'll make something for dinner." She went into the kitchen and pulled out the ingredients for a meal. She thought about how weird it was that Ted had met JC and Wrigley before she had and that they worked in the same place.

Her thoughts came back to her present. It had been fun finding this house for JC. Dr Alice came through with a recommendation. Having a central spot made life easy together.

CHAPTER 29

AUGUST 22, 2017
PALMER, BEVERLY HILLS, CALIFORNIA

almer met Tracy, his PR manager for lunch at The Penthouse at Mastro's. She was a difficult person to work with, always so set in her opinions. Deep mahogany panels lined the walls and the thick carpet absorbed most of the sound from the room. Crystal light fixtures at each booth gave uneven, but flattering, light to their faces.

"So, what do you want from me?" asked Tracy.

Palmer put down his heavy fork and pushed his empty plate away. "I am sick and tired of being attacked for doing my job. I want a story out there that's about them. These eco-terrorists. I want a way to exit. With my shirt still on. It's getting too damn hot. The World Bank announced they won't be investing in fossil fuels is a terrible story. There are too many stories like that out in the public about climate and too many goddamn stories about our reserves and their value vanishing when renewables take over."

"That's no problem, so far as your shirt is already guaranteed in your contract." Tracy laughed, "Maybe you mean you want to smell like a sweet rose? It is hard to keep the focus on 'the war on coal' now that they are shooting back."

"That's not funny. I want you to nail that son of a bitch to the wall." Palmer pounded his fist on the table without noticing. "We need to make him a Ted Kuczynski and flog the living shit out of him in the press."

"I'm not sure that's a good idea. Wouldn't it be better if no one ever heard of him?"

Palmer shot back, "Fox News should be blasting this story to the hills, saying this proves that environmentalists are all dangerous extremists out to destroy the economy, etc, etc."

He cooled off and reluctantly, he said, "I guess." Palmer hated this guy, but maybe silence was golden. This story didn't make him look good. "Well, I don't see what's going to keep someone else from doing this kind of thing."

"That's out of my pay grade, leave it to the government. What I can do is something about the nobility of the coal mine owners, how you lead the miners with care and dignity."

Palmer thought this angle might work, "That's right, now you've got it. Maybe a statue to the men who dig the coal? Something heroic. Maybe on the Mall in DC?"

"I think you are missing the point here. It isn't good to have the focus on the miners. Have you seen Rockefeller Center in New York? You bet you have, everyone has. Now, did you ever see the Ludlow Massacre statue to the coal miners? Probably you didn't read Ivy Lee's *Facts Concerning the Struggle in Colorado for Industrial Freedom* either. You didn't see the statue because Rockefeller's PR firm made him seem like he was the victim. Not the miners shot down by state militia while they were on strike at his mine.

Look how Dick Lockerby uses his victimhood. He is a ruthless, brutal man but he's positioning himself as the victim of powerful outside forces. It's brilliant reframing. Audacious and bold, he shifts the conversation away from the miners who died because of his mismanagement, away from his looting the company while squeezing the miners, and toward his sad childhood or those mean regulators. Boo hoo, poor little rich man." Tracy snickered.

"OK so how do we say that?"

"That's the tricky part. When you think about General MacArthur, George Patton, and Dwight Eisenhower do you think about their raid on the Bonus Marchers in Anacostia? Of course not. Instead, you know the 'I shall return' quote, the movie with George C. Scott, and you remember the likable President." She smiled and added, "We bring good things to life."

He picked up his wine glass, swirled it and put his nose over it to savor the aroma. He took a sip of his cabernet. "Well how about you bring some good to life for coal. And fast." Palmer didn't like being lectured to by his help.

"Fast isn't on our side. Delay is our time-tested strategy. For decades, we've defended simultaneously on three major fronts: litigation, politics, and public opinion. It has always been a holding strategy, consisting of creating doubt about the damage we cause to health and the environment. That way we defeat the charges without actually denying it. And during that time, you've sold a lot of coal."

"OK. So, this madman is saying we're responsible for melting his glaciers. That's hard to prove." Palmer said.

"He's played into our narrative, like a sheep to the slaughter. Finally, proof there is a war on coal." She looked over at Palmer. "Facts aren't on our side either. We don't trade in them; we change the subject to one we'd rather discuss. We have our own stable of 'scientists' who will say exactly what they are paid to say. That doesn't make it true, it just creates doubt. Doubt causes discussion and delay, so we can sell more product. So, what I will work on for you is a story that isn't about this at all but a different narrative between coal, glaciers, and Indians."

Tracy thought for a minute, chewing contemplatively, swallowed, then continued, "Let's see if we can make coal the victim here. Hard working under-appreciated little coal, dug by American heroes. That way he isn't attacking coal, he is defiling our hard-working boys. Keeping them from making America great again."

"Whatever it takes, just fix this. Make it work. I want something now."

"All in a day's work." Tracy finished her meal and smiled, "I'm on the case."

Palmer took out his cigar and ordered a scotch. As soon as she could, Tracy politely left the table. Palmer sat alone and finished his drink and cigar.

His relaxation was disquieted when he thought about the tobacco news. A judge had ordered them to pay for corrective statements in newspapers and on television. He required them to run full-page ads on Sundays in leading newspapers. Plus, statements on TV between 7 and 10pm, five times a week for a year. What was the world coming to? Could this happen to coal? What if some judge told the industry to talk about their business?

When Alpha Coal went bankrupt, internal documents showed they were funding climate denial and exposed the connection to their favorite 'scientist' on the payroll. Would that change the discussion? Or what would happen if they were up against a class action asking for asthma healthcare? His list of demons grew as he puffed. Public attention to this could cause a lot of problems.

Should he cash out now, while he was ahead? Continuing to bet on this 'coal casino' was looking like a dead end. Big money was getting skittish. The World Bank, pension funds, insurance, big players were leaving the table.

He left a ten percent tip and dropped his cigar butt in his wine glass.

CHAPTER 30

AUGUST 23, 2017
LOKI, WHITEFISH, MONTANA

High up in the private mountain resort of Whitefish, Montana Loki, a leathery tanned face and rock-hard body was relaxing poolside. Wearing his aviators, he leaned on the bar that served the swimming pool. He enjoyed soaking up the sun and watching the barmaid's tan legs where they met her short skirt. He heard a door swing open and looked up from his drink.

He saw two young corporate security men from the Coal Institute heading over from the lodge building. They were awkwardly dressed to look outdoorsy and casual but instead they just looked nervous. The one with a mustache waved clumsily on spotting him. Loki lazily waved them over and went to sit at a table under an umbrella. "What is it this time?" Before they could answer, "More importantly, what would you like to drink?" Answering his own query, he condescendingly asked, "Get these boys some Arnold Palmers would you, honey?" He looked at them, "Or would you rather have Shirley Temples?" He chuckled at his imagined cleverness.

They forced smiles and took their seats uncomfortably. "Arnold Palmer sounds good."

The waitress came over and dropped off their drinks and another round for Loki. She gave him an eyeful because he always tipped better if she leaned in and showed her cleavage.

"Now be a good girl and leave us alone for a bit." Loki patted her ass as she turned and smiled at the two. More than happy to leave, she went out on a smoke break.

"We need to get this eco-terrorist off the playing field." The clean-shaven security man pulled a thumb drive out of his briefcase and gave it to Loki. "Here is the whole story about this guy. A complete dossier, everything we have on him. We have his locations in Anacortes, Bellingham, and a cabin outside of Glacier National Park. We will get you anything you need to get this done. Quickly and quietly."

"Anything…. with how many zeros?" Loki asked, his eyes squinted and his smile snake-like.

"Under four. Don't ask. Over that you need to get approval. You can count on Samson at the FBI to feed you what they know as well. Call me if you have any other requests and I'll talk to him."

The other man began, "You see our problem is we really need that tidewater coal terminal. We've got lots of easy-to-dig low sulfur coal in the Powder River but nobody wants to burn it here in America."

The first added, "Thanks to the Sierra Club and Bloomberg's Beyond Coal, half our generating plants are shut down. Lucky for us they are still burning in China and India. We're all set up to put it on a train but getting it across the ocean to market means a terminal, a big one. This is the quickest way we can ship the coal to market. To get the terminal we need public support. That's hard enough, but the Orin is how our coal gets out. If that's not working we don't have product to sell."

Loki looked at them. "I don't give a shit about your problems. What do you want me to do about it?"

"This guy has royally screwed us. We know what he wants. He wants us to stop mining coal. He made his request by burning up four hundred coal hoppers, twenty miles of track, and a hundred thousand tons of coal. That's just not going to happen again. The silo and conveyor alone make this an expensive day. We want you to find this bastard and take him out of the game. His problem is that he thinks one man can make a difference. That's why you have to-"

Loki interrupted, "I heard about that. Nice footage of the wreck on the news. You think he works alone? Seriously? Okay, this is easy. Where is he right now?"

"We are working on that. Some kid helped him. He is a nobody. He's most likely traveling with his uncle back to Anacortes, Washington. Our perp disappeared from the underground science facility in Lead, South Dakota. He might be hiding or somewhere nearby."

"The FBI can't find someone who blew up four miles of trains?" Loki looked surprised. "OK, he must be the master of disguise. I'll find him. Yes, I can help, for all four zeros."

"Remember you cannot call us directly except on these phones. We are available 24/7 for your calls." He handed over an envelope with a couple of cell phones.

Loki took them and held one up to his ear. "Ring ring, what do you have from the big eye in the sky? Where did this terrorist vanish again?"

"All the locations we have, from the pit to the Sanford Underground Lab are on the thumb drive. He goes into the visitor's center and then broadcasts from the conference center to show the world that he took out the trains and a silo because they are melting his glaciers." The agent shook his head, chuckling to himself, "His video file of the broadcast is on the drive."

"He's calling himself Thunder Rolling from the Mountain and some Indian name. His mother was full blooded Blackfoot." the mustachioed man added.

"This will be fun, maybe I should pay you? All I gotta do is look outside a cigar store." Loki guffawed. They squirmed uncomfortably in their chairs.

"Your bank accounts, credit cards, contacts, and some cash to start." The first man handed him a leather pouch. Loki took it and examined the contents. He whistled softly. "So why do you want him dead? Why not just brought in for a trial? His library fines overdue?" Loki chuckled.

"Keep us informed. If you need anything big, ask."

They got up and walked out to their driver waiting in the Suburban. The first man confided, "That guy makes me nervous, thanks for coming along."

"Me too. You know he was one of the Blackwater men who opened fire in Nisour Square in Iraq and killed a dozen civilians with machine guns. He used to tell a story of taking down an Army Ranger and publicly humiliating him while there too. Sicko, but he's good at what he does."

"We've got a new shot for coal with President Karne and after that maybe it is time for me to cash out."

The driver took them back to the Glacier Airport and they settled down with drinks on the Coal Institute's Gulf Stream jet.

CHAPTER 31

AUGUST 23, 2017
TED AND SUN CHIEF, ALBERTA, CANADA

Ted held the steering wheel to support himself. It was hard finding a way to sit without making his chest wounds from the Oh-kee-pah ceremony painful. The long drive into the Blood Tribe in Alberta, Canada had sapped all his energy.

He drove past the small burial yard hosting the white pioneers of Seven Persons. They'd founded the tiny town beyond Medicine Hat when the railroad came through. Lands that the Blood tribes ran to to escape the American pioneers, their mining, and treaties. They forfeited their hunting lands when they did.

He turned into the parking lot of the golf clubhouse, a typical modern ranch style building, and parked next to the shiny red Escalade. He texted Sun Chief to let him know he'd arrived.

Sun Chief, with pot belly and expensive clothes came out and tapped on the door startling him. "Good day to cast, don't you think?" Ted nodded and grabbed his rod and fishing vest from his Bronco. Sun Chief got his rod from his Escalade, put his vest over his dress shirt and string tie, slipped out of his loafers, and put on high rubber boots and a creel. He chirped his car lock and motioned toward the river.

They walked out across the tees and past the green. As the green grass ended the prairie emerged. They clambered down the bank to the gravel bar on the river. Ted noticed Sun Chief was puffing from the effort. A family of ducks launched into the water on their approach. Sun Chief began idly playing his line and then was casting with a Zen ease, sending his fly perfectly onto the water. He continued casting as they talked.

Sun Chief looked over to him, "You follow a strange vision. I saw some news about Thunder Rolling from the Mountain."

"Yes, I know. I made it my responsibility. If not me, who will do anything? I have my reasons."

"Your secrecy is odd. But you were always a private kid."

"It is better this way. I'm grateful for your help."

"We will always be your people." He turned to look at Ted, "You have done a fine thing giving so much to the tribe. All your land and things will be well used."

"I must be free to do what I must do. Things, possessions are an anchor. I'm happy to give them to the tribe."

"You were just a kid when you first came here to visit."

"I remember I was nineteen the last time, just before the Marines. Summer's long days are a good time to enjoy the river, fishing, and swimming."

"I heard you married one of the girls from here. You were both young."

"She died in childbirth along with our baby." Ted lost his footing in the stream and water filled his boot. Pain from the ceremony shot through the wounds. Feelings of loneliness he'd buried long ago washed over him and tears flooded his eyes. He turned upstream, away from view and after a while responded. "I joined the Marines. Seemed like a way ahead."

Sun Chief stopped casting. He stood looking at Ted for a moment and said, "I'm sad for your loss. That is a great sorrow for anyone to bear." He went back to casting.

After a few minutes he said, "You're an odd duck. None of us can figure you out." Sun Chief laughed, "A lot like your white father."

"As I get older I can see that I am. He was a stubborn man."

"Yes, and a good, generous one. I remember him coming here for a visit. He took a whole day to help get a pump working for our farm. It was way out on the back side. He just drove out in that same Bronco you came in today and started working on it." Sun Chief paused, "He was haunted by something."

"I know he was. After his last tour of duty he seemed to withdraw. We spent time together working on broken machines people left out in the fields, even for people he barely knew. He loved to make things work." Ted stopped and the chill of water in his boot distracted him.

He thought of the glaciers vanishing. Their awe-inspiring beauty and their story. To see something so quickly die in front of your eyes tortured him. Then he remembered his wife's laugh, her dimples, and her eyes. Sitting with her as the birth went from joy to death. Training as a Marine was a cakewalk after that.

Sun Chief began to reel in and his face lit up. He played his trout under the sparkling waters in and out of view for the next few minutes. When he finally brought him in, he was delighted.

Ted was impressed. "I want to visit their graves. My wife and our baby are buried near here. So is my favorite aunt." He didn't say more, but his aunt had been one of those rare people who he believed saw him clearly for himself. They had a deep bond.

"Your aunt was everyone's favorite, so generous and kind. What a wonderful woman." Sun Chief put his trout into his aged wicker creel basket. "Ok, let's go."

Sun Chief took a while to get over the river rocks as they scrambled up to the bank to the parking lot. Ted emptied the water from his boot and set his rod in the back seat. Still heavily breathing Sun Chief told Ted to follow in his car.

They drove around a couple of bends in the road to an open field covered with high grass. Sun Chief pulled off the road. They waded through the grass until it opened to a small clearing, the cemetery. It seemed like an afterthought. The hills behind were verdant mounds with wind waves scrolling through the grass. The sun was low in the sky.

Ted went to his wife and baby's gravestone. He brushed the dusty soil and grasses covering it and knelt there for a time. When he rose Sun Chief took Ted to a small wooden cross inside a circle. It had his aunt's Blackfoot name carved on it.

Ted looked up from his aunt's grave and said, "Our Blackfoot women say that this life of plundering the earth means that men can't be men and women can't be women. Everyone is just grabbing for themselves. So the young and weak are always afraid of situations where they are at risk."

Sun Chief said. "My niece works in the coffee shop. She sees the fracking crews and they leer at her. She carries a taser and mace when she goes to her car. She says it is a constant drain being at the counter when the customers act so crudely. It's sad that way out here, in Seven Persons, our women suffer so much violence."

They stood together in silence for a while. Sun Chief started singing a sad lament. Ted turned and walked out to the road.

Sun Chief opened the back of his Escalade. Inside, underneath a worn kaki blanket was a beat-up canvas duffel. They looked at it together and it was filled with smaller zippered bank bags full of cash – hundreds of thousands of Canadian, Australian, US dollars, rubles, and Chinese yuan. There were four passports and driver's licenses as well inside a leather shaving kit. They zipped it closed and Ted took it to his Bronco, stowed it and brought back a tube.

He took the top off and gently pulled out the vertical eagle feather bonnet he received at the Sun Dance in Montana. "You know that Medicine Hat is the English name for Saamis, this bonnet?"

"Yes, I know that. And I know what it means for you to bring it here." Sun Chief said. "You are joining our people closer together."

Ted put it on his head for a moment then carefully took it off and held it for some time. Then he handed it to Sun Chief who gently put it back into its holder. They just stood together in thought and they held hands solemnly in silence. A raven flew over them and gave out a raucous caw. They released their hands.

Ted handed him the keys to his Bronco, smiled and cracked, "Something to drive around on the rez."

Sun Chief took the keys and laughed. "It will fit right in."

Ted smiled, "Maybe lose the window stickers." He looked around and said, "Now I need to buy a car."

"What a coincidence, I have one for sale!" Sun Chief gave Ted the keys to an old Subaru. "Just around the corner. It's past our buffalo jump." He chuckled.

They drove another mile along the river. Fracking wells were visible on both sides. When they got to a lot with a burned-out trailer, there was a dust covered Subaru Outback with BC plates parked in the yard. Sun Chief pointed and said, "All gassed and good to go. She is a sweet ride, not too showy or out of place. We hope you will enjoy your trip. We registered her with the Canadian passport you have in your bag. Still, don't wait around for the formalities when you sell it." They opened the cars and Ted took the duffels and cleared out his stuff from the Bronco.

"Thank you. I am grateful for your help handling the money and documents, most of all your help to realize my vision. I know it may be a problem for you in the future." Ted unzipped one of the pouches and pulled ten thousand Canadian dollars from the stack and gave it to him. "Donate this to the Women's Resource Center for abused women. Put my aunt's name on the donation."

"Yes I am happy to. I guess you already know that they don't have any money."

Ted climbed into the Subaru and the setting sun on the windshield dust made it glow gold. Squirting it off he pulled onto the road and began to drive again, wearily anticipating getting to the Vancouver. The miles clicked by and his Oh-Kee-Pah wounds cried out on each turn in the road. His body ached from the motorcycle drive to Deadwood and the intense focus he'd held over the time between the eclipse and this road. He stayed the night in Calgary near the stockyards with a Blood Indian friend. At first light, he was driving again. This time crossing the Rockies and then on to Vancouver.

That night, Ted leaned lightly against his expedition duffel at the foot of the gangway leading up to a Panamax container ship in Vancouver B.C. The red, horse-shaped loading cranes of the shipyard were bathed in sodium vapor light.

Ted's long day had ended and soft night air flooded in across the water carrying away the odors of the shipyard. Listening to familiar noises of a port at work – the air brakes of the container trucks, diesel motors used to power the huge gantry cranes, yelling, and whistling from dock workers trying to signal each other, and a collection of various other horns and warning sirens intended to be heard over all the other loud noises.

A pasty complexioned twenty-something man with hollow eyes came down to bring him aboard. "Boris says to say hi." He brought out the ship's manifest and some maintenance concerns for Ted before their departure. Ted would be the maintenance supervisor for the entire vessel on its passage to Vladivostok. It was flagged in Angola but the rules of the sea were consistent. No one needed too much information and there was abundant porn, discipline, and vodka for the passage.

Ted went out to the railing and took a last look, soaking in Vancouver's beauty. He looked south past the ferry pier jutting out into US waters and thought of his past life riding his motorcycle with Julia along the shore at Cherry Point, her body pressed tightly against his back with complete trust.

He thought about meeting JC and his goofy puppy, now a fine dog. How he'd grown into a man at ALU. Peter and their working and motorcycle adventures around Sturgis. He was a good man and a true friend. He felt some guilt and hoped Woodrow would find a way to stay clear of trouble after helping him.

Exhaustion overtook his nostalgia. The potlatch, the Oh-Kee-Pah ceremony, all the driving, and sorrow at the graves had drained him. Ted climbed up to his assigned cabin and stowed his gear, he lay down dead tired, maintenance could wait.

CHAPTER 32
AUGUST 28, 2017
LOKI, ALU, ANACORTES WASHINGTON

Loki barreled his Tiger Paw Hummer into the ALU welding shed. JC was grinding a weld smooth with his face shield down and heavy headphones on. Loki ignored him and spotted Peter at a desk toward the rear of the shop. Peter looked up quizzically from his work. Loki walked around to the passenger side and threw open the door displaying Woodrow in the passenger seat. His arms were zip-tied to the ceiling hand grip. Woodrow shrieked out plaintively, "Help me."

Wrigley had been sleeping at the back of the shop and now sprang to his feet. He growled and began a charge across the shop at Loki, who yelled, "Get your dog! Now." Loki reached into his vest and pulled out his pistol. JC looked up at the commotion and dropped his grinder. Then he saw Wrigley was running full tilt at Loki. JC screamed at Wrigley to stop. He didn't slow his charge. JC sprinted and cut him off. He tackled him, throwing himself over Wrigley's head, knocking him to the ground. JC lay on top of him as Wrigley squirmed to get up and go after Loki. JC tightened his grip on him.

Loki lowered his pistol, "Good idea, otherwise you'd be hugging a dead dog."

"Help! Peter, get me away from this guy!" Woodrow screamed across the shop from inside the Hummer. Loki slammed the door in his face.

Peter came over to Loki who asked, "So you think Woodrow here would look good in orange for the next hundred years? How about you put your hands up where I can see them?"

"What do you want?" Peter raised his empty hands up in the air, glancing through the window at Woodrow.

"I'm looking for that friend of yours, Ted or Thunder Roller, who seems to have vanished into thin air."

"I haven't seen him for a week. Last time I saw him was in Deadwood. He hasn't been here. Did you look at his ranch?" Peter asked.

"Oh yes, Beaver Dam was very helpful. He told me all about nothing. Ted's generous donations to the tribe and said he was going to the Sand Hills. He couldn't tell me where that was though. Neither could anyone else." Loki smirked, "Except I'm wondering where Ted built the launchers that threw the thermite grenades into the coal hoppers."

"What are you talking about?" Peter was confused. He didn't know about any launchers.

"Launchers to fly soda cans with thermite in them. You know thermite?"

Peter's face fell, "I lent him my can sealer. I use it for home brew. He didn't say what he was doing when he brought it back."

"Sounds like our boy. Doesn't tell anyone anything. So the launcher got the cans into the hoppers. Where did it come from? Did you make them here?" Loki asked, looking around the shop and added, "Maybe Woodrow will remember when he's back in prison." JC had wrapped his legs around Wrigley who was still thrashing to go after Loki.

Peter was frightened for his nephew, "No, we didn't make them. What are they?" He thought for a minute and then said, "It could have been Boris. He's a mechanical genius. He's in Chicago, runs a chop shop there. He and Ted go way back."

"Now we're getting somewhere. Woodrose here said he'd been to Chicago with Ted but had no idea where they went. Do you have a way to get in touch with him?" Peter nodded and turned to go back to his desk. "No sudden moves." Loki directed and waved his pistol at him. Peter found a contact for the Chop Shop in Chicago.

Holding his hands above his head with the card Peter asked "Could you please leave the boy? If this isn't helpful I'll come with you to help figure this out."

"Aw, how sweet." Loki took the contact for Boris and watched Peter for a minute, "OK, why not. He's been a whiny bitch anyway and it looks like you're as tough as my crippled grandma. You and dog boy." He looked over at JC still wrestling Wrigley.

Loki lazily went to the Hummer and opened the door. In a single motion he pulled out his knife, slit the zip-tie, and pulled down Woodrow's arms, jerked him from the seat, and threw him down onto the shop floor.

"Hope Boris is where you think he is." Loki got in the car, "For your sake." Wrigley finally broke free and chased the car as he drove recklessly out the door in reverse.

Peter went to Woodrow and held his wrists, rubbing them to get the blood flowing. "I'm so sorry. Are you okay? Do you need to go to the hospital?"

Woodrow was sobbing. He shook his head. "No, no hospitals. I don't want to be on anyone's forms."

"I'm so sorry. I had no idea what Ted was up to." He thought for a minute about the drone and the can sealer and Ted's secrecy in Deadwood, or about everything for that matter. The tv news and his sabotage of the trains all fit into place.

Peter went over to JC, "Is Wrigley okay?" On cue Wrigley came back and nuzzled Peter. JC asked Peter if he had known anything about this, Ted's plan they'd seen on TV. Peter shook his head, overwhelmed by the chaos. JC took out his phone and called Julia, "Can you come over and take us home?"

Julia said "Yes, I'll be there as soon as I can pack up here. Are you OK? You sound like something is wrong."

JC tried to hold himself together. "I'm fine. That monster who tripped me at the protest was here. He had Woodrow tied up in his Hummer. He almost shot Wrigley."

Julia responded. "I'll be right over."

Peter put his hands on the worktable, steading himself. He breathed deep, thought for a moment, then phoned Boris. He filled him in on all that had just happened. Boris said he was ready to entertain the company when it arrived.

Peter went back and tried to comfort Woodrow. "It's okay. You're okay. What a goddamn monster. I hope he finds Boris. That'll be the end of him."

Loki used one of the phones the Coal Institute had given him and gave his pals at the FBI an update. "That boy, Woodrose didn't know anything. What a putz. I'm off to Chicago to hopefully find the guy who made the launchers. It should give me a clue about where to look for our Indian."

CHAPTER 33
AUGUST 29, 2017
LOKI, CHICAGO, ILLINOIS

The next day Loki pulled up outside the Chop Shop in a rented Suburban. What a dump he thought to himself. He put his gun into its holster and half zipped his jacket before getting out. The wind blew showers of dirt off the lot.

A bright white light flashed three times short, three times long inside above the office as Loki walked to the door. A loud buzzer blared the same pattern as he went inside. A mechanic wearing coveralls and a respirator pointed him to the office.

Boris was sitting in his chair looking at his monitor as before, but now wearing a cannula in his nose connected by a hose to a portable oxygen tank. Loki crowded up right next to him and looked down. "Pretty big monitor for a chop shop."

"The better to see it with. What can I do for you? I don't think we've met." Boris replied.

"Just tell me where the plans are for the launchers you built for Ted and I'll be on my way."

"Oh, I see." Boris turned in his chair to face Loki but couldn't get around because Loki was blocking him.

"So is this easy or hard?" Loki looked into Boris' eyes with a malicious stare.

"Fuck, what do I care? You want to see the plans, let's go see them." Boris threw his hands up and pointed across the shop to the paint booth.

"You're kidding. What's in the booth?"

"Our clean room. The drive with the plans is in there. I don't often show them off."

"You be my personal guide then. Get up." Loki demanded.

Boris rose from his chair and towered over Loki. He took the loops of the cannula tubing and grabbed the handle to the trolley for his little green bottle of oxygen. He brushed past Loki and walked over to the paint booth. The heavy door opened easily and the brilliant white interior lights blared out into the shop. The positive air pressure engaged as he closed the door behind them.

"This door." Boris pointed to the back of the booth at a small solid door.

"After you, I insist." Loki kept his hand inside his vest near his gun.

"OK." Boris entered the small room and similar lights came on. It was a much smaller booth with a turntable centered under its exhaust hood. After Loki came in, the door closed tight and he turned quickly to see the mechanism.

"Let me get this case. The laptop and drive are inside." Boris pointed at a hardened suitcase under the bench.

"Keep your movements slow." Loki didn't like people opening things up. He reached inside his jacket and pulled his gun from its holster.

Boris raised his eyebrows and clearly explained each action as he moved in slow motion "OK. Here I go. Unlatching the case...opening the lid…. taking out the laptop…. getting the drive." Boris started up the laptop and connected the drive. The startup screen came on with the Chop Shop logo for a few seconds.

Loki felt a sudden, severe headache. He began to sweat, and his vision dimmed. He shook his head, but it didn't clear. He felt his body shake. He began to feel anxious and his breathing quickened. Boris slowly scrolled through the launcher drawing files. Loki pushed off the safety on his gun. As Boris was about halfway through the drawing file section, Loki began to raise his gun, but collapsed before he could level it at Boris. He fell unconscious face first onto the floor, his head smacking hard against the paint flecked concrete. His pistol skittered across the floor. Loki's murder took under five minutes.

"Good night sweet prince, you dead motherfucker." Boris chuckled. He replaced the laptop and drive in the suitcase. Loki remained motionless. Boris picked his gun off the floor, took the bullet out of the chamber, popped the clip out, and put it in his pocket along with Loki's knife, sunglasses, and keys. He left the little room and closed the door. Exiting the larger booth he said "Don't shoot!" loudly knocking the 'shave and a haircut, two bits' pattern on the door with Loki's gun butt. As he opened the door his mechanics smiled and lowered their Kalashnikov machine guns.

Boris put the pistol barrel to his lips. "Shhh, he's resting." He looked around, "Let's find him a comfy place for his big sleep." His men laughed and stowed their weapons. Boris tossed Loki's rental keys to one of them and said, "Let me know when you find his onboard transmitter, maybe two, and his phone. Drive around, then leave his transmitters in something like a car crusher. Bring back his car but get the VINs off and be sure it is clean so we can get to work."

Boris went back into his office and called Peter. "You wanted me to show some plans? I did, but he lost interest right away." He laughed and hung up. He began looking online for totaled Suburbans of the same model year as the one he had watched Loki pull up in on his security cameras. He erased the security footage for the day.

As a couple of guys dragged Loki's body out by his boots, one of the mechanics came around from the back of the paint booth rolling an enormous empty cylinder of carbon dioxide away from the clean room. He put it into the storage cage for empty welding gasses. Boris saw him and said "I guess he couldn't catch his breath? Now he's dead tired. Well, dead for sure." The mechanic snickered and put a chain across the tank to secure it. Boris thought this was just as Ted had said, someone would be coming to ask about this. Not all carbon dioxide gets used to put out fires or carbonate drinks.

Boris arrayed the collection of gear Loki carried. It would all find new owners just like half his Suburban would soon be welded together with a totaled legally registered vehicle. He'd sell it for a tidy sum, and the rest of the car would be sold off as parts. Boris's crew efficiently processed Loki's body in their usual unpleasant way. After bagging his parts in plastic and washing down the table, they loaded the bags with his remains into the back of another Suburban and drove to a construction site.

Waving to the foreman, they drove across to where a crew was pouring piers for foundations. The pile drivers made steady hammering sounds as they drove the piles deep toward bedrock. They backed the SUV up near a rebar cage sticking fifteen feet out of a wet pour. The guy working the concrete pumper waved at them. Taking out several half full sandbags containing Loki's remains they shoveled wet cement into each. Then they took turns flinging them into the center of the rebar cage. After ten minutes, they finished tossing his remains and brought out a bottle of vodka, toasting all around. The concrete poured in on top for the rest of the day as they filled the huge foundation forms for a new office building.

CHAPTER 34
JANUARY 10, 2018
US CAPITOL, WASHINGTON DC

The garish gold paint covered the columns, the ceiling, and even the furniture. Palmer checked into the Karne Krown Kourt just a couple of blocks away from the White House. Expensive accommodations, but it wasn't too much for the Coal Institute to pay, and he expected it would return high dividends. It performed its dual roles perfectly – to line the President's pockets and provide access for guests to the power of the office. Pay and play!

Walking across the marble lobby to meet with Senator Carruthers, he saw Mel standing with him. He felt simultaneously jealous and nervous. He veered off to the rest rooms to collect himself. When he came out, Carruthers was waiting with Secretary of Energy Rick Horren, an enthusiastic sycophant to Karne.

"Gentlemen, good to see you." Palmer expansively extended his massive hand and patted the Senator on the shoulder. Turning to Horren he offered his congratulations on getting the appointment. "You didn't have to close the Department of Energy after all."

Heading to a private meeting room, Palmer quipped, "If coal is so bad for the environment why don't we just burn it all?" The others chuckled. Horren retorted, "If Karne gets a lump of coal in his Christmas stocking, is he happy or sad?" Not to be outdone, the senator finished off with, "Why is coal like anal sex?" To confused looks, he answered "Because people calling it clean aren't taking it up the ass." He roared at his own joke and slapped Palmer's ass.

Once in Carruthers's comfortable office they broke out cigars and brandy and Palmer kicked off their meeting, "We're getting screwed by cheap natural gas. It's driving coal plants into early retirement, sending our projections out the window. Last year US utilities shut down 22 gigawatts of coal capacity. If they don't burn coal, we don't make any money.

Worse, there isn't any new coal generation coming online. Some of the banks are getting weak knees and won't put up money for expansion anymore. Even the insurance companies are dropping us. I've worked RAGA and ALEC but they aren't bringing it back either. We need to sell some coal and we need to do it now. Overseas is our best bet and that means a terminal somewhere, hell anywhere, on the west coast."

Senator Carruthers responded, "All your problems are PBR coal. Our Appalachian market doesn't need it the same way. We have a problem in West Virginia and you're just the man to take care of it. I need you to tell him to drop his run for Senate."

"Dick Lockerby?" Palmer guessed.

"Yes. He's going to split the mid-term vote and we'll end up losing. We can't afford a high-profile loss in West Virginia. Hell, it's our stronghold."

Palmer asked, "Didn't Karne call Lockerby when he got out of jail? Seems he likes the guy. God knows Dick is a big enough brown-noser."

"Yes, and Dick's been making friendly overtures for a while. I've talked Karne out of supporting Lockerby. He sees it could embarrass him badly." Carruthers added his personal reason, "He's attacking me and my wife. They are truly bizarre attacks. I can't support him."

"I know he is off the wall. I'll meet him and let him know to stand down. It won't be fun, he is a vengeful person." Palmer sighed.

Horren broke in, "Let's all agree that we need to sell more coal. Now! What we need to do is give President Karne a script to pitch for us." They agreed and spent the better part of the afternoon working through the details.

When they were ready, Senator Carruthers called and asked the president "Senator Carruthers and Energy Secretary Horren here with Palmer from the Coal Institute, one of your biggest supporters. Thanks for taking our call President Karne."

"Glad you are backing me. What gives? Why did you want this call?" Karne asked. "I've already pulled us out of Paris, taken down the regulations on dumping coal ash and heavy metals in streams, and killed the health studies on mountaintop removal. I gave you everything on your list. I'd say I'm doing some impressive work for coal."

"We want to thank you for all the work you've done to make coal and America strong again. You single-handedly won the war on coal. You really turned this around." Carruthers fawned.

"Yes I did. My administration is full of coal people. I've eliminated coal regulation. I love coal. I say it all the time. Remember me with that gold plated shovel? I dig coal. You know I won West Virginia with seventy percent! That's the best anyone has ever done. But what are you asking for? There must be something you want."

Horren took the lead, "We feel the national security of this country is at risk. We can't let the electric generation plants run out of coal. It could take down the grid and we've been trying to come up with programs to strengthen it.

You know a lot of coal plants are closing, so there aren't as many safe coal-fired plants to make sure that electricity is available twenty-four hours a day, every day." He paused to let that sink in. "Remember when the cyclone bomb hit and those hurricanes? They knocked out power."

"That wasn't good." Karne agreed.

"You just nailed it. Right you are. It looks bad when people lose power. So, we think we might have a solution to make sure it doesn't happen again." Horren added.

"So what do you want me to do to make sure it doesn't? I want to make it special. I will be the one who gives power to the American people. It will be really amazing. So amazing. Power to Americans from me. Really great."

"The Senator and I want to set up a strategic stockpiles of coal, like the petroleum reserve, so every electric generation plant has three months of coal on hand. It will have some costs, but what's the cost of freedom? What's the cost to keep America independent? I'm not sure I want to leave that up to the voters."

"You need my help to do it? Sounds like I just tell them. I'll call it Freedom Energy." Karne was pleased with himself.

"Well, some plants are saying we don't need this, or even they don't like it." Carruthers added.

"OK. Leave it to me. I'll tell them to do it. I'm very powerful." Karne paused, "Anything else?"

Carruthers added "Just one detail. We want Dick Lockerby to drop his Senate run in West Virginia. I know you've been pleased with him and I want to make sure we don't do anything you are against."

"Fine. Lockerby is nothing to me. Tell him he's out." Karne showed his usual loyalty. "Didn't he say something about your wife?"

"Yes he attacked me and you because she works for you." Carruthers said.

THANK YOU FOR BURNING

"Well, he's out." Karne hung up.

Senator Carruthers scoffed, "What a tool." Then he saw Mel had come to collect him. He thanked Horren who excused himself and left. "Thanks, I appreciate it. I'd do it myself if Lockerby were reasonable. There's no point because he wouldn't listen to me." They stood and Carruthers grinned at Palmer. "Thanks for Mel, she's a real asset." He winked.

Palmer wasn't amused, "I'll let you know what Lockerby says. Good work with Karne today."

In the taxi, Palmer went over the files on Lockerby and then went out to Le Diplomate with coal lobbyists who worked the Hill for him. They'd invited the Secretary of the EPA. He made a grand entrance with his SUV motorcade flashing lights, pulling up right in front. Dinner was going to cost a lot more than staying at the Karne Krown.

Palmer gave the EPA Secretary a long list of regulations and exemptions he wanted cut. The secretary was distracted by the attention he was getting from other diners. At the end of the meal, he took the printed list and agreed to get on it.

Palmer was tired when he got back to his room but took time to arrange to meet Lockerby at the Greenbrier. He thought about retirement. It would be good to spend time with people he liked. He went for breakfast at the Krown dining hall, a cavernous, converted building. The fancy plates were the best part of his meal. He went out and met his ride to his chartered private jet.

His limo pulled up in front of the Greenbrier – a truly enormous block of rooms with formal gardens, but so unimaginative it almost looked like a Soviet palace. He used the lobby phone to arrange to meet Dick on the Old White TPC golf course. He was curious to see if it had recovered from the torrential rains that had ruined the course last summer.

Palmer ordered a Ruben sandwich and a soda to drink at the clubhouse overlooking the course. He was just finishing up when Dick showed up. They went outside and got onto their golf cart. Palmer came right to the point. "Look Dick, the President has changed his mind. He wants you to take a break and not run this time. This primary is going to be close and we don't need a split in the party. Could you wait it out? You know, run for Senate in the next cycle?"

Lockerby felt his blood boil. He intoned flatly, "Who do you think you are talking to? I've done more to make West Virginia Karne's than anyone. All the judges and accessors and regulators are mine. I even placed a Supreme Court judge here. Aren't you forgetting the RAGA meeting here, right here at the Greenbrier? I put that together. You know he called me personally when I got out of jail to congratulate me."

"He does like you. He just thinks your negatives are too high for a run this year. Look at Roy Moore's loss to Doug Jones. He was popular and well respected, but in the end, the negatives about his preying on teenage girls drew voters to the polls and we lost a seat. We put in millions and flew in our top men and he still lost. Your negatives are even higher than his because of the dead miners."

"Why would he cut me when I'm the best chance to get rid of that Democrat?"

"It's nothing personal, we just can't afford to lose West Virginia. It sends the wrong signal about coal. As you know Karne is all in for coal. Another Senate race will come up and then we can back you. Sorry."

"It's that bastard, Carruthers isn't it? I knew he'd stab me in the back." Dick was enraged, "His rich little China wife probably turned him against me. She was on the Mine Safety witch hunt after the explosion. She was Secretary of Labor when they screwed me. Like she gives a shit about miners."

Palmer watched a foursome tee off. "Dick, that's not important. We can't take a loss in West Virginia. You are a lightning rod here. The teachers strike shut down the state and they ended up getting their demands met. It spread into a bunch of our states. They are mad as hell and organized. If we put you on the ticket, you'll electrify them."

"Who cares about teachers? I'm talking about the number one industry in West Virginia. Coal. I'm disappointed in you, Palmer. I thought you knew something about what it takes to get elected here. No idea. Look at our Governor. He switched parties like he was changing the sheets and he owns the sheets here, all of them. I don't need you or the party. I can run as independent if I want. Just watch me."

"Like I said, it isn't my call. You have been amazing for coal here in West Virginia. Your success in mountaintop removal and union busting is legend. We aren't forgetting, just telling you to wait. Back off. I can't stress this too much, sit this one out. Things are good for coal politically right now."

Dick's face reddened, "I'm done talking. Go fuck yourself. You can ride this cart to hell for all I care. I didn't spend a year in jail for nothing. I want that Democrat bastard out and I'm going to win and get him. You'll be sorry you crossed me." With that, he rocked the cart as he got out and walked back to the hotel. Palmer watched his angry gait, shoulders hunched over striding on his way to the hotel. He thought about how badly it had gone. If Lockerby would play ball, things would be fine for everyone. Palmer sighed, then continued onto the tee to play his nine holes.

This was a fubar situation. Palmer pulled his driver out of the bag. He set his ball on the tee and hit his drive. When he got off the course he called Carruthers to deliver the bad news, who responded, "Oh hell. This is going to cost us. Is there any way to work with him? I know he wants to run, but is there something we could give him to throw him off?"

"I don't think so. He is a black and white person. Side note, he blames you directly. No compromise is my guess. All right then, I'll spread the word he's out."

"I'll set up a PAC to buy the ad time, something like Mountain Mothers. A name to appeal to the enviros. We can slam him on toxic waste management. Safety too. He has a lot of blood on his hands. Doesn't he get that this is political suicide?" Carruthers asked.

"Don't count him out so easily. He has a decade of installing justices, sheriffs, and local officials and they'll do what he says."

"I don't think we have a choice. We need these ads out now, the primary is only a few months away." Together they worked up a plan of attack. They focused on his negatives, toxic waste, impacts on health, and his fatal mine disaster to get him out of the race. Negative ads work and he was wide open. Leadership was on board now so it was just a matter of loosing the dogs.

CHAPTER 35

JANUARY 15, 2018
JC AND JULIA, SPURLOCKVILLE,
WEST VIRGINIA

JC's heart sank, and as he hung up the phone he looked over at Julia. "That was my uncle Luke. He called to tell me Grammy died." He felt a wave of sadness crash over him. Her presence had been a beacon through all the family turmoil. He instinctively put his hand into his pocket to search for Clem's watch.

Julia came to him and comforted him. When he asked if she would go to Grammy's funeral with him she said of course she would. She called to arrange time off from work. It was lucky they had just hired another nurse so not difficult scheduling her time away.

They took a red eye to Chicago and flew from there into Yeager Airport in Charleston. It was mid-January and the east coast was gripped by a 'bomb cyclone' or land hurricane that had brought frigid weather. Driving from the airport in their rented car JC remembered some of the iced roads from his early days driving. They were treacherous twisted ribbons but they got safely to the church service.

The church was a small clapboard structure painted white, windows frosted on the outside. It was packed with over a hundred friends and family who'd come to pay their respects to her memory. Her corpse was on an open board to be touched by the mourners. A plate of unmixed salt and earth set on her breast following an ancient custom.

She had lived with dignity and compassion and touched so many lives. When they asked for eulogies Uncle Luke and Aunt Mary spoke of her later years and her vitality taking life a day at a time. Singing with the congregation tears poured down Julia's cheeks flowing her grief from losing her mother, Betty. It had been hard to recover from that.

JC felt the weight of leaving. All the loss in his family that drove him to go west reversed polarity and now drew him in closer. Surrounded by his family he realized there were many who he loved deeply and had been missing.

After the service, they joined the procession carrying her casket up to the little wooded cemetery on the way to her cabin. JC remembered walking by with John's ashes, just two years earlier, how heavy the box felt. Grammy's grave was cut into the frozen ground west to east for burial so she could see the coming of the Redeemer.

For her community, burial was an act of faithfulness. One of the miners had brought his concrete saw to cut through the rock-hard ground for her grave next to Clem's. The bitter wind died for a moment as they laid her into the bedrock of the mountain where she was born and bred.

JC walked up to Grammy's mountaintop cabin with Julia for the wake as the sun set over the mountain ridges. It was a magical scene with ice coating each branch and twig. The sun's last rays transformed the silver ice to gold. It was the coldest it had been in JC's memory. He remembered the years with big snowfalls, making snowmen and snowball fights with the other kids. He thought of the time Lo put so much snow down his back he thought he might freeze.

Julia looked up into the arboreal filigree and saw a Snowy Owl perched atop the big Chestnut tree. She was amazed. They live and breed in the Arctic tundra. It was a young female just like the one she'd seen at the waterfall. It swiveled its head and looked down at her imperiously. Rare in its irruption this far south, she stood watching for some time until JC noticed her staring and came over.

"Is this the bird? Like the feather you showed me?" JC was shivering with the cold.

"Yes, it is the same owl. Beautiful aren't they?" Wind gusted and the cold penetrated their clothes. The owl's feathers fluttered and it moved tighter into the tree trunk for protection. They headed into the cabin, crowded, and warmed by so many people.

Under the mantle, a wood fire was burning, JC felt the watch in his pocket and traced the lines with his fingers. The cabin was a handmade treasure. It welcomed the whole family although it was a small building. Everyone had brought something to share and Mary had baked a half dozen tarts from her strawberry rhubarb preserves and her apple butter, and elderberry jam to share.

Later the musicians in the family gathered and sang. A couple of them had real talent, especially the fiddler. Julia joined in on the songs she knew.

They spent the night at Luke's and the next day Julia wanted to talk with him. JC took a call from someone with a job idea and went into the next room. They exchanged pleasantries and then Luke asked her "JC says that you want to know what it will take to stop them? The coal mine owners and their backers." he locked Julia's eyes "You sure?"

"Yes, I'd like to know." Julia was curious what he might offer. Luke thought for a moment then began to tell her.

"Don't mix up the miners with the owners. When the coal miners go into the mines around here, they go in thinking about being strong for their families, the dignity of work, food for their family, and if they're lucky, promises of healthcare and a pension. They just want to be free to live their lives. They take personal responsibility very seriously.

They see exactly how much coal they mined on their shift when they come out. That is a source of pride. What they are not thinking about is what happens when it burns, aside from how warm a fire feels on a day like today. They know what they're doing is good. It is what butters their bread and keeps their family together. If they thought they could do something else and get the same money they would, but they aren't going to stop and go looking. Not until they see the cash on the barrelhead." He looked up to see she was following his thoughts. She was listening intently.

"Now, at the end of coal, the mine owners are like hyenas. They know the beast is dead but circle in to gorge on flesh anyway. Mr. Peabody's mine made him a hundred million this year. You and your protesters are asking for a change that means losing everything these owners have. Look at Lockerby. He took ten million a year while forcing his miners to face death in his hell holes. JC's brother, John, was just one of his victims. Lockerby's career was built on cheating safety so he could squeeze just a little harder.

If they can get more money by going through bankruptcy and washing away the cost of pensions and healthcare, they do. They figure where the clean-up cost is going to be and sell off that part of the business. They don't care that they know the buyer will fail. They don't think about the reality or the physics any more than someone selling cigarettes to kids thinks about them coughing themselves to death.

Right now, the mine owners are thinking about how close to the edge they can skate. With Lockerby, it was saving a few dollars by not allowing his men to put up the partitions, or keep the sprinklers working, or even doing a fire drill. When he went to jail for cheating mine safety over and over for a bit more coal, he didn't feel bad about himself. He thinks that he's right and just. If he can take tens of millions and put that in his pocket, it proves how smart he is.

What your protests are to them is noise. Public opinion or the law could become a threat but I'm not holding my breath." He pointed outside at the wind turbines, "That is a threat. Every turn of those blades cuts a slice off their balance sheet. That's why they've been buying legislators and lawand lying to us using PR firms. It has worked to suffocate clean energy for decades."

Julia interrupted him, "Why don't they just buy up wind and solar? They must know it is the future. They have lots of money and it is a proven source of power."

"Because with renewables they only sell it once and then the fuel is free. They don't want free fuel, no matter if it's clean or dirty. They want dedicated customers who pay and pay and pay.

To stop them the first thing is a demand. Like Fredric Douglass said, "Power concedes nothing without a demand. It never did and it never will." That's not the same as protesting their actions. To demand is to assert a right. It must be made by a credible force equal to their power.

Think of it like going to a party and walking up to the biggest bully and telling him to get out of his seat so you can sit down."

Julia asked, "What about a moral force? The power of millions of us together demanding change. You saw the Women's March. We aren't going away." She emphasized, "The coal owners are people too, they put their pants on one leg at a time."

"Yes, they are people, but they don't care about the earth or other people as much as their profits. West Virginia has less than two million people. A lot of them depend on, or think they depend on, coal. Humans bleed, corporations don't, and yet we let them have a voice.

When they can't make money because no one will burn their coal they'll stop. They know as soon as customers choose renewables they won't get back in the game.

But they will fight to the death. Coal companies are global energy operations. They batter the earth like a pinata, assuming devastation and casualties are part of doing business. Burning coal causes millions of deaths a year because we can't help but breathe.

They care nothing for the welfare of others. They see no harm in flogging the corpse of mother earth until hell freezes or the sky catches fire, so long as they get their money. So, a demand for change needs to be overwhelming."

Julia felt the weight of his arguments. This wasn't a fair fight. Especially for the people she met at the wake. So many stories of smart people leaving the state to find lives elsewhere, so many tragic lives in poverty unable to move.

Luke continued. "Stopping them means stopping them everywhere. They will follow big tobacco's play book if they're blocked here they sell there. Tobacco knew their product was killing their customers and decided that as long as there are children who are unprotected they can keep selling without fear of running out of customers. They've always sold abroad when it is prohibited here. So stopping them burning in America means nothing if they can sell their coal in Asia."

Julia tried to stay positive, "But it is a start. We stopped their access to tidewater in Cherry Point. The whole west coast has refused their terminal requests. The Millennium site refused a coal terminal located there. Powder River Basin coal is stuck with inefficient routes to market."

"That is good, but it is a detail. The death grip of fossil fuels will end. Looking back at the damage caused by their lies and deceit it will be obvious what they did. All their work in order to scrape the last dregs of ancient sunlight's gift into the fires will be on display. What history teaches is that people who act like this are unconcerned with change until the blade is on their throat. And that isn't a protest. That's a credible demand. "

"Thank you. I hear what you are saying. It is sad." His wife came up and signaled the end of their conversation. Julia put her hand on his shoulder, "Thank you." Luke began slowly rocking in his chair again. JC came over and nodded to him.

JC had some news and wanted to tell Julia right away so he guided her out of the room.

CHAPTER 36
JANUARY 17, 2018
JC AND JULIA, SPURLOCKVILLE,
WEST VIRGINIA

They had gone to get lunch at a cafe nearby Luke's. JC was so excited. He told Julia he'd gotten an offer to work on wind turbines using his new welding skills. It would pay a lot and they wanted him to start right away.

Julia was surprised and she could see he was happy with his possibilities.

"I have someone I'd like you to meet." JC steered Julia over to an older freckled redhead. "This is my cousin Bert.

"Hi Bert, pleased to meet you." Julia was thinking about JC's new offer.

"Nice of you to come from so far away to pay your respects. She was quite a grandmother for all of us. Someone to look up to." Bert said.

"I'm sure she was. JC has told me many of her stories. She lived a full life caring for others in her time and made a wonderful family." Julia responded.

JC said. "So Bert is doing something for miners who lost their jobs and are looking for new ways to live. I think you might be interested."

Bert said. "I hope you are interested. A couple of years ago, after waves of layoffs for us miners, I needed a way out. My sister said, 'Why don't you ditch the shovel for a mouse. Learn how to write software?'" He laughed "I thought she was nuts. Coal jobs pay real money, that is when you're working. But she stayed on me and got me to try a coding class.

Turns out, it's something I'm good at! So, I learned a lot and we started making up a program for some other guys. It has grown into a little educational non-profit and we have a graduating class this June."

"That is great. You must be so happy to transform your life. I remember getting my RN and how that opened the world to me. I was a waitress living off tips before and now I can go anywhere and earn a living wage."

"Turns out there are lots of jobs out there in software. It was a surprise to us that working in coal, then changing to coding, isn't as hard as I thought at first. Some of my skills from working the mines carry over." Bert smiled.

"Like what? I don't know enough about mining to guess." Julia asked.

"We work really hard, we're diligent and detail oriented." He said, "And we're extremely team – focused, because in a mine your life and mine are tied together." JC laughed at the mine joke.

"How does that work in tech? I thought all the jobs were in Silicon Valley or Seattle." Julia asked.

"No, it's changed. Tech can be anywhere. We bring a team ethic and when you break programming into small sections, each programmer can live anywhere. We share online."

Bert lit up and added, "I got hired over a four-year grad, somebody just out of college. Oh, another thing, we aren't paying rent in Silicon Valley."

"That is exciting. I'm so glad to hear that there's something new as the old goes away. Some of the folks here don't seem to have those futures to look forward to." Julia said.

"Some guys think that the mines will be coming back. They won't take advantage of the money that is available to learn software." Bert said, "When they go back to mining, they are older and poorer because they were out of work. Now they get paid less, no benefits, or seniority." Bert shook his head, saddened about the harsh reality for those too stubborn to adapt." He'd been talking for a while and so asked Julia.

"So, I hear you're a nurse, and you've helped JC out a couple of times."

"Yes, I'm his guardian angel." she smiled "I've been working in Bellingham for six years at a little clinic."

"Have you seen ours? It's over on Slag Creek. My sister works there. She could use some help. It is so hard to find trained medical people who will work here. We don't pay as much here, so that's a big problem. It gets worse every year for her between black lung and overdoses."

"Send me her address, I'll be in touch." Julia saw the need here was so much greater than in Bellingham. She yearned to do something to help. JC began wondering if there might be a way to stay and help his family here in West Virginia.

Later that night they decided Julia would go back to Bellingham and take care of Wrigley. If she wanted to give Slag Creek a try she would drive Wrigley back in spring. She hated to leave JC but she had to get back to her work. Being separated for a couple of months wasn't so much of a sacrifice given how much JC wanted to reconnect to his extended family.

CHAPTER 37

MARCH 30, 2018
HENRY AND WADE, BLACK THUNDER MINE, WYOMING

Henry stopped his hauler and Wade came on his headset. "So, you up and quit? I don't get it. Why would you break off our beautiful relationship?"

"Hi Wade, you know it isn't you. It's the way you stink up the pit." Henry joked. "I got spooked when that silo came down and the trains all caught fire. Something's not right."

"But how am I supposed to find someone to dump on when you're gone?" Wade chuckled.

"I'm sure you can do it. There's always a bunch of young guys looking to drive heavy metal." Coal thundered into his hauler. "And your half-wit conversation is the talk of the pit."

"Seriously, where are you off to? Going to be a pimp in Deadwood?"

"I've got a job driving oversize for EMP. They deliver windmills."

"Like the little Dutch boys?"

"Nope, they're real big. It takes a whole caravan of oversize rigs to drive the tower sections to the site. One rig per blade too." His hauler rocked under a bucket of coal from Wade. Henry drove off to dump his load.

The alarm beeped as Henry lined up. "The other reason I'm going is the new robot trucks they are testing out. I don't think I can beat them."

"What? Like Iron Man? Or one like Robbie the Robot?" Wade chuckled.

"No, these are the same as my hauler but no driver. There is a guy somewhere in a control room running the whole fleet of them. No drivers at all."

"So that's it, your floozies hooked you on dope!" Wade chided Henry.

"No! I'm serious. I saw a couple of the trucks in the yard and one went past me today over near the entrance wall. I waved. but there wasn't anyone in the driver's seat to wave back." The horn sounded, Henry pulled out from the loading spot again and headed off to dump.

"Couldn't stay away, could you?" Wade chuckled.

"No, you're like a magnet." Henry joked.

"So where is the control room for these robot trucks? I'd like to see it." Wade was curious now.

"I don't know. Nobody said anything about it to me. I just know where they're testing them."

"Who's loading 'em?"

"I don't know, maybe Percy. I think it's the shovel just near the parking lot on the big wall. Shouldn't be hard to figure out."

"Oh, I bet it's Bender from Futurama."

"It isn't funny. These things are real and they're in the pit right now."

"You just send one of them over so I can see it, would you?" With that Wade's overfull bucket showered Henry.

"OK smartass, how about you meet me when your shift ends and we'll take a look?"

"OK fine, see you at the yard." The horn sounded and Henry drove off.

Later in his shift, Henry came back to Wade reporting, "I talked to Percy, do you know him?"

"Is Percy on the new wall shovel? The one near the entry?"

"Yes. He'll meet us at the Coal Hole bar after he gets off his shift for a drink."

"Works for me. See you there." The alarm sounded and Henry drove off.

After their shift Henry and Wade walked into the Coal Hole. They easily spotted Percy seated in the middle of the bar. He stood out because he was twice as big as anyone else. He had a long black ponytail coming down his back. He heard them coming and made his stool squeak as he turned to watch them approach. Behind him, a carved wooden buffalo head was mounted on a plaque between the neon beer signs. "Look what the cat dragged in!" his voice boomed across the bar.

"Hi yourself. How's the wife and kiddies? How many is it now?" Wade asked bluntly.

"None of your business. But I do keep track of the complaints about peckerwoods like you." He sneered at Wade. "Our oldest son has been working on the solar install near the Navajo Generating Station. He said they already put in a hundred thousand panels at the Kayenta Solar Plant."

"That's nothing compared to the power from NGS." Wade bristled whenever solar generation or wind came up. The Navajo Generating Station was an enormous generating plant with three towers. How could a couple of panels make anything like the output?

"That's only the first one. They've got another field of panels ready to go." Percy responded. "It looks like they're done at NGS. Nobody wants to buy it. They can't make money from it anymore."

"You've gotta be joking. That's the biggest generation plant around." Wade didn't believe him.

"No joke. The tribe will get the power transmission lines and now we are building out the generation side with solar panels. Mr. Peabody's coal company isn't very happy because NGS is his only customer for the mine."

The pudgy bartender came over and asked, "The usual, gents?" Each of them nodded.

"I heard that the tribe wants to keep it going." Henry looked confused.

"Oh, there are always some who do. They don't want anything to change, but the coal game is over. Just like working here. I'm just taking what's on the table. There's all this bullshit that's been created saying that the Navajo are going to be devastated, the Hopis are going to be devastated. Hell, we've been devastated since Columbus showed up. Now maybe we will get our water back."

The bartender slid their beers down from the taps.

"What water?" Wade wanted to know.

"Our aquifer water, the water Peabody put in a pipe to make a river of coal. They fill a pipe with coal and use water to squirt it three hundred miles from the mine to the generation plant. The plant uses our water like it is endless. After that, it isn't water anymore, just coal juice. You can't drink coal juice. Our wells have dried up and we can't afford to drill deeper. They have all the water." Percy leaned back, making his stool squeak again, "Sucking all the water out of the aquifer means my aunt drives twenty miles to get water at the Peabody mine because her wells don't deliver anymore."

Henry said, "That's awful."

"Here's the thing – our Navajo Nation lease gives the tribe a good opportunity to transition to renewable energy. When NGS closes, we get 500 megawatts of transmission capacity, a rail line, pumping stations, and support for negotiating rights to Colorado River water. So naturally there's a lawsuit and a bunch of suits trying to buy off the leadership to keep it open."

Henry nodded that he understood how hard it was for Percy. "So, what's new with you two?" Percy asked.

Wade went first. "I'm fine. Same old, same old. Took the grandkids to Disneyland on my break. Henry here says you got some robot haulers and a wall scraper in the pit. That true?"

"Yup." Percy answered.

"What are the haulers doing?" Wade asked.

"The haulers are doing Henry's job. Same hauler, just no Henry. The robot shovel I'm babysitting is clunky but it is doing your job." He looked at Wade and sighed, "I sit there all day while it scrapes the face and dumps coal into the robot haulers." He stretched his arms over his head, "The scraper isn't fast, but it's accurate. The haulers, that's your job Henry, are fast. They line up perfectly every time and they don't need to rest."

"How many of them are there?" Wade was wide eyed.

"Just two right now, but they say they'll save money on account of not being human."

"Well, that ain't good. When did they get here?"

"Oh, about a year ago. There's a bunch of stuff they needed the techs to set up to make them work, but that's all done now. I've seen their plans. They will run the pit with a dozen guys and the rest will be robot slaves. No union, no backtalk."

Wade was speechless. He motioned the bartender for another round.

CHAPTER 38
MAY 13, 2018
JULIA, SLAG CREEK CLINIC, WEST VIRGINIA

ogwoods were in bloom and the fresh leaves of spring made West
Virginia feel new. Julia was giving the Slag Creek Clinic a try to see
if she could stay with JC in West Virginia. They'd had a lot of discussion about the impact they could make during long zoom calls.
Now it was time to see if they could make it happen.

She pulled her stethoscope away from the old man who was hooked
up to a nebulizer "Leroy. you need to use the inhaler. It strains your heart if
your lungs can't get enough oxygen to your blood."

"I can breathe, just not good." he bravely replied, "Inhaler's just
too dear."

"Is there anywhere you can get one?"

"Folks 'round here don't get extras. Food, medicine, but not both. We
just want to take care of our family." Leroy shared matter of factly, but Julia
was alarmed.

"You worked your whole life for the mine, don't you have something?
A pension or healthcare?"

"Not no more. The mine done sold and we was all fired. I got hired back on, when it came back up. But I got no pension and they weren't paying benefits or nothin'. I'm workin' for less, but at least I'm workin.'"

Julia sat down heavily, emotionally sapped, and helpless. She looked around the examination room. Every bit of it overworked and worn. A ring of bare wood underfloor showed through the vinyl tile; encircling the table he sat on. The wear matched the threadbare fabric of Leroy's life and tortured body. She unlocked the supply cabinet in the corner and took out an inhaler and pressed it into his hand. He refused to take it.

"Please, use this." He tried to give it back, "For my sake." She looked him in the eye, and he looked pained, but finally let her press it into his hand. He buttoned up his shirt and left giving her a nod stepping outside.

"See you in a couple days for your rehab appointment" she called as he walked slowly down the steps. She looked at the worn linoleum and thought of her beautiful wood floor in her cabin. It was a big change.

She waited for him to drive off and then went to sit out on the wooden porch. Across the road, the creek flowed past gently around the wrecks of a pickup and station wagon, and part of a house that had washed down in a spring flood. Her white cotton shirt stuck to her skin and the sun baked her dark hair. Even the air felt oppressive, cut only by an insect chorus, an occasional bird, and the small sounds of water running through the sunken wrecks.

A gray Ford Taurus pulled up and a twenty-something sporting a full beard matching his curly red hair got out. He checked his phone as he walked up to the clinic holding an empty cardboard box. "I'm from the CDC, Center for Disease Control, a federal government agency. Is this the Sheets Creek Clinic?" He looked for some kind of sign on the building and at his phone again.

"You are here." Julia opened her arms in a grand gesture of welcome. She remembered her bewilderment when she first came to find it.

"I had some samples from local water supplies sent here and some others collected for me."

Julia took him inside and pointed out a dozen pint mason jars in a box with CDC written in marker on it in the corner. She held one up to the light and it was semi opaque with black flakes floating on the water inside and masking-tape labels. "Here they are but they don't look like water samples." Her stomach churned thinking of drinking anything like that.

"Wow, these are bad.." He took photos with his phone as he transferred them into his box. "Hard to believe these are from the tap. This water isn't fit for human consumption. I wouldn't give it to an animal."

"Why am I not surprised?" Julia shook her head.

"When I went to collect this sample one time, I met this scrawny kid with only one tooth. His mother said Lockerby used the abandoned mine above this kids home to dump slurry water they had used to wash the coal. Soon after his teeth began to dissolve, he'd just lost his baby teeth, and now his adult teeth were rotted. He was excited because he'd be getting dentures soon. He was only eleven for God's sake."

"You're kidding." Julia could barely believe what he was showing her.

"I wish" He said, shaking his head side to side. "She said that Lockerby dumped more toxic water than the BP Deepwater spill in the Gulf of Mexico. Then he had the coal company build a freshwater pipe to his house, not his neighbors, just his house."

Julia replied. "I'm just trying to help people here but they barely accept. There's such a deep fatalism. This water would be a path to that way of thinking."

He shrugged "I get it. They've been screwed for so long, up looks like down, and all some of them believe in is their family, a paycheck or God."

"It isn't hard to understand. I just saw this patient. He looked like he was eighty, but he was only fifty-five. He has black lung, so every breath is a struggle. He has to choose to get food or his inhaler. No one should have to make that choice." Julia said.

He went on. "The perception that people have here is that there is a trade-off between the environment and jobs. It's really not — it's a trade-off between the environment, people on one side, and the profits of a few who like it this way.

Another thing the coal owners love is their fairy tale about bringing energy to poor people. Since most of the world's energy-poor are rural, centralized generation doesn't help much. Mini – or off-grid renewable energy projects usually are faster and more affordable than large, centralized power plants. They serve wealthy urban people who already have infrastructure. Distribution is key, not generation."

Julia sighed, "Well the energy from coal is not helping these poor people."

He added, "Are you going to the town hall meeting?"

"I haven't heard about one. What town hall?" Julia was curious.

"Dick Lockerby is going to have a town hall next week at the Wheeling Fairgrounds."

"I thought that it was a campaign rally. His signs are everywhere." Julia said.

"Well, it's advertised as a town hall. Are you going?" He replied.

She thought about it for a moment, and then said. "Yes, I think I will." Julia didn't have much on her social calendar. She realized that aside from JC's family, her new musical friends, and the teachers she'd met she didn't have one at all.

A couple days later, two women helped an elderly man into a wheelchair and brought him up to the clinic. One of them was an occupational healthcare worker from NIOSH who told Julia "One in five miners have black lung. Way up since the 1970s. Black lung kills miners many times faster than accidents. And it keeps getting worse." They helped him get back to the car after his appointment.

Julia felt the crushing weight healthcare workers carried in these coal communities. It just never got any better, so of course they lost sight of things changing. Hope is a big part of healing.

Thunderstorms swept through, temporarily breaking the stifling heat of summer. The following week, the rain stopped and Julia had an unexpected visitor. A red convertible pulled up to the clinic. Mel took off her scarf protecting her head, reached into the back seat, and put on an enormous hat. She came up onto the porch where Julia was sitting in the shade at a rickety old table eating her lunch.

"Hi, Are you Julia?" She handed Julia her business card. "I'm Melinda Sykes, Senator Carruthers's assistant. I'm here off the record, and I'll deny I came to see you."

"We don't want Lockerby on the ticket and this primary is where to stop him." Mel gauged Julia's interest and continued. "We need your help. Our speaker for Lockerby's rally is sick and can't come. I heard you might be able to speak out." She sat down across from Julia, brushed the dust off the wooden seat, and hung her hat off the chairback.

"Who is 'we' I'm supposed to help and why would I do that?" Julia was surprised that this stranger would be so abrupt and presumptuous. What made her think that she would ever want to speak out at a political rally here in West Virginia?

Mel seemed to have anticipated her questions. "Because you know what a disaster Lockerby is. You care about what happens to people here and nature. We learned that you were active at a rally opposing a coal terminal back in Bellingham, Washington. You already spoke up and sang too. Also, you are a nurse, and can speak to the suffering his representation would cause since you already see the people who suffer the damage he causes."

"Yes, we won that battle. But I'm not from here." Julia responded, "People here know each other and want that trust. That's part of how Lockerby gets his power. He grew up here."

"That's a plus too, for you to speak. The price anyone speaking out about Lockerby pays has a lot to do with how trapped they are here. Coal was the first bonanza for fossil fuels and the people here have internalized generational loss. Over and over, over centuries. You don't carry that weight."

Julia felt apprehensive that she was being drawn into Mel's web. "Won't the voters reject someone like him? He's not talking about anything they need."

Mel looked to see if she was naive or hadn't been following the elections. "He plays to their resentments. Don't underestimate the power of feeling you've been screwed or that someone else is eating your lunch. Especially when it is true. He tells them that environmentalists or regulators are doing them harm and he is protecting them. And he is powerful, he's built a huge network of judges and civil appointees. He's ruined strong men, driven honest businesses into the dirt, and intimidated his miners. Anyone who's worked in coal knows how vindictive he is too."

"So, what exactly do you want from me?" Julia felt puzzled.

Mel explained. "I have our analysis of Lockerby's strategy and the facts to show his real history on a thumb drive." She handed Julia a fat envelope. "All we want you to do is present them in your own words. He has an open mic for questions at his rally, we'd like you to speak out."

Julia took them and set them next to her on the boards of the porch. "I'll think about it."

"That's all we can ask." Mel got up, smoothed her skirt carefully picking a splinter out of the fabric. She held out her hand to Julia "Thanks. Call me." Business concluded, Mel was off.

CHAPTER 39

MAY 20, 2018
JULIA AND JC, WHEELING FAIRGROUNDS,
WEST VIRGINIA

Julia and JC pulled into the Wheeling Fairgrounds and found a spot to park. As they walked through acres of pickup trucks and cars shimmering from the heat toward the gym and outdoor stage, the volume got louder and louder. Litter blew toward them from the overfilled trash drums on wisps of wind.

Julia thought what a strange trip it had been from Grammy's funeral here. She'd decided to stay with JC and he wanted to give West Virginia another chance. His new job working on wind turbines was a huge step forward and she felt he deserved a chance to prove himself.

It had been hard working out the details of their move in the dead of winter. Now they were finally together, living in a comfortable brick house. The yard had lots of room for Wrigley too. Almost heaven.

She remembered falling in love with the wild places here too. Kayaking, climbing, and hiking around in the canyons and frozen streams. She had decided to take the job at Slag Creek Clinic to see if she could do some good. There was so much need here and she had the skills to contribute. The people she met were suffering and this was a chance to give them a break.

Now she'd been invited to be their champion and take on someone she had come to feel was responsible for continuing the misery of the people here. She looked to the stage and saw him.

Dick Lockerby was on stage in his flag shirt and the rally was coming to the day's climax. The singer, dressed in a loincloth, strutted around the stage screaming at the crowd for Dick's opponent to 'suck on my machine gun.' New York FOX News commentator Sean Hannity, British global-warming-denier Lord Christopher Monckton, and Lockerby's own pet scientist, Albert, had all been flown in for the event and lined the stage behind him like so many Disney mascots.

JC thought how this political rally in West Virginia would be strange to the people he grew up with. The usual summer community of his childhood had been replaced by loud angry music, huge BBQs, and kegs of Pabst Blue Ribbon beer.

When he left he felt there would never be anything for him. Now he had so much financial opportunity because of his welding skills. The union here welcomed him in and moved him ahead into positions he would have taken years to occupy in Anacortes. The money he made went a lot farther too. Things were completely new and he felt accomplished.

"Look at this. It's like some kind of carnival." said an older woman wearing a simple cotton dress to her friend. "When I was growing up, West Virginians were respectable and took personal responsibility. Military veterans and God-fearing Southern Baptists and Pentecostals. Some wouldn't allow their kids to use 'damn' or even dance."

On stage, Dick was using all the symbols of patriotism, freedom, and independence as decoration for his run for US Senate. Dick took the mic from the loinclothed singer. "That's about all the All-American fun for this afternoon. Now you all come over to the hall here and hear how I'm going to make West Virginia great." He waved his cowboy hat and pointed to the gym building. He exited the stage with his beefy bodyguards and said goodbye to the out-of-state talent.

Julia felt her stomach knot as she pushed open the glass door to the lobby at the front of the gym. Strengthening her resolve she asked JC to stay back, walked up to the front of the hall and took a seat near the audience mic. She thought about how the smelting industry had lied to her father about his health risks exposing him to asbestos. His coughing and wheezing, and at the end, how he lost his ability to sing. She missed his singing most of all when he died from mesothelioma. Lockerby was the same as her father's bosses. She was still grieving her mother and wished she could have spent more time with her.

The stage had a half dozen identical five by eight-foot signs with 'Dick Lockerby, an American Champion for Senate.' Loud patriotic music played over the PA for a while. A local mine big shot took the mic and told everyone how important it was to elect county judges, sheriffs, and tax commissioners.

JC thought about Lo and how the sheriff let the truck driver who killed her leave the state. It seemed they were all corrupt and didn't do much for the miners or families, just the owners. He felt in his pocket for the watch and remembered how much pride his grandfather had from working for the railroad.

The PA system played "God Bless America." Dick and his entourage swaggered out from backstage parading two cute children all dressed up for the occasion around the stage. He pointed at one of his friends like there was a crowd, but the gym was barely half full. Most of the crowd had left after the music.

Dick recounted his homey stories of his violent and hardscrabble childhood. Tough times forging him into a self-made man. He compared himself to George Washington as a great leader. He went through his litany of how being tough in business is good for everyone and creates prosperity.

He attacked Congress and the Mine Safety people as hurting West Virginia. They were the reason it was hard to keep the mines open.

Julia was sitting near the front looking up at him. When it came time for audience questions, she stepped to the microphone behind a scrawny young woman in a black t-shirt and jeans who began reading a list of campaign contributions from coal and energy companies to Dick's campaign. He looked sourly at her and interrupted, asking that 'no personal comments be made.' When she persisted in reading, a pair of security guards came up to the mic, explained that she could not continue talking. "Drag me out, then." she said. As they physically removed her from the chamber, she cried "Montani Semper Liberi! – Mountaineers are always free!" At the top of her voice. They still could hear her yelling as the guards took her out to the lobby.

The camera crew focused on Julia as she stepped up to the mic and looked directly at Dick, "You ask West Virginia voters to send you to the United States Senate for the next six years to represent their needs, hopes and dreams? Are you truly mad or just suffering from delusion?" Letting sadness and anger from losing her father and mother amplify her voice.

"Your record of caring for people is plain. You don't. Instead, you take all the profit from the mines for yourself and leave the broken men, the widows, the orphans on their own to take care of themselves. You use the State's infrastructure and give nothing back. You don't even live here.

I've seen the fruit of your labors here. Dead and broken men, widows, ruined nature, and your big pot of money.

Your legacy for future generations is flattened mountains, toxic streams, abandoned mines filled with your coal slurry leaching into their drinking water, opioid overdose, ruined kidneys from alcohol abuse, and suicides. You may not prescribe the pills or give out free liquor but make no mistake, their pain has been your gain. On your watch, black lung redoubled after two decades of decline. So much for your care of the miners. You are handmaiden to deaths of despair. Worse than that, your greed trumps your responsibility for the safety of the men in your miners.

Coal is over as an energy source, more expensive than renewables, and uneconomical. When people look back at these last days of coal they will see you as the poster boy for the final chapter of greedy, desperate men grasping for money.

But your longest-lived legacy will be the utter destruction of the natural endowment of this beautiful state. You saw men and mountains as a small price to pay for cash in your pocket. West Virginia's God-given natural wealth plundered so you can drive a fancy car and fly around the world.

So please tell us what you will do for West Virginia that you haven't been doing all along?"

Dick was angry it took his security men so long to come back. They were hustling down the aisle toward her.

Dick leaned into the microphone and fixed his lizard gaze on her, "You aren't from here are you? Did Senator Carruthers send you? I've made people more money in this state than anyone. They are happy to have been part of my team. You accuse me and say I don't care. When the outsiders gave up on coal I stepped in and got the industry working again. How would the miners have lived with no coal mining here? Oh, they had unions, but no work. I've been a civic leader helping to make it work for the honest people." Dick delivered his words mechanically, his head oddly moving side to side, still while his eyes stayed locked on her. The security men stood close to Julia expecting orders from Dick. He was angry and had lost control of the debate.

Julia cut him off, "You think taking your company into bankruptcy, coming out on the other side with your hundred million, while miners lost lives, healthcare and pensions is 'making it work?' These people, who made you rich are hurting because of your leadership. Their health is damaged. They are despairing and turning to anything that will staunch the pain. What are you going to do?"

Dick shot back, "I've brought security, well-being, prosperity, and jobs. The energy coal brings to the world lifts it out of poverty. You don't think that's leadership? Think of the benefits coal has brought us – transportation, steel, and the industrial revolution all rode in on it. If there were a way to get it out without soiling our hands, we would do it.

I get criticized for anything I do. If I bring in new safer technology like big machines that are efficient, and don't risk men's lives in mines, I am accused of losing jobs. If methane gas builds up in one of our mines and explodes, you say I'm a murderer." He looked to the crowd for sympathy.

Julia again cut into his speech "Yes. You are a murderer." The security men stood close to her anxiously waiting for orders from Dick.

"When your mine exploded and killed the miners you claimed that God is guilty for methane gas filling the mine. That's big, even for you. God is the guilty one, not Dick Lockerby! You knew that the coal dust building up before the mine exploded was lethal. You ordered the managers to focus only on one thing – how much coal they got out. You told them to ignore any safety measures that would have eaten into your precious profit. Your failed leadership provided the coal dust that blew them up. Not God or anyone else. You."

Dick was taken aback. He kept his security men off so he could answer but Julia kept talking.

"You pioneered and championed mountaintop removal and you call that progress. It is no such thing. It is a way to get coal that takes a smaller number of miners per ton. You are running a big con job. Externalizing costs, shifting assets, even going bankrupt, are your tools. You take profits by breaking your word to fund pension and healthcare benefits for your so called 'team.'

You have worsened a permanent impoverished population in this state. The money from coal goes to your outsized personal compensation. You represent out-of-state banks who fund your capital-intensive mining. And now you live in Las Vegas! How is that native?

Your management has destroyed any future for jobs because you destroy the mountains and the fabric of life to get at your coal. Once you are done removing the mountaintop, all its trees, flowers, animals, birds, and beauty, what is left? Nothing! Your legacy is dead zones that leach toxins, kill watersheds, foul landscapes, and doom future generations to a wasteland-." The guards were at either arm telling her to stop. Mid-sentence her mic was cut. JC came down the aisle and slowed their way out. The guards told him to back off.

Dick intoned as though it was his turn to speak "The coal industry pays millions in taxes every year into the coffers of West Virginia…"

Julia raised her voice to fill the hall as they backed her up the aisle toward the exit, "Yes it does but the healthcare costs that it saddles the state with are five times that amount every year." The guards mumbled that she needed to come along peacefully. Julia continued, "You deserve full credit for your hard work – you made a hundred million dollars for yourself. But your fortune is built on death and destruction, greed, and deceit." She was yelling now, "You destroyed lives and left a mess of things that will take decades to even begin to recover! For each of the thousand peaks you've leveled, you took a million dollars. Each peak kills miles of streams. Each stream feeds toxins into the rivers." She dug her heels in near the exit.

"You chose the path of greed. Think of the amazing good you could have accomplished in the world with your talents. Instead, you squandered them for more money than you can ever hope to enjoy. Your legacy is poisonous for the State of West Virginia, and to people who hope to live here." She finished as the guards pushed her through the double doors and out of the auditorium.

Dick leaned into his mic and said "People from Senator Carruthers come to try and silence me. I am the victim here. They don't want me to lead you all."

The old miner, Leroy, who Julia had given the inhaler to at the clinic stood and a tech brought him a mic. "You leave that whiny horseshit in the barn, Dickie. That ain't why. She's dead right about you. I worked twenty years for you, in the old days when you weren't rich. I seen you operate – Do as Dick Says. The only thing to you is how much coal come out the mine. You said safety was important, but you made us skip the blast curtains and things to make us safe." His voice trembled.

"You talked for years 'bout how I was on your team. I believed it too. 'member when you needed that tank of toxics dumped. I drove your tank truck out, late at night, just like you said. I took it down to the Tug and poured it in the river. I knowed it was wrong and so did you.

Well, my granddaughter's got the cancer. Six years old dying from the cancer. They told me it is from pollution in the Tug, the same stuff I poured in when you said to." He gripped the chair – back in front of him so hard his knuckles were white.

"You always said you were one of us, from here. Well, that may have been true once but no more. You're no different'n any other carpetbagger comes to take and leave the mess to us." He was shaking with rage "You make me sick and have made me sick. I'm angry for following you and I am ashamed. Ashamed of what I did for you." Some people applauded him. He was still shaking when he sat back down.

Lockerby angrily pointed one of his security men to him and said. "None of that is true. I don't know this man."

Letting go of Julia in the lobby the security men blocked the door back in.

JC came over and embraced her. "Thank you, thank you, I never thought anyone would have the courage to say that to his face. You're brave. I've seen him yell at the grieving families, widows who lost their men in the explosion. They were there to honor their dead and he yelled at them. I've never heard anyone talk directly to Dick like that. You are amazing."

One woman had followed her out, teary eyed, and said, "Thank you. Thank you for standing up and speaking out. We live with this terrible man but no one dares challenge him. He's so vengeful and willing to ruin anyone who gets in his way." Another man who had followed her out into the lobby added "My son died from black lung after working for Dick Lockerby for just twenty years. He was only forty-one years old." And another, "Thank you for speaking up for us. You should run, you know, for office." Julia began to take deep breaths and slowly calmed. These people deserved a voice and she was glad that she had given them one.

A man wearing a red, white, and blue bandana around his neck came out of the hall and beelined to Julia, pointing a finger in her face saying, "You have nothing to say here, you haven't lived our life. That was a disgraceful attack on one of our leading citizens. Go back to where you came from and leave us to manage our lives without outside influence." He left in a huff pushing the door a little too hard.

Back on stage, Dick droned "I'm more Karne than Karne. I'll bring back coal and we will all reap the benefits of jobs and a future for the mines. Freedom to have a good job mining coal." A couple of people from the audience stepped to the mic with note sheets and read positive statements about him. Some of their comments matched his campaign site. Many more attendees left the room.

One of Dick's security men leaned over Leroy's shoulder and quietly whispered in his ear, "You're dead."

A quiet young man nervously told Julia, "My daddy died in that explosion. He went to work before we were up, just like always, but he never came back. I was only ten years old. I was glad to hear Dick say it was an earthquake when it happened. Later all of us who lost family learned about him. I wish I could've said what you just did to him. He might as well have pulled out a gun and shot my daddy. He should be back in jail for murder."

Soon there were as many reporters as supporters and Dick signaled to stop his event. He left with his security men out the back of the auditorium to his limo.

A few of the pro-Dick speakers met the security chief in the lobby who said, "You the guys who came from our ad on craigslist?" They handed back the notes they'd read from and got cash for their performance in return. They left talking with one another about how hard it was to find paid acting work.

Mel asked a reporter she knew to do an interview with Julia and then left the scene.

A woman Julia had met at Slag Clinic came up with her young son, "Oh, I am so thankful for you giving a voice to our suffering. It was so courageous standing up to this horrible man. If enough of us band together we can stop him. Thank you for your courage."

The reporter Mel asked to interview her had been waiting to begin, "So can you tell me why you came today? Obviously you aren't a supporter. Tell us about yourself." Julia spent the next five minutes with him explaining how she had seen the suffering at the Slag Clinic and developed a desire to help.

The support and encouragement left Julia feeling calm at last. "I believe it is possible to have a better world. We first need to stop harming it. It will take a lot more than keeping Dick Lockerby out of a Senate race. We will prevail. People in West Virginia deserve their liberty, independence, and freedom. The reign of coal is over."

She took JC's hand and they walked out together. JC said, "You are incredible. I'm so happy to be with you and that you've adopted this place. I wish you could have met Grammy, she'd have loved your courage."